A WISH FOR JINNIE

AUDREY DAVIS

Enormous thanks, as always, to my family. For believing in me, and putting up with my ranting, obsession with social media and frequent howls of 'I can't do this!' Also, my lovely friends for listening to me wittering on for hours about blog tours, promotional tools and other stuff, all the while pretending to know what I'm talking about. Finally, thanks to two 'special' friends — gin and red wine — for occasionally lubricating the old brain cells. Cheers!

A WISH FOR JINNIE

CHAPTER 1

'It's … erm … rather bijou.' Hannah stretched out her arms and pirouetted around the lounge. The fingers of one hand swiped two of the 'Welcome to your New Home!' cards off the dusty mantelpiece and onto the floor.

'What you mean is there isn't enough room to swing a bloody cat,' grumbled Jinnie, gathering up the cards and dumping them on the coffee table.

Hannah deftly uncorked the bottle of Prosecco she'd brought along to celebrate Jinnie's move to the village of Cranley and poured it into two chipped mugs. Most of Jinnie's possessions were still packed in boxes, stacked in every available corner — which left very little room for anything bar the two friends, a coffee table and two metallic folding garden chairs.

'Look, hun, I know it's not ideal,' said Hannah in a tone of voice that suggested a garden shed would be a better option. 'The thing is, you needed somewhere fast — and cheap — and this fits the bill. Once you're back on your feet, we can find something bigger and better.'

Clinking their mugs together, Jinnie and Hannah sat

down and gazed around forlornly. Maybe it wouldn't seem *quite* so cramped once she'd unpacked everything. But Jinnie had neither the energy nor the motivation to get organised. Her 'get up and go' had 'got up and gone' when her boyfriend of three years (and fiancé of two) announced they were over.

She'd moved in with Mark shortly after they got engaged, delighted to trade her studio flat in Edinburgh for his luxurious three-bedroom flat in the West End. As the owner of a small chain of estate agents, Mark was comfortably off (also helped by having seriously loaded parents). They'd met when Jinnie landed a job at one of his agencies, her normally flawless interview skills derailed by Mark's intense gaze and ridiculously good looks.

Staring into her fizzing mug, Jinnie recalled sitting in Mark's office. He'd sat opposite, tapping a pen on his notepad. She'd fiddled with the strap of her handbag, feeling damp patches forming in her armpits. Every time she'd looked up, Mark gave a warm smile and nod, encouraging her to continue speaking. Which was easier said than done when her insides had turned to baby mush. He'd taken off his tie and loosened the top button of his shirt, at which point Jinnie blurted out, 'Gosh, you're hot too!' And immediately wished the upholstered swivel chair would swallow her whole. Mark had just laughed, pushed aside her scanty CV and offered her the receptionist job.

Nothing had happened for the first few weeks, Jinnie convinced Mark was way out of her league. Until he strode into the office one sunny Monday morning, plonked a takeaway cup of her favourite coffee on the counter and gave her one of his icecap-melting smiles. It was only after he'd left that Jinnie noticed a scribbled message on the side of the cup. *Dinner tonight? Lucca's at 7.*

It had been a relationship fuelled by incredible sex, fabulous holidays and weekend breaks — a world away from

Jinnie's humble upbringing in a council house her parents had scrimped and saved to buy during the Thatcher years. When Mark had slid the exquisite two-carat diamond ring on her finger, Jinnie's heart had soared, along with her thoughts of vintage wedding dresses, making honeymoon love on a four-poster bed in the Maldives, and lots of adorable babies. Well maybe just a couple, as she was already thirty-five and on a biological countdown. And she'd prayed fervently that they'd inherit Mark's ash-blonde hair rather than her mousy hue (which she had highlighted every six weeks), and his aquiline nose rather than hers. Jinnie's was more Roman — or 'roamin' all over your face!' — as her darling younger brother Archie used to say.

There had been times when Jinnie wondered what Mark saw in her. She'd witnessed other women's reactions when he entered a room. And their looks of disbelief when Jinnie clung to his arm, the sparkling ring a warning that he was off-limits. Not that an engagement guaranteed faithfulness. Looking back, Jinnie realised there had been signs along the way. She'd chosen to ignore them. The late nights at the office; the whispered phone calls not meant for her ears. The dwindling of the incredible sex, Mark rolling over and protesting he was too tired.

Now here she was with no fiancé, no wedding and little chance of motherhood in the immediate future. She'd had to move out of the flat and, with nothing in the way of savings, her only options were to move back in with her mum and dad or find something low-budget. The former was a no-no, not because she didn't love them to bits, but because it would be yet another kick to her shattered self-esteem. Thirty-five and living with your *parents*? She'd found this cottage through the agency, one of only a handful she could afford. Particularly as she'd quit her job a week after being dumped, squatting on Hannah's sofa bed in the interim. The final kick in the teeth had been witnessing Mark carrying a takeaway cup of coffee into the office of his latest employee, a statuesque brunette called Kimberley with a cute button nose. A message was clearly scrawled on the cup in black marker pen. Jinnie packed up her belongings and marched out of the door with her head held high, and her heart in pieces. She'd received two months' salary and blown a large chunk on wine, chocolate and a gorgeous little black dress she'd probably never wear. It hung on the door of her poky new bedroom, more mourning gown than party frock.

'Jinnie, I know it's all shite, but once you've got yourself sorted here and found yourself another job, it'll be fine.' Hannah had always been a glass half-full person, while Jinnie veered more towards the 'need a bigger glass filled to the brim' school of thought.

Finding another job was at the top of Jinnie's to-do list, closely followed by saving enough money to allow her to move back to the city. However, with little in the way of qualifications (school really hadn't been her thing), it was unlikely she'd earn enough before retirement age. Maybe she'd tolerate her cupboard-like existence until then, and hope for a place at an old folks' home. Although didn't they cost an arm and a leg too these days?

'Earth to Jinnie, earth to Jinnie,' intoned Hannah, flapping a hand in front of her face. 'You were miles away, hun. Here, have a top-up.' Hannah filled their mugs to the brim and raised hers in a toast. 'To new beginnings and all that jazz. As my dear old mum always says, every cloud has a silver lining. Cheers!'

Jinnie half-heartedly clinked her mug in return. Right now, she felt as if her future was one enormous black thundercloud, prepared to drench her already sodden hopes and dreams…

CHAPTER 2

As villages went, Cranley ticked the usual boxes. Tiny post office cum corner shop (closed for two hours at lunchtime and open Saturday mornings till 11). Quaint olde-worlde pub called The Jekyll and Hyde. Very apt, as the author Robert Louis Stevenson was born in Edinburgh. Doubly apt, as the landlord swung between charm personified and the devil incarnate, as Jinnie had discovered on her few visits there. There was also a tiny hairdressing salon run by Peggy, whose repertoire comprised tight perms or Barbara Cartland-style bouffant dos which could withstand a force nine gale. In her current cash-strapped condition Jinnie couldn't afford a trip to the capital to see the lovely Stephanie, who'd tended to her subtly highlighted mop of curls for years. Luckily, her last visit had been only a few weeks ago, so desperate measures weren't called for yet.

Meandering along the high street, Jinnie took a swig of coffee from her stainless-steel flask. Gone were the days when she'd blithely blow a tenner a day on takeaway coffee — she'd developed a strong aversion to cardboard cups —

with her caffeine fix now courtesy of a battered kettle and a jar of instant.

Pausing outside one of only a handful of shops, Jinnie looked at the window display. A hotchpotch of battered old books vied for attention with grubby mannequins wearing clothing that was less 'vintage', more moth bait. There was a small boutique at the far end of the street, its stock clearly designed for the older members of the community; elasti-cated-waist trousers and flowery frocks that could double up as tents at Glastonbury. Mind you, in the week or so since Jinnie had moved to Cranley she'd noticed that the average age of the population seemed to be late sixties to early seven-ties. Not that she believed older people should dress in a certain way, and she had spotted a few ladies decades her senior rocking skinny jeans and cute tops in funky colours. No doubt they hopped on the local train (which ran fairly regularly into Edinburgh) and came back laden with goodies.

Thinking wistfully of her own lunchtime and after-work shopping sprees, when she'd stagger home with armfuls of clothes and cosmetics, Jinnie sighed. She'd chopped up her maxed-out credit cards on her second day here, and shoved the bills to the back of the kitchen drawer. She needed to start earning money — and soon — but job prospects here were thin on the ground. Jinnie knew her parents would give her money without hesitation, but she wasn't going to ask. They were hardly rolling in it themselves, and they subsidised her brother Archie's musical career. Five years out of university, he was still twanging his battered guitar at open mic nights and producing stuff he declared 'ground-breaking' but not yet ready for the masses to hear. He lived in a tiny bedsit just a couple of miles from their parents and was expert in putting them off from visiting. Just as well, as it made Jinnie's current abode look like the height of luxury.

What little floor space there was played host to Archie's wardrobe, his philosophy being to shed garments like a snake shed its skin. Only when he was down to his last pair of boxers, and even the cockroaches were beating a retreat in disgust, would he haul a bin bag of washing to the local launderette. Or, more often, round to Kath and Rob, otherwise known as the bank of Mum and Dad. Jinnie loved her family, but her younger brother needed to pull his hygienically challenged socks up.

The smell of fresh bread tickled her nostrils as she arrived outside the only bakery/tea room in the village. A Bit of Crumpet was its rather saucy name, inscribed in swirly letters against a cream and pink background. The door was wedged open, the day unseasonably warm for November, and a quick glance inside saw most of the dozen or so tables occupied. A couple of young mums with pushchairs, pensioners tucking into scones or cakes, and a group of women roughly her own age tapping frantically on their phones. Jinnie's stomach gave an almighty rumble, reminding her she hadn't eaten that morning. And last night's dinner of fish fingers and peas hadn't exactly hit the spot.

'Jinnie! What are you doing loitering out there? Come in and try one of my new sausage rolls. Makes those shopbought monstrosities taste like soggy cardboard.' Owner Joanna — 'call me Jo, love' — ushered Jinnie inside. She bent down to remove the doorstop then nudged Jinnie towards a vacant table.

Jinnie had only met Jo briefly twice; once when buying bread and the second time when a dose of the blues could only be fixed by a slice of apple pie. OK, a *whole* pie, washed down by a bottle of cheap plonk which induced both headache and heartburn. Jo was one of those women who you felt you'd known forever, kindness and concern radiating from every pore. Jinnie had given her an edited version of her life story, saying she'd broken up with her boyfriend and was trying to start afresh somewhere new. If Jo was puzzled as to why Jinnie had chosen Cranley, she didn't comment. Now she set down a plate with a gigantic sausage roll and a mug of tea and pulled up a chair.

'On the house, love,' she said, as Jinnie pulled out her purse. Jinnie didn't need to look inside to know there was very little cash. Blushing furiously, she thanked Jo.

'No worries. I know you've been looking for work and there's not a lot going around here. But I did hear of something that might interest you.'

Curiosity piqued, Jinnie leant forward, taking a bite of the sausage roll. Flakes of incredibly light and delicious pastry cascaded down her front. Brushing them away with a napkin, she listened intently.

'You've probably not come across it yet, but there's an antique shop tucked away down a side street near the pub,' said Jo, nodding at a new customer who'd just walked in. 'With you in a sec!' she chirruped before continuing. 'The owner's looking for an assistant, someone to man the till and what have you when he's off gallivanting around the country looking for more tat — I mean, objets d'art — to flog. I think it's only part-time, but it might be worth checking out.' Jo patted Jinnie on the shoulder before heading back to the counter. After fixing a coffee for the customer, she returned with a card in her hand.

'You could ring him, but probably easiest if you just dropped by. He should be there now.'

Jinnie thanked Jo again and finished off the sausage roll, washed down with the rest of the tea. She looked at the card: *Samuel A. Addin, Out of the Attic Antiques*, with an address and phone numbers. Jinnie couldn't imagine herself working in such a place, but job offers weren't going to flutter down from the sky like December snowflakes. There was no harm in going for a chat, was there? Decision made, Jinnie gathered up her things, waved at Jo, and headed off before she could change her mind.

CHAPTER 3

THE DOOR TO OUT OF THE ATTIC ANTIQUES WAS UNLOCKED. Jinnie entered, expecting the jingle of a bell to signal her arrival, but there was nothing. Nor was there any sign of life, although a radio was playing quietly in the background.

'Hello! Is anybody there?' she called out. No response. Jinnie edged further into the shop, which could have doubled up as the set for a low-budget horror movie. The lighting was almost non-existent, and the movement of the door opening had disturbed a layer of dust that hovered in the air like mist over a murky Yorkshire moor. Through the gloom, Jinnie could make out shelves, tables and display cases crammed with all manner of the weird and the wonderful. Well, maybe less wonderful, more 'Who'd pay hard cash for any of this stuff?' She picked up a macabre ashtray shaped like a skull, with the inscription: *Poor old Fred. Smoked in bed. Now he's dead* around its base. Delightful!

The sound of a toilet flushing made Jinnie hurriedly replace the ashtray, in case the owner thought she was about to steal it. As if! She dredged up a smile from somewhere around her lace-up Converse boots, which Mark had loathed. He was a high-heels-and-stockings man (looking at them, not wearing them), and she'd suffered pinched toes and chafed thighs throughout their relationship. Now she could stomp through life in absolute comfort, content in the knowledge that Kimberley would probably end up with misshapen toes and bunions and —

'Hello! Sorry, I was just, um, checking some stock in the back. Were you interested in anything in particular?' The owner — at least, Jinnie *assumed* he was the owner — returned her half-baked smile with a grin that illuminated the murky surroundings. He was not what she'd imagined at all. Samuel A. Addin had conjured up a picture of a curmudgeonly old geezer, clad in fusty tweed and twiddling a fob watch. Instead, he was a forty-something man wearing tight black jeans, a crumpled linen shirt and an air of dishevelled hotness. Was that a word? Jinnie didn't know, but she felt wrong-footed, as if she'd stepped into the lion's den only for the said lion to roll over and demand tummy tickles.

'No, not really. It's just that Jo at the café said you might be looking for some help. And I'm looking for work. I'm not really fussy about what I do — sorry, that sounds rude — but if ever you need somebody...' Jinnie felt an eighties song nip at her ear — Rick Astley? She was too young to remember, but he'd had a resurgence. Gone from painfully unhip to retro cool. If you waited long enough, you came back into vogue.

'Oh, I could definitely do with somebody to look after this place. Actually, someone to clean it up a bit and drag it into the here and now. I'm passionate about old things, but I'm not really an antiques person. Is that an oxymoron? Well, I'm definitely more moron than oxy, but now I'm babbling...'

Jinnie laughed. A full-on belly laugh. When had she last laughed? She and Hannah had had their fair share of giggling about the daft things they'd done, the losers they'd dated.

With Mark ... not so much. Looking back, the laughs had been at her expense. She'd joined in, not really getting — or choosing to get — that she was the punchline. The last laugh for his beer-sodden friends who worshipped at his designer-shod feet, each and every one of them a total tosser. Yes, Jinnie got it now, but it had been a painful journey.

'Right, I can't afford to pay a lot but I don't think you'll find the work too demanding. What's your background ... erm ... we haven't done the introduction thing, have we?' Samuel Addin extended his hand and Jinnie shook it. 'Call me Sam, and I can call you...?'

'Jinnie. Jinnie Cooper. My proper name is Virginia, but no one calls me that these days. My last job was as a recep-tionist at an estate agent's in Edinburgh, but I've also worked in retail and sales.' She felt it best not to mention that her retail experience had been flogging make-up in a department store, and on the sales front she'd spent a miserable year trying to persuade people that their lives would be trans-formed by new windows and conservatories.

'Well, it's almost lunchtime and I'm not exactly run off my feet, so why don't we adjourn to The Jekyll and Hyde for a bite to eat, and then we can work something out. How does that sound?'

Jinnie's stomach gave another ominous rumble. Clearly the sausage roll hadn't hit the sweet spot. She nodded enthu-siastically, and prayed that landlord Ken McCroarty was in happy mode. Last time she'd popped in for a quick shandy, he'd clattered it down with such force she'd feared the glass would shatter.

CHAPTER 4

'What brings you to Cranley?' Sam asked as they ambled along the street.

'Oh, I just needed a change of scenery,' Jinnie replied. There was no way she wanted to bring up the subject of Mark and have Sam look at her with pity. Luckily, he didn't press her further on the matter.

When she revealed that she was living in Brae Cottage, Sam raised his eyebrows.

'That belonged to old Jessie Wilson, a bit of a recluse by all accounts. She died over a year ago with no known family, so the place stayed empty for months until a lettings company bought it for peanuts.' Sam held the door of the pub open for Jinnie, the buzz of customers chatting and jukebox music blaring in sharp contrast to the stillness of the world outside.

'It's not what I'd call my dream home,' she said, 'but it'll do till I find my feet.'

Sam guided Jinnie to a table in a quieter corner, where laminated menu cards were propped up in a wooden stand. Next to the bar was a blackboard announcing today's special to be shepherd's pie. They agreed to go for it, and Sam headed to the bar to place their order, along with a glass of Sauvignon Blanc for Jinnie. She fumbled in her handbag for her phone, a dated Samsung, but upgrading to something fancier wasn't an option right now. There were two messages. One was from Hannah: *How's it going, hun? Big girlie night out planned for next Friday. Be there or be square! Your sofa bed awaits xxxx.* The other was from her mum: *Fancy coming over for Sunday lunch, sweetheart? Archie will be there, so I'll make extra roasties! Love, Mum.* Glancing up, she saw Sam was deep in conversation with Ken McCroarty. Bonhomie exuded from the man as he poured a pint and roared with laughter at something Sam had said. *Maybe he's just taken an instant dislike to me*, thought Jinnie. Perhaps she should pop on some sunglasses and pull up her hood, in case he spat in her lunch.

'Here we go,' said Sam, placing the wine and beer on the table. 'There was only one helping of shepherd's pie left, so I plumped for fish and chips. Kath in the kitchen does the crispiest batter, and the chips are pretty legendary too. You can pinch a couple if you like!'

Was he flirting with her? It had been so long since Jinnie had dated anyone that she felt like she needed a 'how to' manual. She sipped her wine and contemplated the man sitting opposite her. Attractive, for sure, and easy to talk to. What she didn't know — and wasn't about to ask — was his marital status. Although she was sure Jo could fill in the necessary details...

'Grub's up!' A beaming Ken appeared with their food, steam rising from the plates. He nodded a hello in Jinnie's direction, although she wasn't sure he recognised her. After he had left, Jinnie mumbled, 'Jekyll today then.'

'Sorry?' Sam picked up a chip and blew on it.

'It's just he's been a bit off with me when I've come in before,' said Jinnie. 'Like he's got a split personality.'

'He's having a tough time,' said Sam, squeezing a dollop of ketchup onto his plate. 'His wife Mags was diagnosed with early onset Alzheimer's about nine months ago. She's only fifty-four, so at first they didn't realise what it was. She started forgetting things, putting stuff away in the wrong place or muddling up dates. They thought it was due to the … you know … menopause.' Sam stammered over the word, and Jinnie hid her grin by shovelling in a forkful of pie. It always cracked her up how so many men could let rip with all manner of words describing sex or body parts, but couldn't cope with mention of the M word or, in Mark's case, the P word. As in having a period. When she had been crippled with pain or stomping around the flat in a foul mood, he would ask, 'Are you surfing the crimson wave?' or 'Is it rag week?' Torn between irritation and amusement, Jinnie had Googled euphemisms for periods, and discovered there were over 5000 slang terms. 5000! And considerably fewer for penis, apparently.

Dragging her thoughts away from bodily functions, Jinnie said, 'That's awful. Does he have anyone to help him? I mean at home, not in the pub.' She felt rather guilty now for her snap judgement of Ken.

Nudging his chips in Jinnie's direction, Sam shook his head. 'They live upstairs here, and Mags still works behind the bar occasionally, but not for much longer I fear. They're devoted to one another — married in their late teens — with one son, Ed, who's in his early thirties. He works in Carlisle but comes up most weekends to give his dad a break.'

Their meals finished, and Jinnie having managed to polish off half of Sam's chips, they got down to business. They agreed that she would spend three days a week in the shop, dealing with customers in Sam's absence, and giving the place a bit of a clean and tidy up. Sam scribbled down a number on the back of a beermat, and Jinnie nodded. It was more generous than she'd expected, but she'd need to find something additional quickly to avoid sinking further into debt.

'Can you start tomorrow?' asked Sam, waving away her attempt to pay her share. 'I can run through the basics like the till and inventory in the morning, then leave you to it. There's a fair on at Ingliston I'd like to visit in the afternoon. I'm looking for more plates and china. They're my more popular items.'

Jinnie agreed, and they left the pub. Sam promised to dig out his supply of cleaning products, and assured her that she had carte blanche to rearrange stock as she saw fit.

Wending her way home after promising to report for duty at 9am, Jinnie tried not to feel too despondent about her new job. Really, it amounted to being a glorified cleaner crossed with a shop assistant. Then she reprimanded herself for being negative. Sam seemed a nice man and at least she'd be earning something. In the meantime, she had lunch with her family and a night out with Hannah and the girls to look forward to.

CHAPTER 5

'Do you get a lot of customers?' asked Jinnie on Wednesday morning. She'd been welcomed enthusiastically by Sam, with mugs of coffee and fresh croissants from A Bit of Crumpet to start the day.

'Not as many as I'd like,' he replied, stirring two large sugars into his drink. 'But this is really more of a hobby for me. I inherited the shop from my dad when he died, and only started trading myself a couple of years ago.'

'So what's your real job then, if you don't mind me asking?' Jinnie put down her mug and pulled out a handful of dusters and a can of polish from the box of cleaning products Sam had brought from the storeroom. She'd decided to start with a bit of a clean, then move on to rearranging the stock to make it look more appealing. At the moment grimy ornaments and tarnished cutlery were jostling for shelf space with piles of plates, tangled jewellery and ornate boxes in all shapes and sizes. With a little order restored, Jinnie was confident the place could look a lot more enticing.

Sam leaned forward. 'If I tell you, I'll have to kill you.'

Jinnie's can of polish tumbled from her hand and rolled towards a stack of hideous figurines. She lunged forward, fearful of them being knocked down like skittles. Scoring a strike would be a very bad thing.

He laughed. 'Sorry, my sense of humour is a bit on the dark side. As is my real job, which I tend to keep quiet about.' Sam stuck out a foot to halt the can's progress.

Gosh, was he a secret agent, or some kind of undercover cop? She could picture Sam on some covert operation, clad head to toe in black with a bullet-proof vest and an arsenal of weapons strapped to his body. He certainly had the physique for it — not that she was interested in him in *that* way. Nope, Jinnie had sworn off men for at least a year, if not longer. She'd mentally removed the batteries from her ticking biological clock, and warned her mum that the subject was totally off limits.

'Earth to Jinnie … hello!' Sam waggled a hand in front of her face. Steering her thoughts away from men and chubby-cheeked babies, she looked at him expectantly.

'I'm a writer,' said Sam. 'A reasonably successful one, but I like to keep a low profile especially round here. Ken and Mags know, but that's about it.'

Before Jinnie could ask any more, the door opened and a customer entered. At least, she *assumed* it was a customer. It could also be the gasman, or a fan of Sam looking for an autograph. No, definitely a customer, who nodded a hello before rummaging through a box of odds and ends. Definitely at the odder end of the spectrum, as he attempted to untangle a stringed puppet from a knot of stringed pearls. Moving out of earshot, Jinnie whispered, 'So, are you famous? I love reading; maybe I've read some of your stuff!'

Sam grinned, and took her arm, pulling her into the back room. Jinnie's heart did a little jig, totally at odds with her brain saying that men were off limits.

'Moderately so. I write crime thrillers set in and around Edinburgh, but I use a pen name,' said Sam.

As Sam released her arm, Jinnie's heart ceased its jig, and she chided herself for getting carried away. Sam was now her boss and — hopefully — on his way to becoming a friend. Attractive as he was, she didn't need more than that for the foreseeable future.

Peering round the door, she saw the customer waiting patiently at the counter with a stack of plates and a fob watch. 'I'll just deal with him, then you can reveal all,' Jinnie said, then blushed. Oops, unintentional double entendre!

Sam merely winked and told her how much to charge. 'And if he wants to haggle, go for it. But not more than ten or fifteen per cent below the asking price.'

Clearly happy with his deal of fifty pounds, the customer departed, and Sam joined Jinnie again with more coffee.

'So where were we? Oh yes, my pen name. I use the name Alistair Scott. Alistair is my middle name, and Scott because I love the Scott Monument in Edinburgh. It's such an incredible structure, don't you think?'

Jinnie, to her shame, had never given it much thought. She'd always been more focussed on the shops across the road on Princes Street. She knew it was a tribute to the Scottish author Sir Walter Scott, and something like 300 steps to climb to the highest point. She'd never attempted it, preferring to stay on the flat whenever possible.

'How many books have you published?' Jinnie asked. She sipped her coffee and flapped a duster over a dark wood box with an intricate mother-of-pearl inlay.

'Fifteen so far, with another couple in the works,' replied Sam. 'They pull in decent money and I have a pretty faithful band of followers. I just prefer to keep it quiet around here. I'm Sam the antiques man, and that suits me fine.'

He left for the fair a couple of hours later, with Jinnie

vowing to protect his 'secret' identity. With mop in hand, she began scrubbing the grime off the floor, all the while itching to look up Alistair Scott on Amazon…

CHAPTER 6

THE REST OF THE WEEK PASSED QUICKLY. JINNIE FOUND herself enjoying the whole cleaning and reorganising business more than she'd expected. Left mainly to her own devices — Sam was approaching a deadline and only dropped in a handful of times — she'd buffed silverware to an eye-watering shine, hung various pieces of art on the wall, and repainted the wobbly IKEA shelving units with a tin of white gloss. After a few turns of a screwdriver they wobbled no more, and were now home to various knick-knacks and colourful pieces of pottery. Standard lamps and table lights were fitted with bulbs and new plugs, providing ambient lighting throughout. Jinnie had gone to town with Sam's pricing gun where she could, and elsewhere she'd cut rectangles of craft card and used silver and gold pens to write out the prices in her best writing. Customers were still thin on the ground, but a few curious locals had dropped in, having heard both of the 'new girl in town' and the changes taking place.

'Aye, you've done a good job, hen,' declared Janette Cameron, when Jinnie popped into the post office/corner shop for a few things. Janette worked there part-time, and was a colourful and opinionated character. 'It was a right old shite heap before, excuse my language.' Janette looked anywhere between fifty and eighty, with fiercely cropped grey hair, a mouth so tightly pinched that it resembled a cat's arse, and a wardrobe that must contain at least half of Scotland's Crimplene supply.

Determined to also make Brae Cottage more attractive, Jinnie had finally unpacked. That ordeal over, she had covered the weathered sofas with colourful throws, hung the handful of cheap but cheerful prints she owned on the faded walls, and added a few lamps with low-voltage bulbs to turn its inherent gloominess into something warmer. Hannah had often said Jinnie should consider doing a course in interior design. 'You've definitely got a knack for making crap look good,' she'd announced when Jinnie had spent a productive afternoon re-jigging her friend's flat to ward off the post-Mark blues.

In her short time in Cranley, Jinnie had bought stamps and basic groceries from the shop. Milk, bread and tinned soup were essentially her staple diet when she wasn't being treated by Jo or Sam. But Jinnie knew her mum would have a couple of bags of goodies to take away when she visited for Sunday lunch. 'Just some bits and bobs, pet, to tide you over,' she'd say, handing over enough food to fill a Red Cross parcel.

Jo had also been impressed with Jinnie's handiwork at Sam's shop, though less fruity in her choice of language. She'd arrived with a bag of scones and a slab of gingerbread, shooing away Jinnie's protests that she was too kind. 'There's always stuff left over, sweetheart, and I can't bear it going to waste,' she'd said, before oohing and aahing over the transformation. 'What a difference! Sam might not uncover any treasure on his antique-finding missions, but I think he's discovered a true gem in you!' Jinnie had blushed and stammered her thanks, hoping Jo didn't see her as a charity case; some kind of downtrodden waif exiled from her native land (a mere five miles away).

Now it was late Friday afternoon, and Jinnie had the boss's permission to shut up shop, grab her overnight bag and head to the city for a girls' night out. Sam had appeared at lunchtime and handed her an envelope. 'Your first salary from Out of the Attic,' he said. 'Plus a little extra for making the place look a bit less "car boot sale", and a lot more "hidden treasures within".'

Jinnie's bottom lip had quivered perilously as she scrutinised the contents and realised he'd overpaid her. By quite a lot.

Before she could speak, Sam held up his index finger and touched it lightly to her lips. 'Trains cost money, and I suspect your night out might involve a few drinks and a kebab or two.' He smiled. 'Enjoy, but not so much that you decide to abandon me.'

Sam had also waved aside Jinnie's offer to pay for a few things she'd taken a shine to: an Indonesian tapestry wall hanging, a chipped ceramic bowl, and a battered old oil lamp with blackened stones around its circumference. 'They've been kicking around here for ages,' he said, 'and I can't even remember where they came from. Probably a car boot sale. Don't let it slip, but that's one of my favourite scavenging grounds.'

Back at the cottage, Jinnie tossed her toiletries in a bag and paused. The little black dress swung forlornly on its hook, back and forth like a pendulum of misery. It had been an impulse buy, a desperate attempt to cheer herself up after Mark's heartless dumping. The day he'd announced they were over. His actual words being: 'Sorry, but I just don't find you attractive anymore.' They remained seared on her heart, whispered in her ear all the long nights she'd struggled to sleep in the aftermath. The stupid dress hadn't helped. All it had achieved was to further empty her dwindling bank account. Still, she'd bought it and hadn't a clue where the receipt was, so…

Jinnie folded the dress and placed it at the top of her holdall. She'd wear it out tonight with the girls, as they were hitting up a new bar in the West End and Hannah had texted to say the dress code was 'smart'. All she needed were her best pair of black suede heels and a statement necklace to add some bling. Opening her jewellery box, Jinnie pushed aside several necklaces until she found the right one — a thick, twisted silver rope. She lifted it up and —

There it was. Dazzling, beautiful and a heartbreaking reminder of what would never be. Her engagement ring, a cushion-cut solitaire diamond set in a platinum band. Mark had, surprisingly, not demanded it back, and Jinnie had ripped it from her finger the day he told her it was over. She'd briefly considered tossing it into the Water of Leith in dramatic, spurned-fiancée fashion, but common sense had prevailed. She didn't know *exactly* how much it had cost, but several zeros were involved. Perhaps she could sell or pawn it, if her financial situation got worse.

With fifteen minutes before she needed to leave to catch her train, Jinnie unpacked her bag of swag from the shop. She'd hang the tapestry over her bed when she got back. The bowl would look nice on the coffee table, filled with potpourri to mask the damp pong that no amount of window-opening or air-freshener-squirting seemed to eradicate. As for the lamp … it was a sad-looking thing, with several dents in the lid and a layer of filth that would need some serious elbow grease. Why had she taken it? Maybe because its downtrodden, unloved appearance mirrored her own life. All it needed — all *she* needed — was a good old rub-down. A stripping-away of all that was tarnished and tainted. She'd party her socks off tonight, but on *her* terms. If a man came on to her, Jinnie would laugh and chat, but she'd go home alone. Well, back to Hannah's lumpy sofa bed.

Jinnie pulled on her old, comfortable jacket. Mark had called it her 'bin man coat', which had wounded at the time. Now, she didn't care. If she told herself that often enough, she might start to believe it.

She picked up the lamp, and gave it a swift once-over with her sleeve. Then she looked at her watch. 'Oh my!' she exclaimed, picked up her bag, and ran for her train.

Seconds later, a strange *thump-thump-thump* noise echoed around the room...

CHAPTER 7

'Jinnnnnnie!'

Hannah's greeting could have shattered glasses several streets away, and her hug threatened to crush a few ribs too. Clearly, she and her pals had already been imbibing. Through the hallway Jinnie could see a kitchen table cluttered with bottles, and Pink pulsated through the audio system.

Jinnie shrugged off her jacket and accepted a tumbler of something frothy and yellow. *What the hell is this?* She took a sip, grimaced, and headed to the kitchen. A Diet Coke or glass of water was what she needed. At least, for now.

'So, hun, how's life in Hicksville?' hiccuped Hannah. She giggled and pulled mutual friend Shona in for a cuddle. There were five of them hitting the town — Jinnie, Hannah, Shona, Shalini and Jacqui. All were dressed to the nines, bar Jinnie who'd travelled in jeans, T-shirt and Converse boots.

'I'll just pop upstairs and get changed, OK?' she murmured to Hannah, grabbing a can of Coke from the fridge. A few thirsty gulps later, she was stripping off amidst the chaos that was Hannah's bedroom. For a woman who took such care of her appearance, her room resembled a crime scene. One in which a gang of thugs took delight in emptying every cupboard and drawer on the floor, then paused to eat several bowls of Rice Krispies and apply every item of make-up at their disposal before strewing face powder, eyeshadow and blusher across the dressing table. Even the bedding was more crumpled than a paper bag. If Hannah owned an iron, she only used it for clothing.

The black dress looked great, the chunky necklace complementing its simplicity. Sheer black tights and heels completed the look. Jinnie touched up her lipstick, checked she had her purse and went back downstairs. Hannah wolf-whistled, and gave Jinnie a double thumbs-up.

The new bar, Diablo, was a fifteen-minute walk from Hannah's flat. On the way they passed the Scott Monument, and Jinnie's thoughts turned to Sam. What would he be doing on a Friday night? Typing furiously on his computer? Slobbing in front of the TV? Or wining and dining some gorgeous woman? Damn, she still hadn't looked him up online, or quizzed Jo on his background. Not that it was any of her business, but…

'Any talent in Cranley?' asked Hannah as they queued at the bar for a round of drinks. The place was packed, and the other three were circling like sequinned sharks in search of a table. 'You mentioned your new boss, what's he like?'

A barman waved at them, and Jinnie yelled out their order over the din of the crowd. They'd agreed on a kitty, each putting twenty pounds towards the drinks. As it was happy hour the drinks were half price, but she hoped they'd sip them rather than down them.

Hannah nudged her. 'Come on, spill!'

Jinnie sighed. 'He's lovely, but I'm not looking for a man

right now, Hannah. I need to heal myself before I can let someone else into my heart.' Yuck, where had *that* come from?

Luckily, Hannah had already tottered off towards the girls, who'd squeezed in with a group of twenty-something guys — all frayed jeans, checked shirts and man buns, clutching pints and looking bemused at their new companions. Shalini was telling a joke, already creased up before the punchline.

Shona and Jacqui eagerly snatched their drinks from Hannah. Jinnie, behind her, gulped as they, well, *gulped* down half the contents.

'Budge up!' screeched Hannah at the lumberjack posse. How they'd ended up in this place, surely a far cry from their usual post-student haunts, was anyone's guess. Probably the lure of cheap beer, the froth of which adhered to their chins. These were shrouded in beards, or covered in a smattering of wispy hairs which Jinnie's mum would have dismissed as bum fluff.

'Hi,' said Jinnie, for want of something better to say to her hirsute companion. 'I … erm … like your hair. I mean on your head, not the beard. Not that I've anything against beards. They're useful, aren't they?' Oh, for fuck's sake, what was she babbling on about? Useful for what? Hiding toast crumbs? Disguising receding jawlines?

Jinnie wiggled closer, not because she fancied him but because one butt cheek was hanging uncomfortably off the bench. Then she decided to examine his man bun further. Amazing how emboldened one could be after a mere mouthful of a Sex on the Beach. Well, you had to have a cocktail during happy hour. It looked nice and shiny, but — eurgh! — smelt of stale smoke and unwashed socks.

Jinnie retreated, figuring she could perch for a while.

Either Mr Stinky caught the look of distaste on her face, or realised the beer prices were about to double, but he and his hairy mates departed minutes later.

'Slim pickings in here, eh Shona?' Hannah scanned the room, wrinkling her nose up at the male specimens dotted around. They were either huddled in groups or paired up with partners or wives. Nothing new there, and no different to themselves. Out hunting in a pack, although Shalini and Jacqui both had boyfriends.

Hannah rarely stuck with the same man for more than a few months. They either wanted to get serious too quickly, or Hannah would nitpick flaws that even Sherlock Holmes with a supersized magnifying glass would be hard-pressed to find. 'He has a weird belly button!' she complained about one poor soul. 'It looks like a wodge of old chewing gum.' Another had been given the heave-ho because he always hung the toilet roll the wrong way round. 'Anyone who thinks you should access the roll from *below* is not a keeper,' Hannah had declared, arms folded in defiance.

Shalini returned with another round of drinks, jubilant that she'd caught the end of happy hour. Jinnie had watched her crawl through several pairs of legs to get to the bar, and admired her determination. 'Right, ladies, do we hang around after these, or head to Shenanigans?' she asked. 'I'm not feeling the love for this place, and at least there the cocktails won't bankrupt us.'

Not so sure about that, Jinnie thought. She needed to spin out her meagre salary as long as possible, and the train journey to see her parents on Sunday would swallow up another chunk.

Before she could reply, a group of suited men strode past them. Bringing up the rear was an all-too-familiar figure, tie pulled down and white shirt open at the collar. Mark, looking as handsome as ever. Praying he wouldn't see her, Jinnie slid under the table.

'What are you *doing?*' hissed Hannah, leaning down and nearly tipping her Bay Breeze over Jinnie's head.

'Mark's just walked in and I really, really don't want him to see me,' Jinnie hissed back. Even now, Jinnie would look at her reflection and wince at every perceived imperfection. The last thing she needed was to face Mark again and know that he was probably thinking: *Phew, that was a lucky escape! Imagine how ugly our kids would be if her genes won out!*

Popping up like a submariner's periscope, Jinnie was relieved to see that Mark and his mates were at the far side of the bar. Time to make an escape...

'Listen, girls, I don't want to be a party pooper but I think I'll head off. I mean, back to Cranley.' Suddenly Jinnie *needed* to be back in her own poky little place. It might not be big-city swanky, but it was home. And somehow — weirdly — she couldn't wait until morning.

With wails of 'Don't go!' and 'We barely got to chat!' ringing in her ears, Jinnie bolted for the door. She had a spare key for Hannah's place, so she could grab her stuff and catch a late train.

A little over an hour later, Jinnie flopped down on her bed. Kicking off her heels, she fought back a wave of tears. She'd so wanted to have a fun evening out. Just hanging with the girls, having a laugh and putting her sad, financially challenged life in a box marked *Open When Ready.* Would she ever be?

Ready for bed, with a used facial wipe clutched in her hand, Jinnie looked at the oil lamp. It definitely needed a bit of TLC. *Bit like me*, she thought, smiled, and gave it a quick buff with the wipe. *Marginally better.*

Sleep wasn't long in coming. Jinnie drifted off, dreaming

of being carried away by a semi-clad hunk with a wicked glint in his eye. As she rolled on to her back, her gentle snores synchronised with the rhythmic throbbing emanating from the bedside table.

CHAPTER 8

'Pass the spuds, lad.' Rob Cooper ladled gravy over his roast beef. Jinnie's brother, Archie, was, predictably, hogging the roast potatoes, and had already topped up his wine glass for the second time.

Jinnie suppressed a sigh of irritation. They both knew that their parents weren't rolling in it, but they always made a big effort for Sunday lunch — roast beef or chicken with all the trimmings, and a couple of bottles of whatever was on special at the supermarket. Jinnie had brought pudding, an apple crumble she'd picked up from A Bit of Crumpet at a knockdown price, because Jo had insisted it was past its sell-by-date. Which was pretty much how Jinnie felt after Friday night's disaster.

'Chill, Dad,' grumbled Archie, handing over the prized potatoes. 'Mum's made enough to feed the five thousand and still have leftovers.' He added a couple of Yorkshire puddings to his plate, belching loudly as he did so.

'Manners, Archie!' reprimanded Kath, although in a gentle rather than a shocked tone. Jinnie's brother was her miracle child, the one she never thought would happen. Nine years after Jinnie was born, Kath realised her tightening waistband wasn't just down to a love of chocolate and chips. She'd been thirty when she had Jinnie, almost forty when Archie's presence was confirmed during an incredulous trip to the doctor. He was still their blue-eyed boy, even if he treated their home like a free hotel.

'Better out than in!' retorted Archie. He grinned at Jinnie, who rolled her eyes in disgust.

'How's the music going?' she enquired sweetly. 'Is Kanye West quaking in his Yeezys yet?'

Archie's response was another prolonged belch, which once upon a time would have earned him a stern rebuke from their dad. Nowadays, though, Rob's hearing was a bit dodgy, and he rarely bothered to put his hearing aids in.

'Maybe you could record your most attractive burps and release that?' Jinnie smiled. 'With a few techno beats, it might be a whole new genre.'

'At least I'm doing something creative, sis, instead of — what is it now? Working in a scabby old junk shop. Mind you, it's kind of appropriate for an old crock like you!' Archie reached for the wine bottle just as Jinnie flicked a forkful of peas in his direction.

'Right, you two, enough with the sniping! Why can't we just have a nice family meal? Your gran would bang your heads together if she saw you fighting.' Kath sighed. 'It's a shame her gout's been giving her gyp again.' Then she brightened. 'Maybe you could pop in and say hello later, Jinnie. I know she'd love to see you.'

Jinnie and Archie's gran — Rob's mother, Wilma — lived in a tiny bungalow a couple of streets away. She was eighty-six and fit as a fiddle, gout notwithstanding, and a familiar sight in town, wheeling her tartan shopping trolley with *You're a long time deid!* embroidered on the side. She was regarded as a bit eccentric, chiefly because she smoked roll-ups and offered anyone who entered her home a tea-leaf reading.

'Will do, Mum. I'll take her some crumble if there's any left over.' Said crumble was now warming in the oven, and Jinnie would ensure that Archie didn't lick the dish clean.

Before pudding, Jinnie helped her mum to load the dishwasher and put the pots and pans in to soak. Archie, predictably, had sloped off to his old bedroom, from which the melancholic twanging of a guitar could be heard. Rob was in the living room, checking that all the TV shows he and Kath watched were being recorded. Soaps, crime thrillers, wildlife documentaries and game shows — they watched them all, and were frequently confused by the more intricate plot lines. 'No, that's not the one where they found the body stuffed in the chest freezer. You're mixing it up with that *other* one when the scorned husband pours bleach into the wife's fish tank,' they'd squabble, between trying to beat each other on the *Countdown* conundrum.

Jinnie didn't even have a TV. She couldn't justify the £150 licence fee, and she didn't want the licence-dodger people hammering on her door and hitting her with a fine. A pile of second-hand books and her old but reliable Kindle kept her entertained in the evenings, since diving into the pages of someone else's life helped to distract her from her own.

'How are you coping, love? You know … since Mark?'

Kath's hesitant question brought tears to Jinnie's eyes. Seeing him again on Friday evening had ripped away a flimsy layer of the protective shell she'd tried to build up since he'd trodden on her heart.

'I'm fine, Mum, honestly,' Jinnie replied in her brightest voice, swiping a damp cloth over the counter top. 'I know the job isn't ideal, but I like my boss, and I'm going to ask if I can do a few shifts at the local pub. Just till I get back on my feet.' It hadn't dawned on her before, but Jinnie wondered if

Ken could do with an extra pair of hands. She still felt guilty for judging him harshly, so perhaps she could offer some help.

Kath tucked the tea towel over the handle of the oven door, and pulled Jinnie in for a hug. 'Listen, love, if you need some cash to tide you over, you know Dad and I will always see you right. We've got a little put aside for a rainy day, but making sure you and Archie are OK ... that's our priority.'

Jinnie's nose tickled as she fought back a full-blown howling session. *Is this what parenting's all about*, she thought. *Even in your sixties, fretting and scrimping to protect your darling children? Should I just get my tubes tied and save decades of worry and strife?* She wondered if she would ever be fit to be a mother, seeing as she could barely look after herself at the moment.

'Don't be daft. I'm coping, and Mark is ancient history. Anyway, you never really liked him, did you?' On the handful of occasions they'd visited as a couple, Jinnie knew Mark had looked down his perfectly proportioned nose at her humble family home. Yes, he'd always been polite, but still gave off an air of superiority: the lord of the manor gracing his servants with an appearance. In contrast, his parents had welcomed Jinnie with warmth and genuine affection. His snobbery had not been inherited from them.

'I ... well ... I just never thought he was good enough for you, love. Despite his money and his fancy ways. And his eyebrows were too close together. As Wilma always says...'

Beware of those whose eyebrows meet, for in their hearts there lies deceit. Jinnie knew the line well, one of many spouted by her gran. Complete codswallop. She should write her own modern version — *Beware of he who writes on cups, for he will be a total twat.* OK, poetry would never be her thing, but the sentiment was valid. And speaking of cups...

'I'll skip pudding, mum, if that's OK, but I'll just dollop

some into a dish and take it round to Gran's.' Again, Jinnie
felt the pull of getting home as strongly as a magnet.

In the hallway, after kissing her dad goodbye and yelling
upstairs to Archie with no response, Jinnie accepted the bag
of home-baked goodies proffered by her mum. On top was a
dog-eared paperback entitled *Be Careful What You Wish For*.

'Found it in the local charity shop. It's about following
your heart, but never losing sight of what's important,' said
Kath, tucking a loose strand of Jinnie's hair behind her ear.
'Don't forget that you're number one, love, and we're always
here for you.'

Plodding down the road, damp-eyed and lost in thought,
Jinnie realised the straps of the laden carrier bag were
cutting painfully into her fingers. She put it down to change
hands, and the book slid out and tumbled on to the pavement. A fifty-pound note fluttered from its pages, and Jinnie
trapped it with her foot before it blew away. 'Thanks, Mum,'
she whispered, before turning the corner to Gran's house.

CHAPTER 9

'JINNIE! WHAT A SIGHT FOR SORE EYES!' ROARED WILMA, backing into the hallway to allow Jinnie in. This was no mean feat, as the walls were stacked high with old magazines, vinyl records and dog-eared books. Wilma was a hoarder and proud of it, her bungalow so crammed with oddities she would soon be forced to camp out in the postage-stamp-sized garden.

'How are you doing, Gran?' asked Jinnie, pecking her on a heavily powdered cheek. She sidled towards the kitchen, following Wilma who muttered a few expletives under her breath.

'Ach, I'm not bad, except for this stupid gout and a bit of a chesty cough.' Wilma filled the kettle and sat down, gesturing for Jinnie to do the same. She immediately pulled her tin of tobacco and papers towards her, and began rolling a cigarette. Jinnie placed the dish of crumble on the table, and resisted the urge to comment on the wisdom of smoking when poorly. Anyone who dared to mention Wilma's roll-ups or fondness for wine boxes received an ear-bashing. 'I'm eighty-six, and if giving up my vices means I'll be dribbling in an old folks' home waiting for a telegram from the Queen, you can bugger right off!' was her usual response.

Wilma's laptop, a present from Jinnie's parents a few years ago, was open, showing her Twitter feed. Despite, or possibly to stick two fingers up at, her advancing years, Jinnie's gran had embraced social media with frightening fervour. She posted photos on Instagram, rude cartoons on Facebook, and had over 3000 followers on Twitter. Why people would be interested in an octogenarian ranting on about the price of tobacco, the folly of tattoos and how she still thought about sex at least once a day was anyone's guess. And she still persisted in talking about hagtashes, which in Jinnie's opinion was much better than the actual word.

'Right, let's get this brew sorted, then I'll read your leaves.' Wilma spooned tea into the pot and poured on hot water. She swirled the pot around a few times, nodding to Jinnie to fetch cups and saucers. Teabags were an abomination in Wilma's eyes. She had been known to snip them open when visiting friends, always scoffing about their inferiority to the loose stuff.

'More to the point, how are *you*? Found yersel' a new fella yet?' Wilma poured the tea, sparking up her roll-up at the same time.

An acrid plume of smoke drifted across the table, making Jinnie's eyes water. She sloshed some milk into her cup and took a sip. 'Nope, and I'm not looking either,' she said, putting her cup down. 'So don't think you can go fixing me up with so-and-so's grandson.' Jinnie mock-scowled at her gran, who responded by blowing a perfect set of smoke rings.

'Ach, you're well shot of that monobrowed moron,' Wilma said. 'In fact, all you need is a good vibrator and something decent on Netflix. Come to think of it, there's a crackin' site I saw on the web the other day. Free delivery, and returns if not fully satisfied. Mind you, cannae imagine anyone having the nerve to send one back already used!'

Jinnie giggled, well used to her gran's outspokenness. To avoid being subjected to an onscreen array of sex toys, she drained her cup, leaving a teaspoonful of liquid at the bottom. 'OK, Gran, let's see what the future has in store for me.' Well-versed in the ritual, Jinnie took the cup in her left hand and swirled it counter-clockwise three times. She carefully inverted it over the saucer, then turned the cup the right way up, revealing a random pattern of leaves stuck inside.

'Hmm, what do we have here? Pass it over, sweetie.' Wilma gazed into the cup, still puffing away on her cigarette. It was a miracle she could see anything through the fug of smoke. She brought it closer to her nose, using her saucer as an ashtray. 'Looks a bit like … an umbrella.'

Jinnie peered, unable to detect anything more than a shapeless blob. She knew better than to comment, however, as Wilma took her readings very seriously.

'What does an umbrella mean?' she asked, visions of torrential rain and leaking roofs flashing through her brain. Brae Cottage wasn't in the best of shape, and heavy downpours were a year-long feature of the area.

'A new lover,' Wilma replied, eyes flashing with mischief. Jinnie shook her head, determined to steer away from that topic.

'Fine, fine. Let's have another look. While I'm at it, stick that pudding thing in the microwave and we can have a wee slice after.'

Jinnie dutifully peeled off the foil lid and put the crumble on to heat. As she rummaged in Wilma's shoebox-sized freezer drawer for ice cream, a triumphant whoop made her jump. 'Got it!' cried Wilma. 'Clear as day, now I've had another gander. Here, look yersel', Jinnie.'

As the microwave pinged, Jinnie leaned over her gran's

shoulder. Nope, still a shapeless blob, although it might just be — 'Erm, is it a tadpole?' she asked, then instantly regretted it. Judging by the jubilant expression on Wilma's face, she was about to announce that it was a sperm and that Jinnie would be 'up the duff' — another of her gran's favourite sayings — in a matter of months. And that would certainly *not* be happening.

'No, ye daftie! It's a kite. There's the pointy top bit, and the trailing string with a wee bow on it. Can ye no' see it? Never mind, dish up some of that crumble. My tummy's rumbling like the furies.'

With bowls of pudding and ice cream before them, Jinnie and Wilma munched contentedly, the cup's contents temporarily forgotten. Jinnie chatted between mouthfuls about her new job and the cottage, leaving out any mention of Sam lest Wilma go off on another new-man rant.

'Best crumble ever,' Wilma declared, dabbing at her furrowed lips with a tissue. 'My Rob made a smart move, marrying your mum. The way to a man's heart and all that. Do you do much cooking yersel', Jinnie?'

Reluctant to discuss her entry-level cooking skills, Jinnie picked up her cup again and gazed into it. 'Right, so it's a kite, which means —'

'A wish coming true. If you had one wish right now, what would it be?' Wilma coughed heartily, eyed her tobacco tin wistfully, then picked up a glass and leaned towards a box of Cabernet Sauvignon perched at the edge of the table. 'One for the road?'

Jinnie shook her head as Wilma filled the glass to the brim. She had no idea what she would wish for. To have Mark back? No, no and a thousand times no. To find more direction, more purpose in her life? Probably, but baby steps were enough for now: getting back on her feet, financially at least, and then seeing where things led. A wish for global peace, an end to famine and all the other horrors she witnessed on the news? Jinnie was sure that millions of people wished for these things daily, to no avail. And what were wishes, anyway? Just vague little wisps of hope that rose and popped, as fleeting as the bubbles in a champagne glass.

'I don't have a wish, Gran. Except to be healthy and happy. And for you, and Mum and Dad, and Archie and Hannah, and everyone I know and love, to be OK. That's it. End of.'

To her horror, Jinnie's eyes filled with tears, and one spilled over and dripped on to her T-shirt. She dabbed at it with her finger, aware of Wilma's concerned stare. A moment later, her gran had shuffled over and wrapped her tobacco and perfume-scented arms around Jinnie's heaving shoulders.

'Everybody has a wish, sweetie. It's just you don't always know what you want — or need — until someone points you in the right direction. Save it for now. When the time's right, you'll know. Trust me.'

A short while later, Jinnie gathered up her stuff and hugged her gran tightly. It was time to head back to Cranley and all it had — or didn't have — to offer. She'd speak to Ken about some bar work, and her sparkling ring might just find its way to a reputable pawnbroker.

'Don't be a stranger, sweetie,' said Wilma. 'You know I'm always here, a wee bit deaf and full of shite, but you wouldnae want a gran who knits and bakes, would yae?'

Jinnie shook her head. She was glad of her badass Gran, with her antisocial habits, serious attitude, and obsession with tea leaves. The logo on her bag, about being dead for a long time, summed up her take on life. If only Jinnie could be even a tenth as brave...

'Take care, Jinnie,' said Wilma, shoving the uppermost pile

of teetering magazines back into position. 'My door's always open for tea, sympathy and wine. And dinnae forget my favourite motto.'

Jinnie smiled as she kissed her gran goodbye. In unison they chanted: 'Whit's fur ye'll no go by ye!' *If things are meant to happen, they will*. With the phrase running through her mind on a loop, Jinnie headed for the station.

CHAPTER 10

'HOW WAS YOUR WEEKEND?' SAM ASKED WHEN JINNIE ARRIVED for work on Monday morning. He was standing on a ladder, attempting to hang a glittering chandelier. As he wobbled alarmingly, Jinnie steadied the bottom of the ladder and tried not to stare at his exposed stomach as his shirt rode up. Toned, lightly tanned and with a pleasing amount of body hair. Jinnie had always had a bit of a thing about body hair. A tantalising glimpse of chest hair protruding from an open-necked shirt got her a little hot and bothered. Strange, really, as Mark's chest had been smooth as a baby's bottom, while his own bottom was surprisingly hirsute by comparison.

'Not bad,' she replied, stepping aside as Sam climbed down to safety. 'The girls' night out was a bit of a damp squib, but it was lovely to see my folks. Oh, and my gran is an absolute hoot. I want to be just like her when I grow up!' OK, maybe without the smoking and the tea leaves, just with that devil-may-care *joie de vivre.* 'What did you get up to? Were you writing?'

Jinnie had quickly managed to look up Alistair Scott on

Amazon before she left her Mum and Dad's. Blimey, he had *hundreds* of five and four-star ratings, and was clearly raking in some decent money if his rankings were anything to go by. Her personal favourite review, though, was a one-star moaning that 'I haven't read it yet'. Honestly, people could be so stupid!

'A bit of writing, yes, and a short FaceTime chat with my son,' said Sam.

Damn, thought Jinnie, *he's married! Or is that an assumption too far?* 'Oh yes?' was all she said.

'He's in his first year at Stirling University, and pinning him down for a catch-up is no mean feat,' Sam continued. 'I sometimes message him to ask if he's still alive. Still, he's doing well, and hopefully he'll manage a visit here at some point soon.'

'Oh, does he speak to his mum more often?' The words were out before Jinnie could stop them, and she felt her cheeks warming up. 'I mean … sorry, none of my business, I just wondered…'

Oh, help. Sam's normal cheery expression had vanished, and his demeanour had turned distinctly glacial. Maybe she'd died in a horrible accident, or run off with her hunky gym instructor. Or maybe, just maybe, Sam simply didn't appreciate Jinnie sticking her Caesar-like nose into his private life.

He was silent for a moment, then a sad smile crept across his face. 'Yes, I think he does. We're divorced and don't communicate much, although we try to maintain a united front when it comes to Sean. That's my son, our only child, and the best thing to come out of a less-than-happy marriage. Now, who's on brew duty?'

Jinnie busied herself making coffee and arranging custard creams artistically on a willow-patterned plate. She felt bad for asking about Sam's wife, yet ridiculously relieved to know they weren't together. What was *that* all about? Hadn't she sworn off men for the foreseeable future? Jinnie needed to have a stern word with her libido. Along the lines of *Down girl, get back in your box pronto.*

They worked companionably for the rest of the day, selling a few bits and pieces to some tourists who'd ventured further than the capital. A Japanese couple snapped up the chandelier for an eye-watering sum, declaring it perfect for their apartment in Osaka. They didn't even flinch at the shipping costs.

At four o'clock Sam shooed Jinnie out, telling her to drop by the pub. 'Ken's too proud to ask, but I know he'd welcome some help if you need a bit of extra cash. He's a big softie really, and having you behind the bar might draw a few more punters.'

Jinnie blushed at the compliment and strode off to The Jekyll and Hyde, fully intending to chat to Ken. But as she approached, a car screeched to a halt by the main door. A tall, bearded man leapt out, to be greeted with great enthusiasm by Ken. His son Ed, perhaps. Her guess was reinforced by Mags appearing behind Ken and hugging the stranger with gusto.

Not wanting to intrude, Jinnie made her way home for a slap-up tea, courtesy of her mum's food parcel. Home-made chicken and leek pie followed by sticky toffee pudding. Carbs be damned! A little light reading might be in order too, although Jinnie doubted *Be Careful What You Wish For* would hit the spot. She'd had enough talk of wishes over the weekend. Right now, her only desire was for tasty grub and a bit of peace and quiet.

Two hours later, Jinnie was nursing a giant food baby and had tossed aside a novel. It was a romantic comedy, a genre she normally enjoyed, but the heroine was so sickly sweet and the hero so dull that she couldn't bear to continue. Instead, she dragged herself upstairs with the intention of hanging the tapestry she'd procured from the shop. No potpourri yet for the bowl, and the lamp still looked forlorn and neglected. Luckily she'd snaffled a tube of metal polish from Sam's array of products, which was sitting on the kitchen counter. Could she be bothered to fetch it? Ah well, at least another trip downstairs would burn a calorie or two…

With polish and cloth in hand, Jinnie sat on the bed and picked up the lamp. There wasn't much she could do about the dents, but restoring some of its former lustre would help. Carefully she squeezed a dollop of polish onto the cloth and began rubbing. Immediately a patch of shiny gold appeared and … hang on … was it her imagination, or did the lamp just *move*? Tentatively Jinnie rubbed the lamp again, and it vibrated in her hand. With a shriek she jumped to her feet, and the lamp bounced, then rolled across the floor. Heart pounding, Jinnie watched it come to rest below the window.

Suddenly the lamp started spinning at high speed, then rose from the floor, disappearing in a whirling grey cloud of smoke. Jinnie gasped, and squeezed the polish tube so hard it squirted down the front of her blouse. Unable to tear her eyes away, she backed up slowly, fell backwards onto the bed and banged her head on the wall. 'Ouch!' she squealed, at the same time as a disembodied voice emitted a similar cry of pain. *What the—?*

As the mini cyclone subsided, Jinnie made out a vague shape which shimmered and grew, the outline becoming more distinct. More … *manlike*. This could *not* be happening, it simply wasn't possible, except…

'You wouldn't happen to be a masseuse, would you, pumpkin? Because my muscles are, like, *totally* in knots.' The apparition, for want of a better word, stretched its arms and proceeded to perform a series of side bends. 'Ooh, the agony! Actually, some of that Deep Heat stuff might do the trick. Got any to hand?'

Jinnie gawped, unable to utter a single word. Surreal didn't begin to cover the situation and … where the heck did *pumpkin* come from? As the final traces of smoke dispersed, she saw a rather scrawny figure, clad in billowing purple silk harem pants. His upper half was bare, and whiter than a Scotsman stripping down after a long, cold winter. Wait a minute, surely he wasn't a —?

'Jinnie!' her unexpected companion shrieked, slapping his forehead with a bangle-strewn arm.

Wait, wasn't that *her* line? 'You're a … genie, right?' she stammered. 'I mean, the lamp's a bit of a clue, now I think about it. Oh, hang on, you just called me by my name, didn't you?'

With a sweeping bow, he moved closer. Jinnie stood and faced him. Up close, he had finely-chiselled features, accentuated by a wispy goatee beard. His eyes were the colour of amber, and his full-lipped mouth curled somewhere between a smirk and a scowl.

'Darling girl, that term is *so* outdated. I prefer personal wish-fulfilment assistant, although it is rather a mouthful. Probably easier if you call me by my name: Dhassim. It means "the idolised", by the way.'

Hmm, thought Jinnie. Judging by his widening smirk, Dhassim hadn't been at the front of the queue when modesty was dished out. Which wasn't really relevant right now. How was this even *possible,* and how did he know her name?

Before Jinnie could speak again, a loud gurgling sound emanated from Dhassim's stomach. 'Before we get into all the wish-fulfilling nitty-gritty, would you be an angel and rustle up a little snack? Being cooped up in a lamp for centuries plays havoc with the digestion!'

And so Jinnie found herself rummaging in the bathroom cabinet for some muscle-soothing gel, then preparing a cheese and pickle sandwich, all the time wondering just *where* this was going to lead…

CHAPTER 11

JO PULLED A TRAY OF FRESHLY-BAKED PASTIES FROM THE OVEN, cursing as yet again she burned herself in the process. She'd invested in longer oven gloves, but still managed to add to her collection of scars on a regular basis. She adjusted her glasses, and scrutinised the angry red mark.

'Maybe I need a suit of armour,' Jo grumbled under her breath. Certainly not a chastity belt, as it had been a very long time since anyone had tried to get her into bed. OK, there *had* been one occasion two years ago. She'd taken herself off for a much-needed mini break in the Scottish Highlands, and got chatting to a handsome stranger over a glass of single malt. With a log fire roaring in the hearth, enough tartan to kit out the cast of *Braveheart,* and the Proclaimers singing about walking ridiculous lengths to be with a loved one, Jo had felt all squidgy and desirable. Well, by her third glass of whisky, at least.

Her handsome stranger — 'The name's Pete' — seemed like the perfect gentleman. Until he'd opened his overnight bag to reveal his 'n' hers latex suits and a couple of feather dusters. 'Are you up for a bit of slap and tickle?' he'd asked. Jo was torn between slapping him, bursting into tears, or ordering another whisky. She'd opted for another drink which she took to her room, its peaty (excruciating pun alert) scent mingling with toothpaste and mouthwash. No, you weren't supposed to drink *after* brushing your teeth, but Jo had felt the need to sip the comforting liquid as she sat in bed and pondered her disastrous love life.

She'd come close to marriage once, in her early thirties, but as the wedding day approached Jo had got cold feet. In fact, make that toe-numbing frostbite. Her fiancé, Graham, was kind, but a complete marshmallow when it came to life and people. He never stood up for himself, even when his bosses at work treated him like something unpleasant stuck to their shoe, and as for his mother, Felicia… Jo shuddered at the memory of the woman who had never cut the apron-strings. More like traded them for industrial-strength rope to secure her compliant son. Graham was always at her beck and call, and they chatted on the phone at least four times a day. She wasn't ill or frail in any way: simply a control freak who'd made it clear from day one that Jo wasn't good enough. While Graham had been devastated when Jo broke off the engagement, Felicia had probably ordered champagne and balloons to celebrate.

Running her burn under the cold tap, Jo reflected on all that was good in her life. She'd bought A Bit of Crumpet five years ago, as a fortieth birthday present to herself. Over two decades of working in hospitality and catering had earned her both a wealth of experience and a decent pot of money, which she'd invested in a solid range of stocks and shares. Although originally from the west coast — by the bonnie banks of Loch Lomond — Jo had always had a soft spot for the east and Edinburgh. When the premises came on the market, she hadn't hesitated. Cost-wise, they were a fraction of anything in or near the city, already packed with similar businesses. Cranley was sleepy — downright soporific at times — but it had charm and individuality. So Jo had focused on making A Bit of Crumpet a home-from-home kind of place, serving traditional fare with an emphasis on quality. No skinny lattes or weird herbal brews here, just plain old teas, coffees, cakes and savouries.

'Morning!' Her first customer of the day, Ken McCroarty, slumped into a chair, tiredness etched on his face. Jo liked Ken, whose occasional gruffness masked a kind heart. Dealing with his wife Mags's decline was taking its toll, and Ken had admitted to her the other week that he was struggling to sleep. Mags had started wandering in the night, and once Ken had found her at 3am, shivering and confused in the beer garden.

'Morning, my lovely,' Jo replied, drying her hands and switching on the coffee machine. 'How strong d'you want it? Strong, eye-popping or waking the dead?'

'The last one, Jo,' said Ken, placing his wallet and phone on the table. 'Ed surprised us yesterday, so he's holding the fort while I visit my suppliers and get a few bits in the city.' He sighed. 'Mags was thrilled to see him, then she asked him four times in twenty minutes how long it had taken him to drive over. And the other day she ran herself a bath, then completely forgot about it. Luckily I got there before it brought the ceiling down.'

Jo poured Ken's coffee and placed it in front of him, along with a still-hot pasty. Ken regarded her with bloodshot eyes and a weary smile. 'Just what the doctor ordered. What would we do without the baking queen of Cranley?'

Before Jo could reply, the door opened and Sam strode in. *Two of Cranley's finest gents in the space of a few minutes*, Jo thought to herself. One most definitely and devotedly married, the other … well, who knew? Sam was very easy on the eye, but he kept a low profile. Only she and Ken knew about his writer alter-ego, for instance. Although perhaps he'd confided in Jinnie too? She was a sweet girl — well, woman — who'd clearly escaped to Cranley after a disastrous relationship. Jo was keen to get to know her better, but didn't want to seem pushy or interfering.

'Hi, Sam. Is it takeaway for two, or are you flying solo today?' Jo saw Sam gaze hungrily at the pasty Ken had virtually demolished.

'Just one of those,' he answered. 'Jinnie's not in again until tomorrow. We agreed she'd work Mondays, Wednesdays and Fridays. Speaking of which, did she come and see you, Ken?'

Ken looked puzzled, and Jo concentrated on sliding a pasty into a paper bag.

'Erm, no, she didn't. Why would she come and see me? I get the impression she doesn't like me very much. Not that I like *myself* that much, these days. Ed says I'm a grumpy old git, and he's not wrong.' Ken licked a finger and dabbed at the remaining crumbs of his pasty. Without a word being exchanged, Jo took his plate and added a second helping.

'Sorry, shouldn't have spoken out of turn.' Sam counted out some coins and handed them to Jo. 'Jinnie's looking for extra money, and I thought you might need a part-time barmaid. She's a hard worker, I can vouch for that, and —'

Ken swallowed his bite of pasty. 'Aye, that would be a big help right now. When you see the lass, tell her I said so. Right then. Jobs to be done, people to be argued with. Later, folks.' He got up to leave just as customer number three entered the building.

'Jeez Louise, do I need cake,' announced Janette Cameron, shaking out an umbrella. 'It's pissing doon out there now, and my blood sugar levels are cryin' out for assistance. That'll do, Jo,' she said, pointing a pudgy finger at a chocolate fudge cake under a glass dome.

Jo cut a generous slab and passed it over the counter.

'And a pot of tea too, there's a dear. I've the morning off, so I'm treating mysel' before I catch the train into town. Need some new bras — these puppies have worn out the old yins!' Janette jiggled her ample bosom with both hands, while Ken and Sam watched in amused horror.

Jo carried the tea over to the table where Janette had plonked herself, winking at the two men.

'I'd give you a lift, Janette,' said Ken, 'but I'm visiting my suppliers before I head to Edinburgh.' He didn't quite succeed in hiding his look of relief. A car journey spent discussing bra sizes and styles probably wasn't his idea of a fun-filled outing.

'Nae worries, Ken,' said Janette. 'I'll just take my time here and keep Jo and Sam entertained.' She gave her chest another Les Dawson-like waggle. 'So, I cannae decide between balcony or cleavage-enhancing. Mind yae, my cleavage disnae so much need enhancing as scaffolding!'

Ken was out of the door at lightning speed, followed rapidly by Sam. A few more customers appeared, sparing Jo from any more underwear chat. Janette was a likeable soul, but could talk the hind legs off the proverbial donkey.

After the lunchtime rush, Jo whipped up a batch of scones and a lemon drizzle cake. She normally closed around five, but decided to shut up shop early. Perhaps she could pop in and see Jinnie on the way home. The poor girl always appeared to be starving. Jo wondered how she was coping, both financially and in terms of having a friendly shoulder to cry on. *No,* Jo decided, *that was definitely overstepping the mark.* Better to invite Jinnie out for a drink, or round for supper one night. All she probably needed right now was a quiet life...

CHAPTER 12

'Ooh, baby, baby,' sang Dhassim. He might be 'the idolised', but he'd have received a massive thumbs-down on *Pop Idol*. Tuneless didn't cover it as he bopped around, baggy trousers flapping and upper body glistening. Jinnie had been less than impressed to find he'd snaffled her expensive gold-flecked body oil and smeared it all over his torso. He'd also devoured all her bread, cheese and leftovers from Monday evening.

Now it was Tuesday afternoon, and Jinnie harboured evil thoughts of cramming him back in the lamp. She was ready to scream. Not from fear, or horror at the madness of the situation. No, her grip on sanity was slipping because he was *driving her mad!* Not only had Jinnie been nagged into rubbing Deep Heat into his knotted limbs, but she had had to endure endless tales of 'wish fulfilment' spanning hundreds, if not thousands, of years.

'There was this mediaeval chick — can't remember her name — who dreamed of marrying the local lord. No idea why — he had a face that could turn milk sour. Whereas her boyfriend was a *hunk* of burning love. Just didn't have any dosh. Shallow, or what?' Dhassim flounced across the room, indignation written across his face. 'I granted the wish, they tied the knot, then she spent most of her marriage sneaking off to shag her boyfriend behind the cattle sheds. Until His Nibs cottoned on, and then it was…' He drew a bony finger across his throat, Adam's apple wobbling in sympathy.

By all accounts, Dhassim had been granting wishes for longer than he could remember. Some more successfully than others. He had no recollection of how he'd ended up living in a lamp (Jinnie didn't feel so bad now about the size of Brae Cottage), or why he'd appeared in her life.

'Aren't you supposed to have a master?' she asked. Her knowledge of genie mythology was limited to childhood stories and the Disney cartoon. And Dhassim bore little resemblance to Robin Williams' wise-cracking sidekick. He wasn't blue, and his physique was more stick insect than buff fantasy figure. Mind you, being crammed into an oil lamp didn't leave much scope for bicep curls or crunches.

Dhassim had, thankfully, stopped warbling along to Jinnie's CD collection, and was now nosing in the fridge, sighing dramatically at its meagre contents. 'Yeah, I guess so, although it looks like I now have a *mistress*.' He shot her a look that made her toes curl more than his satin slippers.

As a diversionary tactic Jinnie tossed him a packet of cheese and onion crisps from her handbag. *Damn, there goes the emergency snack supply.*

Ear-bending crooning swapped for nails-on-blackboard crunching, Dhassim sashayed his way upstairs.

Jinnie followed, her temper gaining momentum. 'Listen, Mr Wish-Fulfilment Assistant, I'd really prefer if you didn't treat every inch of my home as your own personal space. In fact, I wish you'd just disappear!'

The words were out before she could stop them. Jinnie held her breath, expecting Dhassim to vanish in a puff of smoke. That would be a shocking waste of a wish, assuming he really did have the power to grant them.

Nope, he was still there: standing outside her bedroom, arms folded and bottom lip protruding. 'Pumpkin, you have hurt my feelings. Here was I, thinking we were getting along so well, and then you say something like that. Ouch!'

Dhassim swivelled around and flounced into the bedroom. Ye gods, the man was camper than a row of tents! And Jinnie still didn't appreciate the 'pumpkin' term of endearment.

Dhassim eyed the lamp, still lying beneath the window, then turned his attention to Jinnie's abdominal trainer, now serving as a makeshift drying-line for her knickers. He swept them aside, wiggled beneath the instrument of torture, and proceeded to count down his progress.

'One, two, three … oof … four, five, six… How did I get *so* out of shape?' Huffing and puffing, he kept going until Jinnie kicked it out of the way.

Undeterred, Dhassim turned over and assumed the plank position. 'Honeybun, you really need to play nice if you want me to hang around,' he whined. 'And wishing that I'd disappear is a no-go area. Now, count me down from one hundred.'

Gritting her teeth, Jinnie did as he asked. Dhassim swayed and wobbled, whistling as he struggled to remain balanced. Remarkably, he made it to the end, and collapsed in a heap on the worn-out rug she'd placed under the abdominal trainer.

Jinnie crouched down and faced Dhassim as he hauled himself upright. 'Look, I appreciate your need to get fit, but can we *please* talk about how this three wishes thing works?'

To her dismay, he let rip with a honking laugh. '*Three* wishes? Wherever did you get that idea from? Oh dearie me, don't go believing all that movie and book nonsense.'

Dhassim admonished Jinnie with a *tut, tut* finger. 'We genies *have* evolved, you know. Nowadays it's all about granting wishes in accordance with their relevance, and in the name of equality, we expect something in return.'

This was getting worse by the minute! What on earth (or wherever he'd materialised from) could Dhassim expect from her? Surely he wasn't … he couldn't … be hinting at some kind of relationship? As in coupling up and making the beast with two backs? And Jinnie wasn't thinking of a camel…

Dhassim rummaged in his capacious trousers. If he so much as *mentioned* a magic wand, Jinnie was ready to run downstairs as fast as her wobbly legs would allow. But he eventually produced what looked like a pedometer. A very glitzy, blingy pedometer, the kind she imagined one of the Kardashians would use, assuming they ever ran anywhere. Dhassim clicked the little button on the top a few times, and the gizmo made a noise like a pub gaming machine, all bells and flashing lights.

Jinnie moved closer, leaning over Dhassim's shoulder to see what the screen showed. All she could make out was a series of numbers flashing past at high speed. Gradually they slowed, the glowing digits coming into focus.

'Hmm, looks like my WIFI has selected the economy package,' said Dhassim, frowning at the screen. 'Ah well, that makes things a little simpler.'

If Jinnie's mind had boggled before, it was now doing veritable cartwheels of confusion. What did an internet connection have to do with anything? Was Dhassim somehow connected to an ancient mythological version of the web? He certainly wasn't hooked up to her network, since the internet was another thing on Jinnie's 'can't afford' pile. She relied on external resources when she needed to look anything up.

'This,' Dhassim announced, 'is a Wish-Instigating Finder

Instrument.' *So bugger all to do with the internet, then.* 'It detects and calibrates the emotional energy waves present between the genie — *moi*, of course — and the wisher, picking up on buried desires and latent longings. Then it uses a series of complex algorithms to produce the maximum number of wishes available, the timeframe in which they may be granted and — cue drum roll — what little old me gets out of it!'

Worlds populated by demons, dragons and other fantastic creatures had never been Jinnie's thing. She was a realist, with a side order of pessimism. Now she was facing a mythical maniac more akin to Doctor Who than a benign spirit with wish-fulfilling powers. *Maybe he's got a sonic screwdriver handy*, thought Jinnie with a smile. After all, the kitchen cupboard doors were hanging off their hinges.

But is he benign? A faint, tickling thought of mischievous if not downright nasty genies made Jinnie shiver. What if Dhassim wreaked havoc with her life, turned it upside down and left her penniless and heartbroken?

Wait, no. That had already happened.

'Erm, I hate to be an ignoramus, but what's the economy package?' she asked, not sure she was ready for the answer.

In response, Dhassim did an impressive backflip, landing inches from Jinnie's quizzical face. 'Simples, sweet cheeks. We have two months to get to know one another better. During that time my faithful friend will flag those lil' old wish moments, and yours truly will make 'em happen! We are going to have such *fun*!'

CHAPTER 13

ED MCCROARTY LUGGED ANOTHER CRATE OF BOTTLED BEER UP from the cellar. He'd been working solidly since 8 am, his dad otherwise occupied for the day. He usually visited his folks at least one weekend a month, but since his mum's decline he'd vowed to spend more time with them. His full-time job as a graphic designer allowed flexible working hours and he had holiday leave to use up, so taking time off in December wasn't a problem.

Mopping sweat from his brow, Ed grinned at his latest tattoo: a black sundial with a cloudy background, drawn so that it almost appeared 3D. It was his fifth in the past two years, and wouldn't be his last. Neither of his parents were thrilled by them, but Ed was nudging thirty and felt the need to live a little dangerously.

He'd been a sickly child, bullied at school for having his nose stuck in a book or being off games. His early teens hadn't been much better, even when the bouts of chronic bronchitis eased off. Ed had been a late bloomer, dodging the communal school showers, with his peers sprouting hair and developing 'down there', whenever he could. It wasn't until he went to college that his sluggish hormones sprang into action. Within a matter of weeks he'd lost his virginity, got blind drunk — the two events weren't unrelated — and started growing a beard. Ed loathed working out but enjoyed running, and his physique was now a source of pride — along with said beard, which he trimmed himself outdoors once a week (better lighting and less mess).

Taking a break for a protein shake and a banana, Ed checked his phone. There were two messages from Cheryl, his girlfriend of the past two months.

Hope your mum's doing OK. Tony's being a total twunt as usual. Tempted to tell him where to stick the job. Miss you C xx

BTW, you deffo back next weekend? Cal and the crew planning a house party. U wouldn't want me looking for a new man, would you? ♥

Ed sighed and bit into his banana. Cheryl was fun to be around, but had a tendency to be overdramatic. She worked as a reporter for a small chain of provincial newspapers in the Scottish Borders, just a short distance from Ed's home in Carlisle. Not a week passed without her complaining about the deputy editor, Tony, who she was convinced had it in for her. According to Cheryl, he would haul her over the coals for the slightest thing. Missing hole punches, a few typos in a news story, failure to buy milk and biscuits when it was her turn. Ed hated confrontation; life was too short for all that crap. He'd buy a new hole punch, apologise for the typos, treat the entire office to posh cakes, and possibly bring in a cow to deal with the milk issue. OK, an exaggeration — but Cheryl's histrionics were a bit wearing. And her friends, Cal and his 'crew', were a little too fond of pill-popping and talking more existential bullshit than Ed could stomach.

'Morning, love.' Mags wandered into the kitchen, hair unbrushed and dressing gown gaping in the middle.

Glimpsing more mum-flesh than he'd like, Ed stepped towards her and retied the belt firmly.

'I'll make you some tea and toast,' he said, grabbing the kettle and filling it. 'White or brown?'

'Can I have a boiled egg?' Mags asked, sitting down and massaging her face. 'It's been ages since I had one.'

Ed didn't point out that she had a boiled egg with toast soldiers nearly every morning. He, his dad and the staff had an agreement never to correct Mags's mix-ups or forgetfulness.

Leaving his mum with her breakfast, Ed went to welcome the team for the day. Young Jamie and Rose were on bar duty, and husband and wife duo Ray and Liz were tasked with putting together the pub grub which attracted customers from far and wide.

Liz checked the menu board. 'Right, we're on for black pudding with bacon bonbons, haggis with whisky cream, macaroni cheese, and chargrilled chicken breast,' she said. 'Oh, and spicy chickpea burgers for the veg-heads.' She rubbed her hands. 'Ray is doing the sides and a couple of desserts, so let's get cracking.'

Ed enlisted Jamie to get more supplies from the cellar: mixers, soft drinks and boxes of crisps and nuts. He tried to strike up a conversation, but this was greeted with little more than Neanderthal grunts. Jamie, just turned nineteen and living at home with his mum, could never be described as chatty. His over-the-bar banter was limited to 'What can I get you, mate?' and 'You want ice in that?' Mags treated him like another son, though, insisting that he was 'probably on the spectrum somewhere.' By all accounts, his home life wasn't easy. Rumour had it that his mum Angela suffered from serious depression and washed down her medication with large quantities of cheap vodka. Ed had only seen her once, pacing outside the pub waiting for Jamie to finish his shift. She'd looked normal enough; though how could you judge someone on one brief sighting? The only sign of disharmony had been when Angela had attempted to sling an arm around Jamie's shoulders. Jamie had reacted violently, shrugging it off as if it were a dangerous snake.

'Hey, have you seen that new horror series on Netflix?' asked Ed, in a last-ditch attempt to instigate a chat. 'Scared the crap out of me. Even Stephen King gave it the thumbs-up.'

Jamie hoisted a crate of tonic water onto the bar before fixing Ed with a look that was midway between sad and puzzled. 'We don't have Netflix and Mum doesn't like scary stuff. It, like, freaks her out.'

Conversation over, Jamie carried on arranging bottles and hanging snack packs. Ed sighed, dug out his phone, and replied to Cheryl.

Mum's OK, still muddled but Dad's doing his best. Keep the peace with Tony, at least till you get something else lined up. And I'll be back at the weekend. Let's see how it goes. E xx

'Nice tattoo.' Ed nearly dropped his phone. Jamie had spoken! His gaze was fixed on Ed's forearm, and the sundial he was so proud of.

'Thanks, mate, it's new. I've got a few others if you'd like to —' If you'd like to *what?* Take a peek at my arse? Have me strip off my shirt — hell, my entire outfit — so you can admire my body art? Ed coughed, opened a can of Diet Coke, and glugged it back. 'Never mind. Bring up the rest of the stuff. I'm off to get changed, see you at eleven.' Ed felt as if he'd slipped back into his old self: an awkward, don't-fit-in boy with a massive inferiority complex. Or was looking at Jamie like looking in an old mirror, the reflection reminding him of his own adolescent struggles?

Ed made for the stairs, meeting his mum on the way. She'd dressed, although her choice of clothing was more appropriate for the height of summer: a flimsy sundress and flip flops. He made a mental note to grab her a cardie from her room. And maybe a hairbrush too.

'You're up early!' Mags cried, clasping his face in both hands. 'My handsome boy, even with a beard. Are you even old enough to *have* a beard?'

Ed kissed her cheek, a waft of her signature perfume almost convincing him that all was well. His lovely, funny, generous mum, always there for him. Sitting up through the night when he was convulsed with coughing, or scraping projectile vomit off his bedroom wall after a wild night of booze and all-you-can-eat (and throw up) buffet. Patiently helping him with his homework, hugging him tightly when frustrated tears coursed down his face, telling him he was better than the bullies. His dad was brilliant too, just in a quieter, more introspective way.

As Ed carried on up the stairs, his mum called out after him. 'I'll just help myself to some breakfast, darling, and then we can catch up with all your news. It's so lovely to have you home!'

CHAPTER 14

Jɪɴɴɪᴇ ʏᴀᴡɴᴇᴅ sᴏ ʜᴀʀᴅ ᴛʜᴀᴛ sʜᴇ ᴛʜᴏᴜɢʜᴛ sʜᴇ ᴍɪɢʜᴛ dislocate her jaw. Sleep had been in short supply, as Dhassim's ceaseless chattering had carried on into the small hours. Only when she emerged from the bathroom, wielding her toothbrush and foaming at the mouth, did he quieten down and nod off.

Sadly, his chosen place of slumber wasn't back in the lamp, but curled up like a cat on the ancient rug by the foot of the bed. The night before he'd slept on the sofa, but complained it was too uncomfortable. Torn between ordering him into the kitchen (if only she had a dog basket, or similar) and letting sleeping genies lie, exhaustion won the day. But no sooner had Jinnie closed her eyes than Dhassim started snoring with all the fervour of a Black and Decker power tool.

'Rough night?' asked Sam.

Jinnie nodded as she tried and failed to stifle another mega-yawn. 'You could say that. Bad dreams. I probably shouldn't have eaten cheese before bedtime,' she replied. Much as she'd like to confide in someone, Jinnie felt sure

Sam would call the men in white coats if she revealed what was happening. When she'd woken up that morning, feeling headachy and nauseous, she'd half-expected — hoped, even — that it had been a nightmare. But no, there Dhassim was, busting some yoga moves and looking completely at home. 'That lamp you gave me … have you really no idea where it came from?'

Sam put down a notepad he'd been scribbling in, and gave Jinnie a questioning look. 'Sorry, I can't honestly say, although… Let me check something.' Sam wandered into the back room, reappearing with a box of index cards. 'I know, not very twenty-first century.' He laughed. 'I've just never got the hang of spreadsheets and all that malarkey. My computer's for writing, researching and online shopping. I hate going shopping, unless it's stuff for here. Especially clothes.'

Wherever Sam sourced his wardrobe from, he did a good job. Today's ensemble was a V-neck plum-coloured jumper (possibly cashmere, Jinnie thought), and dark cords. With his reading glasses and distracted air as he rifled through the cards, he reminded Jinnie of Clark Kent. Mild-mannered gent by day, all-conquering superhero by night. Not that she had a clue *what* Sam got up to in the evenings. And it probably didn't involve Lycra and phone boxes. *Focus, woman!*

'I don't keep track of everything I purchase or pick up, but I have a vague recollection that this was an unusual one.' Sam paused, then produced a card with a flourish. 'Got it! It was a couple of years ago, from a house clearance in Musselburgh. An elderly lady whose husband had died, and she was downsizing.'

'Why was it unusual?' asked Jinnie, peering over his shoulder. His handwriting was appalling, like a spider dipped in ink tap-dancing across the card.

'They'd spent some time living in the Middle East, and they'd accumulated quite a collection of artefacts. Most of it was of little value, although there were a couple of carpets worth a fair bit. I pointed her in the direction of a reputable dealer to sell those.'

A man of integrity! Jinnie's respect for Sam went up another notch. Not that it could *go* much higher, but even so…

'I'd completely forgotten, but she was desperate to get rid of the lamp. Practically thrust it into my arms when I arrived.' Sam's brow furrowed, memories clearly pushing their way to the fore.

'Why?' demanded Jinnie. Had Dhassim materialised in front of the poor old dear too? She couldn't imagine some widowed pensioner coping well with a genie interrupting her denture-cleaning routine. Not that she necessarily *had* dentures. Her gran still had most of her own teeth, even if they were on the yellow side.

'She said she hadn't seen it for years.' Sam shrugged. 'It was in a box in the garage with other junk. When she took it out, she claimed it — moved.' His expression was one of good-natured disbelief.

Jinnie assembled her features in a suitably shocked fashion. 'What did she mean? It's a lamp, for goodness sake! Did she drop it, or something?' That might account for the dents, at least.

'No, she was adamant that it vibrated in her hands. That gave her a real fright, so she threw it back in the box.' Sam grinned, clearly convinced that the old lady had imagined it. 'Why are you interested? Don't tell me it's spooked you, too!'

Jinnie buried her head in a box of old books Sam had picked up on his latest mission. She didn't want him to see the telltale flush rising from her neck to her cheeks. She wasn't good at fibbing, never had been. Her stammered excuses for missing homework had got her into more trouble at school, while her friends' creative fabrications had left her in awe. It was the same with Archie. He could lie through his teeth to their parents, his angelic countenance in contrast to Jinnie's scarlet hue.

Clutching a dusty tome that weighed a ton, she stood up. 'Of course not. I just thought it might be valuable after all. It, erm, polished up a treat.' Feeling another rush of heat, Jinnie mumbled something about needing the loo. Sam turned away as a customer entered and she beat a hasty retreat.

Sitting on the toilet, the ancient book balanced on the basin, Jinnie was thankful she didn't actually need to perform. If she had, tearing pages from *The Cook's Oracle* for wiping purposes would have been necessary, since as per bloody usual the toilet roll was conspicuous by its absence. Didn't men notice these things? Even Mr Perfect Pants Mark had been guilty of using the last sheet and leaving Jinnie to put a new one on the holder.

'We're out of loo roll,' she announced, as she came back in.

Sam pulled a 'bad me' face and left the customer browsing through a pile of old prints. 'Sorry. It was on my to-do list, along with getting some decent biscuits for break time. Give me five minutes, then I'll pop round to Janette's.'

He looked so contrite, like a scolded puppy caught weeing on the carpet, that Jinnie pulled her best martyr face and grabbed her bag. 'No worries, I'll go. Chocolate digestives or fig rolls? Budget, or quilted for extra softness?' As if Janette's emporium offered anything so luxurious. The digestives would be chocolate-free and the loo roll one step removed from sandpaper.

Sam peeled a tenner from his wallet and handed it to Jinnie. 'You might want to swing by the pub too, and have a word with Ken.' He gave her a significant look. 'I know he'd appreciate a bit of extra help.'

Did he indeed? Jinnie had the distinct feeling she'd been

the topic of conversation between the two men. Not that it mattered. She needed more money, and a way to escape from her unexpected house guest.

'OK, I won't be long. Anything else you need?'

Sam shook his head, watching the customer approach the counter with a sepia print of Edinburgh Castle.

Jinnie grabbed her bag and headed for the door. As she pushed it open, Sam called out after her. 'Make sure Ken offers you a decent hourly rate! And I just remembered — there were two of them.'

'Two of what?' Jinnie turned around, clueless as to what Sam was talking about.

'The lamps,' he replied, rolling the print up with care. 'When I got the box back here, I found a second one.' He frowned. 'Not sure where I put it, though.'

Jinnie wandered along the main road, her mind whirring at hyper-speed. There was *another* lamp? What did that mean? Perhaps nothing or maybe — oh God — maybe there was another Dhassim…

CHAPTER 15

'CAN I NO' TEMPT YE TAE SOME TUNNOCK'S TEACAKES, HEN?'
said Janette, ringing up Jinnie's other purchases. 'I happen to
know Sam's partial to them. Even if ye cannae dunk them in
your tea like the digestives!'

Jinnie nodded, and Janette added a pack of the iconic
chocolate-coated treats to the bag.

'You're looking nice today, Janette. Is that, erm, a new
top?' Instead of her usual Crimplene, Janette wore a fuchsia-
pink number with a plunging neckline. If she bent over,
Jinnie feared her breasts would make a bid for freedom.

'Aye, it is. I had me a wee trip to Edinburgh to get some
new undies. Saw this in Primark and thought to mysel', time
for a change. Got it in blue and orange too!'

Leaving Janette admiring her cleavage, Jinnie headed to
The Jekyll and Hyde. She contemplated a quick detour home
to see what Dhassim was up to, but decided against it. She'd
left him fiddling with his wish gizmo, muttering something
about a malfunction.

It was just after eleven, and the pub was still deserted

apart from an old man nursing a pint in the corner. There was no sign of Ken, just the tall, bearded man Jinnie had seen the other day, who had looked up from scribbling on a blackboard.

'Hi, I was hoping to have a word with Ken, if he's around.' Up close, Jinnie noted a definite similarity between the two men. Both had slate-grey eyes and close-cropped black hair. Ed's eyes — assuming she was correct — were twinkly and friendly, whereas Ken's were often steely and unwelcoming. Build-wise, Ed was much broader, and his arms each bore a tattoo.

'Sure, he's out the back. Can I say who's looking for him?'

'Jinnie. Jinnie Cooper.' They shook hands, Jinnie glad that his handshake was strong and firm. She hated limp hand-shakes, or 'wet haddock flappers' as Hannah called them.

'I'm Ed, the ne'er-do-well son of Ken and Mags. Pleased to meet you.'

Jinnie had never been a fan of facial hair, and especially not the beards currently in fashion, which could provide homes for several orphaned chicks. Nor did she like tattoos, even though she actually had one. A butterfly on her left shoulder blade, done in a moment of madness when she was twenty, egged on by Hannah and the gang. It was tiny and faded now. Still, Ed seemed a nice person, and she wouldn't judge him on his beard and body art.

'Dad! Jinnie's here to see you,' hollered Ed. 'Can I get you a drink?' he added, at a normal volume.

'Just an orange juice, please.' Jinnie perched at the bar, watching Ed retrieve a bottle from the fridge. He removed the lid and poured it into a glass, adding a scoop of ice.

'Hello there! I've been expecting you,' boomed Ken, much more like the friendly man she'd encountered while having lunch with Sam.

'Um, well, I was wondering if you could offer me some part-time hours,' gabbled Jinnie, aware that Ed was within earshot and grinning enthusiastically.

'Give her a job, Dad,' he chimed in. 'We could do with a bit of glamour behind the bar. Jamie's face could turn milk sour, and you're hardly an oil painting yourself.'

Ken mock-frowned at his son, then nodded at Jinnie. 'I certainly could. Have you any bar experience?'

Aside from propping one up on a regular basis?, thought Jinnie. Not really, although she had spent one summer working at a local music festival, doling out watery pints to sloshed revellers. Upmarket gin and tonics and elaborate cocktails were beyond Jinnie's current capabilities, but how hard could it be?

'A little,' she said. 'I'm a hard worker and a fast learner. Honestly. If you hire me I promise I won't let you down.' *Well, that didn't sound remotely desperate, did it?*

'I'll teach you the ropes, Jinnie,' said Ed. 'I'm around for a couple more days. When can she start, Dad?'

Ken scratched his head, lost in thought.

Ed pulled a clipboard from behind the bar and stuck it under Ken's nose. 'Look, Dad, Jamie's working day shifts, and so is Rose. I was going to ask one of them to cover tomorrow evening, but how about you start then, Jinnie? Say from seven till eleven, and we can take it from there. Sunday night's a possible too, but I can't guarantee that right now.'

They agreed a rate that wouldn't have Jinnie's bank manager jigging with glee, but it was better than minimum wage. Hopefully, if she didn't make a complete hash of things, she could do a few more shifts. And working alongside Ed might be fun. He seemed like a decent sort, as did Ken, despite her earlier impressions.

'How did it go?' asked Sam, as Jinnie sauntered in with

her bagful of sweet treats and toilet rolls. 'Well, judging by that smile.'

'The good news is that we have biscuits *and* tea cakes.' She produced the items with a flourish. 'The bad news is the Andrex puppy would run a mile from Janette's cheap bog paper. And I'm doing my first shift at the pub tomorrow night, and feeling a wee bit nervous.'

'You'll be fine,' Sam assured her. 'The Jekyll and Hyde has a good reputation, and I know they treat their staff well. Free grub too, I believe!'

The rest of the day passed pleasantly. Sam and Jinnie happily munched their way through most of the tea cakes, and served a couple of customers. In a quiet period, Sam confessed he'd hit a brick wall with his latest novel, having decided to introduce a romantic element. 'My previous stuff has been quite dark. All mutilated bodies and police knee-deep in their own personal demons.' He gave a self-conscious laugh. 'Mind you, my ex would say I don't have a romantic bone in my body. I was hopeless at buying gifts, and never remembered Valentine's Day.'

Jinnie smiled sympathetically, doubting she'd be able to read one of Sam's books. She liked her books frothy and fun-filled, not dripping in blood and gore.

'Romance isn't about that, is it?' she said. 'It's more about the little things, the gestures that mean something, rather than buying fancy stuff or feeling obliged to go overboard on a date that's just a commercial con.' Mark was guilty as charged, presenting Jinnie with underwear that said more about his dubious taste than her personal preference. And as for his choice of Valentine's card... Enormous, padded and dripping with faux sentiment. Like the engagement ring, which still languished in her jewellery box...

'You might just have inspired me,' said Sam. 'Romance with a side order of reality. Less hearts and flowers, more —'

'Tea cakes and toilet roll.' Jinnie reached over to brush a flake of chocolate from the corner of Sam's mouth. 'Because we all need a little sweetness, and we all need to wipe. Right?'

CHAPTER 16

Jɪɴɴɪᴇ ᴇᴀsᴇᴅ ᴛʜᴇ ғʀᴏɴᴛ ᴅᴏᴏʀ ᴏᴘᴇɴ, ᴜɴsᴜʀᴇ ᴡʜᴀᴛ ᴛᴏ expect. The first thing she heard was her vacuum cleaner, accompanied by what could best be described as the sound of a cat being strangled. It was coming from upstairs. She dumped her coat and bag and trudged towards the noise, any hope that Dhassim might have found another mistress or master fading away.

Entering the bedroom, Jinnie found Dhassim shimmying around the room, singing some unknown number and looking a lot like Freddie Mercury in the "I Want To Break Free" video, minus the boobs and moustache (and the vocal ability). He was manoeuvring the ancient upright vacuum her gran had given her. 'An anniversary present from your granddad, God rest his soul,' she'd said. 'Romantic gestures were never really his thing.'

The tatty old rug was receiving a good going-over, at least until its tasselled edge got snagged in the machine. Dhassim switched it off, muttering expletives in a foreign tongue. As he bent over to untangle the threads, he saw Jinnie and let out a high-pitched scream. 'Girlfriend, do *not* creep up on me like that! My little heart is thumping.' He placed a hand on his chest and panted like a mother about to give birth.

'Sorry.' *Not sorry.* Why should Jinnie apologise, when he was the one who'd invaded her life? She didn't want — didn't need — a genie hanging around. Even one intent on cleaning, which had never been Jinnie's forte. Who was that old bloke she'd read about? The one who said something like: 'After the first four years the dirt doesn't get any worse'? She'd never been *that* bad, but Jinnie's philosophy was to do the bare minimum and keep the lights turned down when visitors arrived.

'Why are you vacuuming? Shouldn't you be fixing your wish thingummy?' Said device was plonked in the middle of Jinnie's bed, next to a screwdriver and a can of WD40.

'All done,' announced Dhassim with a smug smile. 'Just needed a little lubrication. Speaking of which, I am totally parched. Any chance you could rustle up something cool and refreshing?'

Jinnie stomped downstairs, Dhassim hot on her heels. 'I suffer from shocking allergies, you know,' he huffed, adding an ostentatious sneeze for good measure. 'Dust is the devil, and your house is a veritable health hazard.'

In the kitchen, Jinnie tossed him a box of tissues, and Dhassim honked heartily into one. Opening the fridge, Jinnie took out a couple of beers — on special at Janette's as they were approaching their use-by date — and levered off the caps. 'Cheers,' she said.

Dhassim eyed the bottle dubiously before taking a gulp. 'Hmm, interesting flavour, although I'd have preferred something a bit more exotic. Don't you have any rosewater or fresh mint?'

Yes, thought Jinnie. *My kitchen is crammed with exotic ingredients.* Baked beans, sliced white bread and budget cornflakes. Ooh, and not forgetting a bottle of Ribena. It evoked childhood memories of being tucked up in bed with a cold and her mum bringing her a hot mug of the blackcurrant drink.

Within minutes it was obvious that Dhassim wasn't a drinker. Giggling inanely, he performed a series of break-dance moves. Either that, or he was having a seizure. Not sure whether to laugh or cry, Jinnie left him to it and went into the lounge. Right now she wished she had a telly, just to watch some mind-numbing rubbish or wildlife footage of lions tearing apart a wildebeest. That would suit her current mood. Then thoughts of David Attenborough narrating the gruesome scene were quickly displaced by another thought: *What the actual hell...?*

Jinnie blinked, unable to process what now took up almost one wall of the cottage. A friggin' ginormous television, one of those fancy curved numbers. On the coffee table was a remote control with more buttons than Jinnie had ever seen on such a device. Tentatively, she pressed what appeared to be the on button, and the screen burst into life. At least, there was a colourful bouncing ball icon which ricocheted from one edge to another, then burst like a bubble. Speaking of bouncing balls... Dhassim sprang in front of the screen, jigging from one foot to the other.

'Whoopsie! Looks like my little chickadee's first wish got granted.' His expression was one of contrition mixed with mischief. Wordlessly, Jinnie handed him the remote and watched as he fiddled and clicked until an actual picture appeared. A handsome Hollywood hunk, going in for a serious smooch with an equally gorgeous actress. Jinnie would have preferred a bit of animal chomping, but that wasn't really the issue here.

'When I wished I had a telly, I didn't really mean it,' she

said. 'Anyway, how did you know what I wished for? I didn't say it out loud.'

Dhassim changed channels. This time the screen was filled with images of a hippo thrashing around in a river, with a crocodile's teeth clamped around its body. OK, either he was a mind reader, or —

'It's not me, cupcake. My WIFI is definitely having a wobble. Here, you play with this.' He handed Jinnie the remote. 'I'll see what's going on.'

Jinnie sank into the sofa as Dhassim bounded upstairs. He was back in a flash, the errant piece of kit in his hand. 'Hmm, it looks like it's upgraded to the premium economy package all on its ownio.'

'Meaning?' Jinnie eyed the device suspiciously. It was beeping and flashing manically, and Dhassim was muttering under his breath while he examined it. He finally went for the scientific approach of bashing it repeatedly on the coffee table, adding a few more dings to the table's battered surface.

He looked up. 'This shouldn't be happening,' he said.

No shit, Sherlock, thought Jinnie.

'It's giving you bonus wishes! Like, it's tuning into everything you wish for. That's not how this baby is supposed to work.' He shook it, then put it to his ear.

'Meaning *what*, exactly?' Jinnie's temper was starting to fray, and her tummy was rumbling. Two Tunnock's teacakes and a vat of coffee didn't exactly constitute a balanced diet. There was a macaroni cheese in the freezer with her name on it, assuming Dhassim hadn't already scoffed it. Not that she'd shown him how to work the microwave, but Jinnie suspected he'd have figured it out. Or chiselled through the meal with his pointy little teeth.

'Well, it should only grant wishes that you directly ask me for, and which meet the guidelines laid down in the Charter for Harmonious Upstanding Genies. That's CHUG, for short.'

Jinnie had had enough. Dhassim could take his WIFI and CHUG and stick them where the sun didn't shine. She was tired, hungry and wondering how she'd fare on her first evening behind the bar. Plus the whole second lamp thing was messing with her brain. She wasn't going to ask him about it right now; it was all too much. What she really wanted to do was confide in someone about what was going on. But who? *Not Hannah*, she thought decisively. Hannah would wee herself laughing (literally, the girl had zero pelvic floor control). Her parents? They didn't need the added stress of thinking their daughter was a sandwich short of a picnic. Maybe Gran? If she believed in tea leaves as a tool for foretelling the future, why not a genie? Then again, Gran wasn't getting any younger and the shock might —

'Just be careful for now. Until I figure out what's going on with my faithful friend.' Dhassim lovingly stroked his WIFI, which made a mewling sound.

Leaving him flicking through the channels, Jinnie dragged herself upstairs to bed. The microwave meal had lost its appeal. Instead, she'd found a packet of peanuts and made herself a mug of hot Ribena. Snuggled under the duvet, she heard Dhassim howling with laughter at something on the box. *Great.*

There was a set of earplugs in the bedside cabinet drawer, picked up years ago when she'd gone to a concert with the gang. Jinnie hadn't worn them then — how boring-old-fart was it to muffle the sound of awesome music? — but now she needed to mute the guffaws from below. She squidged them into position, and the sound of her heart beating amplified threefold. Grumpily, she pulled them out and willed herself to sleep. *Deep breaths in, deep breaths out. Think calm, rational thoughts. Do not eat any more peanuts, especially as you cannot be arsed to brush, never mind floss, your teeth.*

As Jinnie tried to drift off, two images flitted through her mind. Solid, reliable and easy-on-the-eye Sam. Then — this one was *so* off the wall — tattooed, bearded Ed. Polar opposites. Night and day. Someone she was attracted to (if she allowed herself to go down that road) and another who was fun, friendly and keen to help.

Jinnie rolled over, prodding peanut shards from her teeth with her tongue, and thought about getting up. But it was dark, the bed was warm, and the thought of having to converse with Dhassim filled her with dread. He knew nothing about her day-to-day life. Whatever his role was, they'd have to find a way to get to know each other in the coming weeks, or months.

Be careful what you wish for.

Jinnie punched her pillow, then punched it again. She pressed her cheek against the scrunched-up fabric and groaned. *I want to sleep! Please, gods of all things to do with shut-eye, let me sleep!*

Moments later, all was quiet downstairs. Jinnie flickered in and out of consciousness, something nudging her awake. Tomorrow. Her first night at The Jekyll and Hyde. She had to perform. She had to be good. She wished she could be an ace bartender...

CHAPTER 17

'You look nice.' Ed smiled as Jinnie approached the bar, blushing at the compliment. Ken had assured her there was no dress code as such — smart/casual, he'd said — but she wanted to make a good impression on her first shift. A black faux-leather skirt that ended just above the knee, teamed with a fitted white shirt and chunky boots.

'Meet Ray and Liz.' Ed gestured to a middle-aged couple, clad in aprons and looking distinctly hot and bothered.

'Good to meet you, Jinnie,' said Liz. Ray nodded in agreement. 'We're the galley slaves, for want of a better description, and we need to get on with tonight's menu so we'll catch you later.'

Ed showed Jinnie where to hang her coat and bag, then they returned to the bar. It was just after seven and still very quiet, but Ed explained that it would fill up as the evening progressed and people were attracted by the food.

'We've a few stalwarts who always come in for the beef and Guinness pie. It's pretty special; Liz makes the lightest puff pastry you can imagine.'

Trying not to drool at the thought, Jinnie took her place

behind the bar. Ed pointed out the various beer pumps and spirit optics, as well as the fridges and selection of wines.

'Here are the measures for the wine — small, medium and large — and the cocktail shakers,' he said. 'We don't serve that many, but — Oops, spoke too soon.'

A group of girls in their early twenties burst through the door, giggling and nudging each other. Despite the bitter cold, they were dressed for an Ibiza nightclub: tight, sleeveless dresses, and more fake tan than a *Strictly Come Dancing* contestant. Jinnie couldn't help noticing one had run out of tan at her calves; her stiletto-clad feet were snowy white.

'Hiya, Ed,' smouldered one of the girls, flicking her long, blonde hair away from her face. 'Didn't know you were in town, otherwise I'd have come in sooner.'

'How's your mum?' enquired another, a wodge of pink gum visible as she chewed with open-mouthed fervour.

'She's not too bad, Kylie,' Ed replied. 'Good days and bad days. Now, what can I get you ladies?'

As they flicked through the drinks list, Ed whispered, 'Don't worry, I'll deal with these. You sort out those two' — he indicated a couple of men in paint-splattered overalls — 'and I'll fix the complicated stuff.'

Taking their order for two pints of Belhaven, Jinnie angled the glasses and began to pour. As she did, her toes began to tingle, and the feeling rose rapidly to her fingers. The sensation grew, as if an electric current was passing through her entire body.

Jinnie thrust the pints at the men and nudged a startled Ed aside. 'I've got this,' she declared, reaching for a couple of cocktail shakers. 'OK, two Zombies, a Sex On The Beach and a White Russian coming up.'

Like a human whirlwind, Jinnie spun around and measured out the ingredients. Peach schnapps, vodka, cranberry and orange juice. She flipped a bottle in the air, twirled, and caught it behind her back. Oblivious to the gasps around her, Jinnie filled a shaker and agitated it at hyper-speed. On to the next one. Rum, brandy, more juice and a dash of grenadine. Swivelling her hips to an imaginary beat, she shook, and shook some more. Grab a glass, up it goes, catch it in the other hand. Drinks poured, on to the next one. Bailey's, vodka and — dammit, where was the cream?

'Jinnie, stop. Please ... stop. You're making me dizzy.' Ed placed a hand on her arm, his other holding an opened carton of cream. She lunged for it, but he moved it out of reach. As she scowled at him, the tingling began to fade.

A smattering of applause rang out around the bar. 'It's bloody Tom Cruise in a skirt!' one voice called out.

'Woo hoo, darlin'. You available for private parties?' shouted another.

Jinnie's vision swam for a few seconds, and she felt her legs give way. In a flash Ed wrapped an arm around her shoulder and walked her around the bar to a stool. Jinnie breathed deeply, her nose pressed into Ed's denim shirt. He smelled of something warm and spicy, with an under-note of cedarwood. Nice. Was it his deodorant or aftershave? She leaned in closer and —

'Erm, Jinnie, why are you sniffing my armpit?'

Oops. She raised her head to find Ed with tears in his eyes. Tears of mirth rather than misery, she hoped. Yep, Ed was laughing, little crinkly lines emphasising those deliciously dark eyes.

Getting to her feet, the feeling of faintness already passed, Jinnie saw that her audience had lost interest and were back to the serious business of drinking and eating. Well, *most* of them.

'Any chance we could *have* our cocktails?' whined the blonde girl, looking distinctly put out. Jinnie couldn't tell whether that was because she hadn't been served yet, or she disapproved of Ed getting too close to her.

Finishing off the White Russian and working the till, Ed waited for Jinnie to return to the bar. 'Are you OK?' he asked. 'If you need to sit down a bit longer, grab something to eat…'

'No honestly, I'm fine. Sorry. Got a bit carried away, wanted to make a good first impression, you know how it is.' Except *he* probably didn't. Jinnie didn't have to be a genius to work out who (and what) was responsible for her new-found skills. She'd bloody throttle Dhassim when she got home.

'Well, that was one amazing show. The locals haven't been so entertained since Janette Cameron got hammered and treated them to her special Scottish version of the can-can. I thought you didn't have much experience?'

Dig yourself out of this one, thought Jinnie, racking her brains. 'I found a recipe book at home, for drinks and cocktails, and I, um, had a little practice run. Couldn't find a shaker, mind you. Had to improvise with a coffee flask!' She smiled sweetly, aware of the tell-tale flush signalling another porky-pie. Hopefully Ed wouldn't notice, or put it down to her wobbly moment.

'Hmm. Well, you did say you were a fast learner, but that was pretty incredible.'

Before Jinnie could say any more, Ray appeared carrying two plates of pie with a side of buttery mash. 'Get that down your necks,' he said. 'Heard a lot of whooping and cheering through here. Did we miss something?'

Jinnie and Ed looked at each other, and Jinnie shook her head slightly. She'd had enough embarrassment for one night. Quick on the uptake, Ed simply said Jinnie had showed remarkable dexterity with a cocktail shaker.

'Huh, she wasn't *that* good,' huffed Blonde Girl, who'd drained her drink and was scrolling through the list with a glittery pink talon.

After devouring the pie and mash and serving a steady stream of customers, Jinnie glanced at the clock. Almost eleven and the end of her shift. She'd enjoyed trading banter and, most of all, chatting to Ed. Working with Sam was fun, but his clientele rarely paused for a natter. Ed was easy-going, open — he'd talked about his mum and how hard he found her condition — and attractive. He was the complete opposite of Mark, but perhaps that was a good thing.

'See you Sunday?' he asked.

Jinnie shrugged on her coat, buttoning it up to face the bitter cold that awaited her. 'See you Sunday,' she replied.

Digging her hands deep into her pockets, Jinnie strode towards home. Time to confront Dhassim, and figure out where her life was going.

CHAPTER 18

SAM WAS MAKING SNAIL-LIKE PROGRESS WITH HIS LATEST BOOK. Sometimes the words flowed, but this evening was like wading through wet cement. He took another sip of whisky, hoping it might lubricate his stagnant brain cells.

Things hadn't got off to a great start with a call earlier from his ex-wife. She'd been on a rant about their son, Sean, following a visit to see him at his shared digs in Stirling.

'He's living in total squalor!' Lucy shrieked down the phone. 'I went to use the bathroom and I have never seen anything more revolting in my life. Hairs everywhere, and the toilet was a health hazard. I had to hover in case I caught something. And the kitchen… Well, the concept of washing up must be alien to them. Dishes stacked high, and encrusted with God knows what.' She paused before delivering the punchline. 'You need to *talk* to him, Sam!'

Mother and son had a strained relationship. Growing up, Sean had been a bit of a daydreamer and struggled academically. His passion was writing — like father, like son — while other subjects such as maths and science went over his head. Lucy was something of a tiger mum, relentless in her quest to push Sean to greater heights. She questioned his teachers' abilities at parents' evenings, poor Sean squirming beside her. Sam tried to get along when he could to play good cop, but he felt helpless in the face of her ferocity. Instead, he focused on spending as much time as he could with Sean of an evening, when Lucy was out wining and dining clients or honing her physique at the gym. They'd work through past papers and online exercises, Sam reassuring his son that straight As and a degree didn't guarantee a happy life. What mattered was finding something you loved doing, and following your dreams.

The little differences between he and his wife, which seemed insignificant in the early, heady days of their relationship, gradually developed into unbreachable chasms. Lucy accused Sam of being too soft with Sean, obsessed with his books, and uninterested in her. He pleaded guilty as charged, and they agreed to separate. Sean chose to stay with Sam for his final year of school, knuckled down in the run-up to his Advanced Highers, and secured a place at Stirling to study English. Lucy moved back to her home town of Dumfries, and was now in a relationship with a fellow financial advisor.

Sam had managed to appease her by promising to have a word with Sean. When he'd visited Sean, the flat hadn't been *that* bad. It wouldn't win any health and hygiene awards, but they were students with better things to do than clean loos or soak grimy saucepans. Sam suspected, perhaps unfairly, that Sean had deliberately left the place in chaos to wind his mum up to the max. He was good at pushing her buttons: payback for all the years she'd pushed his.

The whisky glass was empty. He topped it up, and ate the last cheese-topped cracker that constituted his supper. Sam typed another sentence, read it back, and deleted it. The cursor blinked at him mockingly. *Give up, loser.* With a sigh, he saved the file and closed the computer down. What he needed was some company: an escape from the rambling old house that was too big for one person, and echoed with the ghosts of happier times.

Wrapped up in his favourite tweed coat and heavy scarf, Sam headed to The Jekyll and Hyde. Frost sparkled on the pavement, and his breath condensed in front of him. He wondered if Jinnie would be working. The thought that she might brought an unexpected glow to his frozen cheeks. She was a lovely girl — woman — whose presence in the shop had made a big impact on Sam's life. Going to work, knowing he'd see Jinnie several times a week, made him happier than he'd realised. He enjoyed her company and good humour, and she was undoubtedly very attractive. Since splitting with Lucy, and Sean's departure for uni, he'd convinced himself that being on his own was what he wanted. Lucy had loved hosting lavish dinner parties, filling the house with loud, opinionated people who talked over one another and oohed and aahed over the food. Little did they know that his ex-wife could barely boil an egg, hiring caterers to prepare everything in advance.

Yes, Sam had believed that a solitary existence — the lonely life of a writer — was right for him. Now, he wasn't so sure.

The warmth of the pub enveloped him like a blanket as he pushed open the door. A tantalising smell hung in the air: meaty and mouth-watering, with a hint of spice, reminding Sam of his pathetic snack earlier. His good spirits drooped a little when he saw who was behind the bar. Young Jamie, dour as ever, and, surprisingly, Mags.

'How are you, my lovely?' she chirruped as he approached. 'And how's Lesley? Haven't seen her in ages.'

Sam knew who she meant. He assured her that Lesley was fine and fumbled for his wallet. Damn it! In his haste to escape, he'd left it on the hall table. 'Sorry, Mags. I seem to have come out empty-handed. Would it be OK if…'

Mags smiled and waved away his attempt to explain. 'Tell me what you'd like and square up next time you're passing. You'll be having something to eat? The menu this evening is on the … on the…' A look of frustration crossed her face as she pointed at the blackboard. 'It's on that black thing.'

Sam ordered Thai green curry and a pint of lager. He glanced around the room, recognising a few faces, including Jamie's mum, Angela. He didn't know her really. They'd exchanged hellos and she'd called into the shop once or twice, looking for knickknacks. He was aware of the rumours surrounding her. Alcohol problems, mental health issues, the usual fodder for a village that thrived on idle gossip. She was on her own, gazing into a glass of clear liquid as if it held the answers to all the universe's problems. Sam looked for a spare seat, but the pub was crowded and he didn't fancy eating at the bar.

'A penny for them?' Sam dropped into a chair beside Angela, foaming pint in hand. Up close she looked tired. There were purple shadows under her eyes, and her hand trembled as she reached for her glass.

'Oh, hi there.' Her greeting was unenthusiastic, and Sam considered making his excuses and moving. Then Angela gave a watery smile, and raised her glass. It was half-empty, and a folded crisp packet lay in front of her.

'Can I get you another?' Sam asked. 'And I've just ordered some food if you fancy joining me.' He wouldn't normally be so forward, but something about Angela's solitude and sadness had touched a nerve.

'That's so kind of you. I'm not hungry, but another one of these would be lovely. It's a soda water and lime, by the way.' Angela's expression — *I know what you were thinking* — made Sam flush with guilt. He hurried to the bar and ordered her drink from Jamie, just as Mags appeared with his plate of curry.

'There you go,' she said, setting it down. 'Last serving, so it's your lucky day.'

Sam returned to the table with the food, drink and an extra set of cutlery, just in case.

'Thank you.' Angela accepted the glass and they toasted each other. He took a mouthful — absolutely delicious — and gestured to the spare fork and knife.

'Try some? It's a lot better than a bag of smoky bacon.'

Angela looked on the verge of refusing. Sam took another forkful and she hesitantly picked up the spare fork and followed suit. As she chewed, her eyes abruptly filled with tears.

'Oh, gosh, is it too spicy for you? I'm sorry, maybe take a drink to wash it down.' Sam felt terrible now, as if he'd tried to poison the poor woman.

'No, it's fine,' Angela replied, sipping her soda water. 'The food's perfect, it's just … you being so nice.' She looked down. 'I guess I'm not used to people being nice to me.'

As if on cue, Jamie loomed above them, gathering empty glasses and glaring at Sam and Angela. 'All right here? Hope you're not overdoing it, Mum. You know what the doctor said.'

Pink spots appeared on Angela's cheeks. Jamie had spoken abruptly, and Sam guessed she was also embarrassed at the mention of a doctor. 'Thanks, Jamie, but I'm OK. Sam and I are just chatting. I am allowed to chat to people, you know.'

With a not-very-discreet roll of the eyes Jamie stomped back to the bar, glasses rattling on his tray. Angela sighed and rubbed a hand over her face. 'I love that boy to bits, but there are times I could gladly strangle him. His heart's in the right place, but he acts like he's the boss of me. Understandable, I suppose, since he's never had a dad and ... well, I haven't always been the perfect mum.'

When he'd wished for some company, Sam hadn't *quite* imagined this turn of events. Still, if Angela wanted to offload her worries, he could at least lend a sympathetic ear. They polished off the curry between them, Angela talking between mouthfuls.

'I had Jamie when I was very young. Sixteen, in fact. The father was a bit older and legged it as soon I said I was pregnant.'

'That's tough,' said Sam. He and Lucy had been in their early twenties when they married and had Sean. *Too young*, he thought, with the benefit of hindsight, *but sixteen?*

'My mum did what she could to help, but it wasn't easy. Specially when we realised Jamie had some learning difficulties. Money was pretty tight. Still is, but I've tried my best.'

Not knowing what to say, Sam squeezed her hand; then Angela snatched it away. 'Sorry, I'm rambling on and I should be getting home.' She stood up. 'Thanks for listening, and for the food and drink.' Before he could respond, she grabbed her things and almost sprinted to the door.

Sam decided to call it a night. Waving at Mags and Jamie (who nodded curtly), he left the pub. Some mind-numbing TV and another whisky would hopefully point him in the direction of sleep, and steer his thoughts away from two very different women...

CHAPTER 19

'GIRLFRIEND, THAT IS SOOOO FUNNY!' DHASSIM HONKED AND hooted like a demented duck on drugs when Jinnie relayed her tale of cocktail-making chaos. She had tried to look cross, but looking cross was difficult when her 'roomie' was rolling around on the floor, clutching his sides. He'd been sound asleep when she got back from the pub, and despite her earlier anger and embarrassment, she'd refrained from giving him a kick.

'When you're *quite* finished.' Jinnie gave him her best stern headmistress look, but her cheeks were wobbling with barely-contained mirth. The situation was so insane, so out-of-this-world bonkers, that it was a wonder she wasn't writhing around on the floor with him. Not in a sexual way, of course. Dhassim was quite cute, but getting it on with a genie? No, not happening. Whereas writhing around with Sam, or Ed…? *No, no, no!*

'Honeybun, any chance of us eating soon? My stomach feels like my throat's been cut.' Ugh, he really needed to stop with the cutie-pie names. They were making Jinnie feel nauseous.

'My name is Jinnie. Please just call me that.' She rummaged in the cupboard for something to have for breakfast. The cheap and not very cheerful bran flakes she'd picked up at Janette's looked like something you'd sprinkle in a cat litter tray, and didn't taste much better.

'Fine, *Jinnie*,' grumbled Dhassim, pronouncing her name 'gin knee'. 'So what are we having? Hmm, you've got flour, eggs and milk. I could whip up pancakes. Got any syrup?'

Jinnie was due at the shop in half an hour. Luckily, Dhassim was as adept at pancake-making as she'd been at cocktail-shaking. Within ten minutes they were feasting on a mini mountain of the goodies, topped with sugar and a squeeze of lemon.

'What are you planning on doing while I'm out?' asked Jinnie. Her humble abode was gleaming from top to bottom, since Dhassim was a dab hand at everything from hoovering and dusting to polishing and scrubbing. His lamp now took pride of place on the mantelpiece, which reminded her —

'I told you I found your lamp at Sam's shop,' she said, hunting for her house keys and lipstick. Pouting in her compact mirror, she applied a double coat of Vixen Rose. Which, along with a touch of foundation and lash-lengthening mascara, was purely for her own benefit. Not to impress anyone else. No sirree.

'Yes, I believe you did,' replied Dhassim, dabbing his mouth with a piece of kitchen towel. 'And…?'

'Well, there were two of them. Sam can't find the other one, but he's adamant they came as a pair.' Was it her imagination, or did his bronzed face (he'd nobbled the last of Jinnie's fake tan) turn paler?

'Really? How interesting, although I'm sure it's just a coincidence. The world is full of lamps that look similar. You just struck it lucky getting the one which contained little old me!' Dhassim flounced into the lounge and the theme song from *Friends* blasted out. He'd already binge-watched four seasons, and declared himself in love with Jennifer Aniston.

'I POPPED into the pub last night,' said Sam, when Jinnie arrived at work. He was painstakingly unwrapping old plates and stacking them on a shelf. 'Thought I might see you there.' His tone was casual, but he didn't quite meet Jinnie's eye. Was there the tiniest spark of interest there, or was she reading too much into things? Even if there was, Jinnie had enough on her own plate coping with Dhassim and the whole wish conundrum.

'Ken's asked me to work Tuesday and Thursday evenings for now,' she replied. 'And I might get the odd weekend shift too.' At ten pounds an hour the money wasn't brilliant, but at least she might be able to go a bit more upmarket on the breakfast cereal.

They worked companionably for the rest of the day. A smattering of customers came and went, some only to browse, but a nice set of silver candlesticks and an intricately woven table linen set left the building.

'Have you met Angela, Jamie's mum?' Sam's question took Jinnie by surprise, and made her wonder if she was totally off the mark thinking he might be interested in *her*. Perhaps Angela was the one.

'No. In fact I haven't met Jamie yet, although I think we'll be working together at some point,' she replied. 'Is she nice?'

A devilish voice inside her head whispered, *Say no. Tell me she's a miserable old harridan with bad breath and appalling dress sense.*

'She's lovely. Not that I really know her. We just got chatting in the pub and, well, I get the feeling she could do with a friend.'

As opposed to a boyfriend? *How old is she anyway*, wondered Jinnie. If she had a son in his late teens, surely she must be well into her forties. Mind you, Sam must be of a similar age if Sean was in his first year at uni. Not that age mattered. Her granddad, Wilma's late husband, had been fifteen years younger, and they'd been blissfully happy until the day he keeled over on the bowling green. 'Died doing what he loved,' Wilma always said. 'It was either that or mid-shag, and I'm awfy grateful I didnae have tae call out the doctor for that scenario!'

'I'm sure I'll bump into her at some point,' said Jinnie. 'It's not as if Cranley is a teeming metropolis. Give me a few more weeks and I'll be on first-name terms with everyone.'

Making a mental note to find out more about the mysterious Angela, Jinnie returned to the task in hand: flapping a duster over items that were destined never to leave the shop. I mean, did *anyone* want a World War One gas mask? Or a Russian samovar, when nowadays you could pick up a kettle for under a tenner? Still, there was 'nowt so queer as folk', another favourite adage of her gran's. Not technically Scottish, but Wilma didn't care about the origins of her expressions, only that they got across the message. Anyway, people bought things — even old things — because they were drawn to them. Not for their practical use, necessarily, but because they pleased them aesthetically. Why else had Jinnie been drawn to the lamp?

As she fiddled with the gas mask, and sent a silent prayer of thanks to those who'd strived to create a better, safer world — what would they think now? —, Jinnie paused. Which had come first? Meeting Sam, definitely. The lamp had appealed to her, but only as something to add a touch of retro charm to her spartan cottage. And yet, were those things somehow connected? Was Jinnie always destined to walk through the door of Out of the Attic Antiques? Why had the lamp, and its elusive partner, ended up there in the first place? Was Sam somehow part of the puzzle, and if so, how?

'Bugger!' Jinnie's ponderings were interrupted by a crash as one of the plates hit the floor, fragments scattering everywhere.

Sam shrugged and picked up the scruffy brush and pan he kept on hand for emergencies. 'To all the plates I've broke before,' he sang, scooping up shards with ease. 'Sorry, both for the terrible singing and the appalling grammar.'

Jinnie smiled and bent to pick up a couple of larger pieces, careful not to cut herself. She tossed them in the wastepaper basket, Sam adding his collection of fragmented china. They did a final check, satisfied that no shards were left to cause injury to passing customers.

'I hate breaking stuff. But when it isn't beyond repair, I don't mind.' Sam was looking at the bin, but his words were directed at Jinnie. 'A chipped plate, glasses that don't quite match. Things don't have to be perfect to work.'

Was there an underlying message there? Jinnie didn't know what to think. Was Sam hinting that Jinnie was 'damaged goods', or was he referring to the lovely Angela? Or was he simply saying that things didn't need to be pristine to bring pleasure?

The doorbell chimed and a woman entered the shop. She looked in her mid-thirties, although deep lines furrowed her brow. She wore no make-up, and her limp blonde hair hung damply round her face. She was shivering — hardly surprising, as her lightweight jacket was more suited to a sunny spring day — and chewing her bottom lip.

'Angela!' Sam approached her with a warm smile. She responded with a nod, lips resolutely turned down. *Speak of the devil*, thought Jinnie. Not that she looked remotely demonic, more downcast and nervous.

'Hi, Sam. I wondered if I could have a word. In private.' Angela's gaze took in Jinnie, who immediately busied herself dusting more things that didn't need dusting.

The pair shuffled over to the far corner and began muttering together. Jinnie strained to hear what they were saying, but could only pick up the odd word. A definite 'sorry' from Angela, a 'don't worry' from Sam, and what might have been 'fancy a quickie'. Jinnie hoped she'd misheard the last one.

'Jinnie.' Sam called her over and Jinnie went to join them with all the enthusiasm of a dog going to the vet. 'This is Angela, Jamie's mum. Angela, this is Jinnie, my wonderful assistant and part-time bar person at the Jekyll and Hyde.'

They shook hands. Angela's was ice-cold and trembling. Up close, Jinnie thought she was very pretty beneath the pallor. Sam had said she could do with a friend, so despite some reservations, she decided to go for it.

'Nice to meet you, Angela. I'm fairly new around here, so perhaps we could get together sometime? My mates are all in Edinburgh so I get a bit lonely.' *Except I have a demented genie at home waiting to grant me wishes, and I keep thinking about Sam and Ed in ways I really shouldn't.*

'Erm, sure. That'd be nice.' Angela seemed taken aback at the suggestion, whereas Sam was nodding like one of those toy dogs on a car dashboard. For good measure, he clapped his hands together and looked in danger of breaking into a little jig.

'Excellent! I'm sure you two will get on like a house on fire. Right, anything take your fancy in the shop today?'

Apart from the man himself, thought Jinnie grumpily. And where did that stupid expression come from, anyway? What did a blazing building have to do with people getting along with each other?

Phone numbers exchanged, Angela spent a few minutes

browsing before leaving empty-handed. She had more colour in her cheeks, but still seemed like a woman with the weight of the world on her shoulders.

'You're a good person, Jinnie Cooper,' said Sam. 'I'm a firm believer in small acts of kindness, and that was definitely one.' He gave Jinnie a look of such exquisite tenderness that her insides liquified. Or was that just the after-effect of too many pancakes for breakfast?

'Yup, that's me, Saint Jinnie of Cranley. Full of goodness. Bite into me and feel your teeth ache with sugar overload.' *Oh, help.* Where had *that* come from? Not only did she sound horribly sarcastic, she'd actually suggested that Sam bite her. And even worse, the thought of that was causing havoc internally.

'Would you mind if I skipped off a bit early? I've got a bit of a headache.' *Not true, but I need a cold shower, a reality check and a quiet evening with Dhassim. An oxymoron, perhaps, but better the devil — or genie — you know.*

'Sure, no problem.' Sam's expression was now one of concern. 'You get home and have a rest. I'll probably shut up shop early too. I need to knuckle down and get writing before my publisher sends me an abusive email.'

They said their goodbyes, and Jinnie left. She paused outside the shop for a moment, staring at the sky. It was streaked with clouds, and full of infinite possibilities. Adventures to be had, if you had the courage. *Spread your wings and fly away.* Jinnie sighed, and headed home.

CHAPTER 20

'ARE YOU OK?' JO WAVED HER HAND IN FRONT OF KEN'S FACE. He was in a trance, his cup of coffee and Danish pastry untouched.

Ken started. 'Sorry, Jo,' he replied. 'My head's in a proper guddle. Another rough night with Mags, I'm afraid.'

It was just after eight, and there were no other customers in the café. Jo had been in since six, baking and prepping for the days ahead. She'd close up on Christmas Eve and re-open on the fourth of January. In the past she'd booked a short trip over the break — Belgium, Iceland, Tenerife for a bit of warmth — but she had nothing planned this year. With both her parents long gone, and friends scattered all over the UK, Jo knew she'd painted herself into a lonely corner. Whether by accident or design, she'd chosen a solitary existence. Her customers were often the only people she spoke to on a daily basis, apart from best friend Carole who'd gone to primary school with her —as well as Brownies, Girl Guides and the local pub that didn't check their age when they ordered Pernod and blackcurrant. How they'd howled with laughter after flirting with a few blokes, only to realise their mouths were stained with inverted purple fangs! Carole lived in Somerset now, two husbands down and currently dating a former champion bodybuilder whose Facebook profile was filled with photos of him flexing various muscles. They chatted on FaceTime every few weeks, but hadn't seen each other in ages.

'I'm a good listener, if you want to offload,' said Jo, fetching her mug of tea and sitting down.

Ken smiled wanly, picking the edge off his pastry. 'There are days when I convince myself that Mags is better. Well, not exactly *better*, just not any worse. Then something else happens, and I know things will never be the same again.'

He related last night's episode. He had woken at 3 am and found Mags's side of the bed empty. He'd checked everywhere, including the beer garden, but there was no sign of her. Eventually he heard footsteps overhead. Mags was in the attic, and had pulled the wobbly ladder up after her. It had taken all his powers of persuasion to get her to lower it for him to come up. He found her rummaging through ancient suitcases, looking for a dress to wear at Christmas.

'God, it broke my heart, Jo. She was pulling out stuff from aeons ago. She found a dress, crushed purple velvet, that she wore for a photo portrait with Ed when he was little. She kept saying it was perfect; but it won't fit her now. Then she got upset when I tried to get her to come down. She started screaming for Ed, and hitting me with her fists...' Ken's eyes filled up, and he bowed his head.

Jo patted his arm, unsure what to say. 'If there's anything I can do,' she offered, aware how inadequate the words were.

'Thanks, Jo.' Ken produced a crumpled hankie from his pocket and blew his nose. 'I know it sounds horrible, but there are times I need to escape, in case I lose it. I love Mags, but it's like watching her gradually fade from view. And there's nothing I can do to stop it.'

Jo had no personal experience of dementia, but Carole's gran had suffered from it. Admittedly she'd been much older than Mags when diagnosed, and she had gone downhill very rapidly. Jo remembered, to her shame, the two of them giggling when the poor soul turned up at Carole's wearing her bra over her blouse. There'd been other episodes, when she put house keys in the oven and dirty dishes in the cupboards. Later she became quite aggressive, and swore profusely — all the more shocking as she had been a sweet old lady, who thought 'bum' was a rude word.

Just then a couple of regulars arrived, and Jo hurried back behind the counter to serve them. Out of the corner of her eye, she saw Ken finish his drink and head for the door. 'Wait a minute,' she called, pushing the tray of coffees and scones towards the customers. She came out from behind the counter and approached Ken, suddenly nervous about what she planned to say. Not that she'd really *planned* it; the idea had popped into her head.

'Listen, if you need some space — not here, it's too hard to chat properly — why don't you come round to mine one evening?' she said. 'I could make supper, and we could talk about anything you like. Mags, the pub, why toast always lands buttered-side down…'

If Ken was surprised at the suggestion, he didn't show it. Instead, he took Jo's hand and gently squeezed it with his own warm, lightly calloused one. 'That's a lovely thought, Jo,' he replied. 'The problem is finding an excuse to leave the pub. Or rather, explaining to Mags where I'm going.'

Because it might seem a bit odd to say, 'See you later, darling, just off to spend the evening with another woman'. Jo bit her lip, feeling like an idiot. But she wasn't suggesting a date, for heaven's sake. Just a chance for two people to relax over some food and a glass or two. And it wasn't because she was lonely, or had feelings for Ken. Absolutely not…

'Let me check the rota for the next few days,' Ken said. 'Ed's hoping to come back soon and Jamie's keen for extra shifts, so I might be able to bunk off. I'll just say I'm meeting an old friend. Which we are. Excuse the "old" — I mean me, of course.'

Jo got out her phone and they exchanged numbers. A moment later, and he was gone.

Walking back behind her spotless counter and wiping it down again, Jo wondered what she'd set in motion…

CHAPTER 21

Dʜᴀꜱꜱɪᴍ ʜᴀᴅ ᴀꜱꜱᴜʀᴇᴅ ʜᴇʀ ʀᴇᴘᴇᴀᴛᴇᴅʟʏ ᴛʜᴀᴛ ᴛʜᴇ WIFI ᴡᴀꜱ now functioning normally, and only wishes said out loud, in front of him, and which received a steady green light, would be granted. The only teeny, tiny problem was … what to wish for? Jinnie wished for things every day. Heck, people were always wishing for things. *I wish the ironing pile would disappear. I wish those extra pounds I gained over the holidays would melt away. I wish my boyfriend hadn't dumped me for someone with a nicer nose.* Wishes were, by and large, no more than a gripe about trivial matters. Unless you were talking about the big stuff. And Dhassim had already made it clear that his powers didn't extend to solving world problems or making her rich beyond her wildest dreams. Anyway, Jinnie didn't want to wish for money. Unless it was to help someone else —

'OK, I've thought of a wish: a proper one, this time. Don't get too excited — it's a bit mundane — but I wish I could fly.'

There, she'd said it. The thought of boarding a plane filled Jinnie with skin-creeping terror. She'd done it once several years ago with the girls, who'd nagged and cajoled her into a boozy weekend in Magaluf. In the build-up to the trip Jinnie had had nightmares about bomb-touting terrorists, security staff frisking her and finding drugs secreted in places she hadn't thought possible (not that she *did* drugs, but still), and worst of all, the aircraft plummeting from the sky. She'd watched the movies and read the news reports.

Even the process of passing through an airport terrified her. Jinnie had taken some over-the-counter medication that was meant to calm you down before the flight. She'd checked and double-checked that her liquids didn't contravene the rules (including a small flask of brandy Hannah insisted would take the edge off), and told herself repeatedly she was more likely to be hit by a bus than die in a plane crash. All to no avail. She'd snivelled and sobbed throughout the journey, and the supposedly fun-filled trip had been dominated by one thought: *I have to do it all again.*

'Don't they have planes for that these days?' Dhassim flounced over to the TV, the picture freeze-framed on Rachel and her annoyingly bouncy hair. 'Long tubey things with wings, and good-looking men and women who fetch you drinks and snacks?'

Jinnie had given up trying to figure out how Dhassim knew so much about the modern world. By all accounts he hadn't escaped the lamp in over a century, yet he was remarkably up to speed on twenty-first-century life. Everything from politics to climate change, film stars and pop music. As well as his crush on Brad Pitt's ex, he was possibly The Spice Girls' number-one fan; proof that his taste in music was as bad as his singing ability. If Jinnie heard one more 'zigazig ah', she'd stuff Dhassim head-first into the bloody lamp.

'Yes, they have planes. I wasn't thinking of flapping my

arms and hoping for take-off,' she huffed. 'I'm afraid of flying, and it's a bit of a pain when my friends go off on holiday.' As a concession to Jinnie's phobia they'd taken the Eurostar a couple of times to Paris. That had been lovely, but Mark had been largely dismissive, saying her fear was irrational (weren't all phobias irrational?), and suggesting she took a day-long course to get over it. She'd got as far as booking one in Edinburgh, then chickened out at the last minute.

'Let me check my trusty gizmo,' said Dhassim, giving Ms Aniston a last, lingering look before switching off the TV. He whipped out the WIFI, and instructed Jinnie to repeat the wish.

'I wish I could fly,' she intoned solemnly.

There was silence, then a series of jingles and chimes.

'Bingo! We are good to go. Your wish is granted.' Dhassim flashed one of his killer smiles that made Jinnie forgive him almost everything. But she didn't *feel* any different. And as she had neither the time nor money to fly anywhere any time soon, how would she know it had worked?

'Ma chérie,' — Dhassim was also a fan of all things French — 'it's a beautiful evening. And remember that for every one of your wishes, your genie extraordinaire gets a little something too.'

Jinnie frowned. If Dhassim thought for one second that she was going to book a romantic holiday abroad with him, he could think again. In any case, she was pretty sure he didn't have a passport.

'With you in two shakes,' he said. He thundered up the stairs, two at a time by the sound of it, reappearing a minute later with the mangy old rug rolled up under his arm. 'I can tell by your face that you doubt your loyal servant.' He shook out the rug, and placed it on the floor. 'So, what better way to prove that you've conquered your fear — and make me a happy little bunny — than to go for a spin on this?'

He could *not* be serious! Hell would freeze over before Jinnie would get on that *thing* ... and then what? Hover outside the window and scare a few locals to death? Plus it might be a beautiful night, but the temperature had dipped below zero. Hypothermia definitely wasn't on her wish list.

'Is it Persian?' asked Dhassim, smoothing out a few crinkles and knots where the vacuum had almost shredded the rug's fringe.

'Erm, no. It's from IKEA.' As if Jinnie possessed anything as valuable as a Persian rug! The only thing of value she owned was that damned diamond ring, and she was still dithering over what to do with that.

Dhassim stroked his goatee in a thoughtful manner. 'Geography is not my thing, sweet — Jinnie. Is that in Turkey? No matter. You and I are going to *fly*!'

He reached out his hand, and despite every fibre of her being screaming *This is insane,* Jinnie took it. Together, they stepped onto the rug.

As they did, the lounge window swung open and an icy blast of Scottish air filled the room.

'Shouldn't we get some jackets, or blankets?' They hadn't moved an inch, yet Jinnie was already trembling. Partly through cold, partly terror, except ... was she really scared? Or was this feeling excitement, the anticipation of doing something completely bonkers? A once-in-a-lifetime chance to soar through the skies without a seat belt, sick bag or in-flight shopping?

'No need,' said Dhassim. 'Where we're going, we don't need blankets.' And right on cue the rug twitched, levitated, and steered them through the window and out into the inky night sky. For an IKEA rug, it moved like a Swedish dancing queen.

Up, up, up they climbed, the village shrinking to doll's-house proportions. Jinnie clung to Dhassim's hand, aware that she was incredibly warm. She felt like a small child on Christmas morning: snug in bed, but indescribably thrilled about what lay ahead, and itching to see all the magic the day had in store.

'Look, Jinnie. Just look!' She hadn't realised her eyes were closed. *Don't you dare close your eyes, not for this!* She opened them, and gasped.

They were gliding above the city of Edinburgh. Below, sparkling lights were already in place for the build-up to Christmas. Above were the twinkling stars of a glorious winter evening, like diamonds stapled to a swatch of black velvet.

'Enjoying yourself?' Dhassim regarded her with his intense amber eyes.

Jinnie nodded, no words adequate to describe the feelings flooding through her. She had never felt so energised, so alive. Whatever else life had in store, this was a moment she would relive forever. Oh, wow, now they were just above —

'The Scott Monument. I did a little research, Jinnie. My WIFI does more than grant wishes, you know. And you *did* mention a certain connection between it and your boss, Sam. Aha, now you're blushing!'

Oops. Jinnie had forgotten mentioning Sam and the reason for his pen name. And perhaps she had babbled on a little too enthusiastically about him.

'I'm not blushing, it's the cold air,' she retorted. 'Sam's my boss and a nice man, but that's it.'

They swooped and soared over the floodlit castle, Jinnie still grasping Dhassim's hand. She wasn't afraid, not in the slightest. This was a truly magical experience, seeing the sights of the city she loved but had never taken the time to appreciate fully.

The rug headed towards the Firth of Forth, giving an incredible view of the Forth Bridge. If they kept going, they'd end up over the North Sea. Suddenly the carpet did a three-point turn (Jinnie had always struggled with those, which was probably why she'd failed her driving test five times), and they headed back towards Cranley. The whole journey had taken less than twenty minutes.

As they glided above the high street, the carpet began its descent. Then as they drew close to The Jekyll and Hyde, Jinnie spotted a familiar figure approaching the door. It was Ed, illuminated by the street lamps and the light spilling from the pub windows. Before she could stop herself, Jinnie leaned over the edge of the rug and called out his name.

'What are you *doing?*' squawked Dhassim, pulling her back to the middle.

Like a souped-up sports car the rug went from cruising to warp speed, propelling them over the pub roof and towards Brae Cottage. Jinnie giggled at Dhassim's stern expression. She knew she'd been naughty, but doubted Ed had heard or seen her. He'd told her earlier that he'd be around most of the holidays, which pleased her more than she cared to admit.

They sailed back through the open window and landed somewhat inelegantly in the middle of the lounge floor. Within seconds Jinnie was shivering, the adrenalin rush of the adventure replaced by bone-chilling cold.

Still with a face like thunder, Dhassim grabbed a fleecy blanket from the sofa and threw it over her shoulders. 'Do not do things like that!' he admonished. 'If other mortals witness my magic powers, I will be banished for evermore to genie purgatory. And that is *not* where I want to spend the rest of my days, honeybun.'

Jinnie apologised, and let the sickly term of endearment

go unchallenged. She hugged Dhassim, thanked him for an incredible evening, and headed for bed.

By the time Dhassim hauled the rug upstairs and made himself comfortable, Jinnie was snuggled up in her favourite cosy pyjamas and nudging towards sleep. She felt bone-weary, exhausted, but exhilarated. It had truly been a night to remember.

CHAPTER 22

Ed was on the train back to Carlisle. He hated leaving his mum, even though they chatted on FaceTime once a week. His dad was doing his best, that was clear, but the strain was showing. Ed had always believed his parents' relationship was rock-solid, unbreakable, but what happened when the person you knew inside-out began to change?

In the few days he'd been home, he'd sensed Ken's tension each time Mags muddled something up. Just a look — never directly at Mags — or a gesture that signalled his frustration. Banging down a cup or a book just a little too hard. Taking himself off to another room, to put some space between them.

Stirring his takeaway coffee and pulling chunks from a crumbly blueberry muffin, Ed opened another message from Cheryl. He was officially in her bad books, having declined to attend the house party with Cal and his crew.

I don't see why you can't come. Surely work can wait? You're turning into a grumpy old git C ☺

Ed had used his time at home as an excuse, saying he had to catch up with stuff. It wasn't strictly true, but a night with that lot would involve a fair amount of booze and other substances. He steered clear of the latter, but sinking a good few drinks was the only way to cope with their inane wittering.

The 'grumpy old git' comment made Ed smile; it reminded him of Jinnie talking about her first impressions of Ken. She'd been embarrassed at how wrong she was, and Ed enjoyed their easy banter behind the bar. He was still baffled by her cocktail-making prowess — surely no one could learn *that* quickly? — but he was glad she was working there.

And he'd definitely see her when he returned for the holidays. Ed had booked off the whole festive period from work. He knew it was time for a change, but wasn't sure what direction to take. Perhaps be his own boss, and find a partner who was more in tune with his needs. Whatever *they* were. Cheryl was like a primary-school band, all discords and skinned knees. He wanted something calmer, more soothing to the soul. Soaring violins. Gently-twanging harps. Tinkling bells.

Jinnie. Or was he reading too much into things?

* * *

As an olive branch, Ed had agreed to meet Cheryl for a quick coffee. He spotted her straightaway, sitting by the café window glued to her phone. He also clocked another male customer giving her the once-over. That wasn't surprising. Cheryl, with her striking scarlet hair and porcelain complexion, stood out in a crowd. Very easy on the eye, but much harder on the ear.

'Did you miss me?' she cooed, leaning in for a kiss. Ed responded, noting that her admirer looked distinctly put out.

'I'm still not sure I should forgive you for bailing,' she murmured. 'All work and no play makes Ed a very dull boy.'

Fetching them both cappuccinos, he sat and listened as Cheryl grumbled about Tony at work. She'd been reprimanded again for being late, and as a punishment — in her opinion — been assigned council meeting duty. 'I'll need bloody matchsticks to prop my eyes open,' she whinged. 'Boring doesn't begin to cover it. All they do is drone on about budgets and cost-cutting and where the funding's coming from for the latest community project. That little weasel Eric ought to do it, but he's such a total arse-licker…'

On and on she ranted. Ed nodded at appropriate moments, but his thoughts were elsewhere. Staring at Cheryl's constantly moving mouth, her face blurred and her features became those of Jinnie. Loose dark curls and lightly tanned skin, with hazel eyes that sparkled when she laughed. And that smattering of freckles across her nose…

'Ed. Ed! Are you listening?' Cheryl snapped her fingers in front of him, and Ed jolted back to the present. 'Honestly, you abandon me all week, refuse to come to a party with me, then act as if I'm not even here.' She folded her arms defensively, tossing her hair for good measure.

'Sorry, sorry,' mumbled Ed. 'There's just a lot on my mind with Mum, and work's piled up over the past few days. I'll make it up to you soon, promise.' Now wasn't the time to mention he'd be away over Christmas *and* New Year.

When Cheryl finally paused for breath, he gave her a quick update on Mags and pub life in general. He didn't mention Jinnie, convincing himself it was only because he barely knew her. Which was true, but that didn't explain why she kept occupying his thoughts.

'Right, I'd best be off,' announced Cheryl, draining her cup. 'I promised Cal we'd do a supermarket run for booze and snacks, and we need to use my car because his failed its MOT.' They kissed again, and Cheryl pulled him close. 'I'll try to behave, but don't blame me if some hot bloke melts my defences,' she whispered. 'While the cat's away, and all that.' Off she skipped, leaving Ed with a half-empty cup and the feeling that maybe that wouldn't be such a terrible thing.

Back at his flat, Ed cranked up all the radiators and put on an extra jumper. It was already mid-December, and the temperature had dropped dramatically. He made himself cheese on toast with a liberal splosh of Worcester sauce, and settled down at his desktop for a few hours' work. His latest assignment was a series of brochures for an upmarket hotel chain, featuring everything from luxurious suites to in-house spa facilities. He scanned through a file of photos: opulent rooms with swathed four-poster beds; candlelit table settings with ice buckets and arty floral arrangements; impossibly beautiful people wearing fluffy white robes and satin eye masks, reclining on chaise longues.

An oozing wodge of cheese landed on the keyboard, and Ed cursed. Fetching some kitchen roll, he cleaned up the mess and closed the file. His heart wasn't in it. And his head was most definitely somewhere else.

CHAPTER 23

'Come in, come in,' urged Jo, desperate to shut the door before another Baltic blast penetrated the house. It had been snowing on and off for most of the day, although the long-term forecast said it would turn milder. A white Christmas looked unlikely.

'Thanks, Jo.' Ken shrugged off his heavy overcoat and scarf, hanging them on one of the pegs in the hallway. 'Jeez, it's bitter out there; the pavements are getting treacherous. I reckon it'll be a quiet night at the pub. Folks will want to keep warm indoors.'

'I doubt it,' she replied, gesturing towards the kitchen. 'The old diehards will be digging out their skis. A wee flurry or two won't deter them from their pints and chasers.'

The kitchen was toasty warm, the radiator blasting out heat and Jo's prized Aga adding to the feeling of cosiness. The table was set for two. Nothing fancy, just cutlery and paper napkins, as she'd decided lighting candles would be a step too far. A rich beef stew with dumplings was simmering away, and a bottle of red sat uncorked and breathing on the counter.

'Smells incredible.' Ken sniffed the air appreciatively, still rubbing his hands to counter the cold. 'I'm glad I only had a cheese sandwich for lunch.'

He had messaged Jo that morning. She'd read the text immediately, convinced it would be a polite rejection. What had she been thinking, inviting a happily married man round for supper?

Probably too short notice, but I could be free this evening. Mags is out with a couple of friends, and Rose and Jamie are on duty. No worries if you're busy. Ken

Jo's fingers had hovered over the phone, torn between *That's great! Drop by around 7* and *Sorry, plans tonight, maybe another time.* The former had won, but only because she'd given herself a stern talking-to. They were friends, double-underlined and typed in bold. Ken was having a really tough time, and in all the time she'd known him, he wasn't one to confide in others. Apart from herself, and maybe Sam. He might not wear his heart on his sleeve, but Jo was perceptive enough to know that heart was battered and bruised.

'So who is Mags out with?' As far as Jo was aware, Mags and Ken were a tight-knit unit. Even before her diagnosis Mags had seemed to spend virtually all of her time in the pub, apart from the odd night out with Ken (and Ed). Then again, she might have a group of friends Jo knew nothing about. Perhaps she was in a book club, or they just liked to meet up for a drink or a bite to eat every now and again. Jo felt she was in no position to pass judgement on someone's social circle. Or lack of one.

'Lindsey and Ruth. They're the wives of a couple of locals, both quite new to the area,' said Ken, accepting a glass of red. 'They've been really kind since — you know, and they're good with Mags. Other friends going back years have found it harder to cope. Some have drifted away, always making excuses why they can't visit. It's almost as if they think Mags might be contagious.'

Jo put the plates in to warm, and produced a platter of deli meats, olives and cheeses to nibble on. 'That's awful, but people are strange when it comes to illness. It's like folk who say they can't stand visiting someone in hospital because they find the smell and the atmosphere upsetting. As if anyone *enjoys* being in hospital!' Jo speared an olive with vigour, indignant that Mags's so-called friends could be so thoughtless.

'It is what it is.' Ken sighed. 'I told you before, I'm struggling to cope myself at times. I just want my Mags back, but I know that's never going to happen. Sorry, I bet you're wishing you'd invited someone more upbeat to eat with you.'

'Hmm, like Scrooge?' Jo donned a pair of oven gloves and wrestled the stew from the oven, her glasses steaming up in the process. 'Dammit, can't see a bloody thing!' she exclaimed.

Ken leapt to the rescue, seizing a couple of tea towels and manoeuvring the hot dish on to the hob.

'Thanks,' said Jo. 'You'd think in my line of work I'd be a bit more proficient when it comes to oven-wrangling.' She wiped her glasses and left the stew to rest, joining Ken in polishing off the nibbles.

'So, tell me to mind my own business — people frequently do — but how come a good-looking lady like you doesn't have a man in her life?' Ken topped up their glasses, his gaze steady and curious. Other women might be offended by his directness, but not Jo. She had chosen to keep her private life under wraps, but hadn't she invited Ken around to share confidences? Mind you, she could have a little fun first…

'Well, it's probably because I'm gay.' Jo watched Ken's mouth form an 'oh' shape. 'I haven't met the right woman yet, although I've had my eye on Janette for quite a while. It's that pink and white-checked overcoat, I think. Gives me goosebumps every time I see her in it.'

Getting to her feet before she burst out laughing, Jo started dishing up the stew. Ken got up too, and gave her a playful nudge.

'Oi!' she scolded. 'Watch out, unless you'd rather wear your dinner than eat it.'

Ken picked up the tasting spoon and blew on it, before putting it in his mouth. 'Heavenly,' he pronounced. 'Unlike the wee devil who made it. If you're gay, I'm the tooth fairy. And before you get the wrong idea, I don't have a prejudiced bone in my body.'

Piling dumplings on the plates, they took their places. Ken tucked his napkin into the top of his jumper — 'I'm a hellishly messy eater' — and they each waited for the other to take the first mouthful.

'Your dumplings look incredible,' said Ken.

There was a pause as they eyed each other, then they both erupted with laughter.

'I think we're straying into *Carry On* territory,' sobbed Jo. 'You'll be complimenting me on my baps next.' She pointed at the basket of bread rolls, waiting to soak up the excess sauce.

'Aargh, stop, woman!' Ken snatched at his napkin and dabbed at his eyes. 'I came here for a peaceful evening. Now you're twisting my words and making me laugh, and it's *exactly* what I need right now. Exactly what I need.'

Jo picked up her fork and stabbed at a chunk of beef. She managed to spear a carrot too, and used her knife to cut a sliver of dumpling. All stalling tactics, because she felt, she *felt* — what did she feel? Glad that they were so relaxed in each other's company, of course. She was happy that they could laugh together, be a bit silly, tease one another. It was basic human interaction, nothing more. It didn't *mean* anything: at least not anything that could be frowned upon. Unless you were a card-carrying member of the 'men and women can never just be friends' brigade.

'So, you didn't buy me and Janette as a couple? That's a pity.' Time to simmer things down, and keep humour to the fore.

'As I said, I didn't believe a word of it. Well, you had me going for a split second, but Janette…'

Jo gave a reproving stare. 'Beauty is in the eye of the beholder. I happen to think that Janette is a total gem, with a crusty exterior which belies her inner sparkle. Any man or woman would be blessed to be with her.'

'Aye, right.' Ken buttered a bap and plunged it into his stew. 'Don't get me wrong, Janette is a pillar of the community, but I happen to know she has a black belt in macramé.'

More hilarity ensued, Jo developing a stitch in her side from the constant laughter. Ken related some comic tales from the pub, and Jo pitched in with exploits from her younger days.

'Seriously, you climbed out of a bathroom window to escape a date just because the poor chap had bad breath?' Ken chortled, upending the bottle to share out the last of the wine.

'That was the icing on a very unpalatable cake,' Jo replied. 'He also had wandering hands syndrome. It was like being attacked by an amorous octopus. I legged it to the loo, and figured the only way was up and out. Wouldn't fancy my chances now, mind you.' Jo patted her hips, aware that she was more curvy than fat. Not that she was fishing for compliments or anything…

'As I said, you're a good-looking woman who still hasn't explained why she's single, but I'll shut up now.' Ken mimed pulling a zipper across his mouth.

'No big secret,' said Jo, clearing away the empty plates. 'I just never met the right man, but that's OK. I love my life, simple as it is, and I don't have to answer to anyone. I'd never settle for second best. If I met someone, I'd want what you have.'

No sooner had the words left her mouth than Jo felt like kicking herself. What she *meant* was having a relationship as solid and loving as Ken and Mags's. Instead, judging by Ken's downcast demeanour, she'd just reminded him that he was losing the love of his life little by little each day.

'Sorry.' Jo started rinsing the plates, her back to Ken. 'That came out wrong. I didn't mean to upset you, I —'

Ken lifted her soapy right hand from the washing-up bowl and squeezed it. 'You didn't. Jo, coming here tonight has been a tonic. Truly, it has. I was wondering if I'd forgotten how to laugh, but you've shown me I still can.'

Slowly Jo withdrew her hand, and dried it on the towel draped over the Aga handle. The atmosphere in the room had changed. There was an intimacy, an electricity that hadn't been there before.

Perhaps Ken sensed it too. He mumbled something about getting back before Mags returned. Jo refused his offer of helping to do the rest of the dishes, and he fetched his coat.

'Thanks, Jo.' Winding his scarf around his neck, Ken shuffled from one foot to the other. Jo wanted to hug him, but her arms remained welded to her sides.

Finally Ken gave her an awkward half-hug, and a kiss that landed on her forehead. 'I hope we can do this again sometime,' he said. Jo smiled and nodded, and with another gust of icy air, Ken was gone.

Leaning on the closed door, Jo told herself that nothing had happened. Everything was fine; *they* were fine. Just friends. If she said it often enough, she might just believe it.

CHAPTER 24

CHRISTMAS EVE

Twas the night (or rather, the day) before Christmas, when all through the house things were supposed to be quiet as a mouse. *If only!*

Jinnie was upstairs trying to blow-dry her hair, which always did the opposite of what she wanted. Even the grinding noise of her close-to-death hairdryer failed to drown out the sound of Dhassim caterwauling in the lounge. He'd discovered the joys of YouTube, and was working his way through a catalogue of Christmas songs with lyrics bouncing along the bottom of the screen. How she'd survived the past couple of weeks was nothing short of a miracle. At least she'd been busy at the shop, and a few shifts at the pub meant she wasn't totally skint.

'Give me strength,' Jinnie groaned, the barrel brush doggedly refusing to part company with a clump of hair. Through her squeal of pain, she heard Dhassim launch into an equally painful rendition of 'I Wish It Could Be Christmas Every Day.' No bloody way. Not if it meant putting up with *that* racket.

She stormed to the top of the stairs. 'Could you turn it

down, please! I am getting a headache and I've got a lot to do before I see my family tomorrow,' Jinnie hollered, still trying to untangle the brush.

The volume dropped marginally, and there was a brief reprieve before Dhassim launched into a Cliff Richard sing-a-long.

'Bugger the mistletoe, pass me the wine,' thought Jinnie, back at her dressing table and abandoning her styling attempts. She scooped up her hair with a scrunchy and chugged a mouthful of orange juice. Pity it wasn't a Bucks Fizz, but there'd be a few celebratory drinks later at The Jekyll and Hyde. Maybe even some mistletoe, although Jinnie didn't plan on kissing anyone.

Pulling on some jogging bottoms and a well-worn sweat-shirt, she clumped downstairs in her fake Ugg boots, which unfortunately smelled like an overripe cheese. You get what you pay for; wasn't that the old adage?

'Ah, Jinnie, I am loving all these Christmas songs. It really is the most wonderful time of the year!' Dhassim grabbed her hand and twirled her around as Mel and Kim warbled about dancing around the Christmas tree. Despite herself Jinnie bust a few moves, glad that years of watching *Strictly Come Dancing* had taught her something.

'I do not understand, however, why someone sings about seeing their mother kissing Santa Claus,' panted Dhassim, demonstrating a couple of sharp heel leads. 'From what I gather, this Santa is a rather rotund man who somehow manages to squeeze down chimneys to leave presents. That is puzzling enough, but why would a married woman kiss him? Surely that would be classed as infidelity?'

'No, the thing is...' Jinnie stopped, not sure she could explain the truth about Santa. Dhassim was a genie; why shatter his illusions about a jolly bearded fellow with a penchant for whizzing through the sky on a reindeer-driven sleigh? Her own belief had been dealt a fatal blow at the age of nine, when she'd woken up to spy her dad fumbling with the stocking at the end of her bed. Jinnie had kept up the pretence of believing for several more years because she knew Rob would be upset to discover he'd been rumbled, and ignored Archie's snide remarks about her stupidity.

Hannah and Shona were coming to Cranley for a bite of lunch at A Bit of Crumpet. Before they arrived, Jinnie wanted to wrap her presents for family and friends. Later, they would head to the pub for a few festive drinks — Ray's home-made mulled wine was legendary for its potency — before the girls headed back to Edinburgh.

'Dammit, why is the Sellotape never where I thought I'd put it?' Jinnie grumbled, scrambling through the 'man drawer' in the kitchen, as comedian Michael McIntyre dubbed it. Sure enough, it contained random keys for mysterious locks, a hotchpotch of tea lights and candles, and bundles of expired store loyalty cards and other rubbish. But not the bloody Sellotape. Jinnie finally located it at the back of the drawer where she kept tea towels and packs of paper napkins.

'You still have not explained to me about the kissing thing,' said Dhassim, hovering in the doorway.

Jinnie grabbed the bag of wrapping paper propped up in the corner, and took a pair of scissors from the utensils holder. 'Another time,' she replied. 'Look, could you be an angel and help me wrap stuff? I'm going to be late meeting the girls if I don't get a move on. I still have to get changed and do something with *this*.' She waved the scissors perilously close to her badly-coiffed head. Maybe that was the answer. Chop it all off, à la Carey Mulligan. Except Jinnie feared she'd end up more Cary Grant: manly rather than gamine.

It turned out the genie was a genius when it came to

wrapping (of the gift variety; his attempts at rapping musically were ear-bleedingly bad). Jinnie sat back and watched as the presents were transformed into packages worthy of an expensive Christmas ad photo shoot.

As Dhassim snapped off the final piece of tape with his pointy teeth, Jinnie got to her feet. 'Brilliant, thank you! Right, I'm off to get tarted up. I just wish I had perfect hair, instead of a bird's nest perched on my head.'

Before she could move an inch, Dhassim whipped out his WIFI. He gave her a quizzical look as the device flashed and beeped. As wishes went, it wouldn't win any awards for inventiveness, but Jinnie had no doubt it was shared with millions of women around the world. 'Go for it,' she said.

The steady green light appeared, and Jinnie's scalp felt as if a million tiny ants were performing a Lindy Hop on it. She winced, then hit the stairs as fast as her pins-and-needles legs would allow.

As she approached the dressing table, Jinnie squeezed her eyes shut. Her vision of perfect hair might differ greatly from Dhassim's. He'd been kicking around a very long time, so who knew? It might be a towering, pomaded homage to Marie Antoinette, or a heavily lacquered beehive from the Swinging Sixties. Oh God, would she have to spend the rest of her life sleeping upright and bulk-buying cans of hairspray to maintain the look?

'Wow.' Jinnie wasn't often lost for words, but her reflection rendered her speechless. Staring back at her was a woman with hair so sleek, so glossy, so utterly *perfect* that it would make hair models weep with envy. Not a strand was out of place. Jinnie shook her head vigorously, then watched in wonder as every strand fell back into place. Even the dark strip of neglected roots had miraculously disappeared. It looked like expensive trips to Stephanie were a thing of the past — and those terrifying thoughts of putting her head in the hands of Peggy the high street perm-queen forever banished.

'Hubba hubba!' cried Dhassim when Jinnie returned, wearing a purple velvet dress she'd picked up in the sales several years ago. 'I believe that is the correct terminology for complimenting a woman on her looks.'

Possibly in a 1950s movie, thought Jinnie, but accepted it graciously. 'Right, I'm off to meet my friends, and I doubt I'll be back till much later. Will you be OK?' She felt guilty leaving Dhassim alone so much, but she could hardly take him with her. 'Hey girls, meet my very own genie of the lamp! Amazing what you can pick up in the shops these days.'

'Do not worry your pretty little head,' Dhassim replied. 'I have found many Christmas movies to watch, and I have more delicious haggis to partake of.'

Jinnie had snapped up a few battered tins of Scotland's national dish at Janette's. At first Dhassim had looked on in horror as she scooped what resembled dog food into a pan. But once heated, he'd taken a tentative taste and declared it 'magnifique'.

'OK, enjoy.' Gathering up the girls' presents and her coat, she left as Bing Crosby and David Bowie harmonised to 'The Little Drummer Boy', and Dhassim enthusiastically *pa rum pum pum pum*-ed along.

CHAPTER 25

Jinnie, Hannah and Shona huddled at a table in the café, fingers wrapped around steaming mugs of hot chocolate. Hannah had brought along a hip flask and added a generous splosh of rum to each one.

'At this rate we'll be sozzled before we hit the pub,' said Shona, just as Jo arrived with their food.

'Get this lot down you and you'll be fine,' she said, passing them plates of Scotch pie and baked beans.

'I can feel my waistband straining just looking at that,' groaned Hannah. 'Do you make these yourself?'

'I do indeed,' said Jo. 'Only the finest ingredients, not like some of the dodgy ones you get elsewhere.'

'And there's cake for afters,' grinned Jinnie, pointing at the glistening array of cupcakes, éclairs and other sugar-filled goodies.

'The diet starts on January 1st,' declared Shona, cutting into the pie. 'I'm just not saying which year!'

It felt good being with her friends, catching up on gossip and exchanging beauty tips. Both Hannah and Shona had oohed and aahed over Jinnie's hair, demanding to know which products she used. She'd smiled in her best Mona Lisa fashion, and moved the conversation on to the girls' favourite topic.

'I thought he might be a keeper, but when he made this funny noise' — Hannah did a fine impression of a stuck pig — 'during sex, I knew it was over.'

'Anyone on the scene for you?' Jinnie asked Shona.

'Nah, I'm in the same boat as you. Who needs a man when you've got great mates and pie!'

The conversation turned to Shalini and Jacqui. Both were still loved-up, with Jacqui hinting that boyfriend Kev might be about to pop the question.

'What question's that, then?' said Hannah, scooping the last of the beans into her mouth with the knife. For such a picky woman, she had a few dodgy habits herself. 'Will you move in with me, do my washing, and keep the fridge stocked with beer from here to eternity? Oh, and I'll put a ring on it, but don't expect to glide down the aisle any time soon.'

Jinnie play-slapped her cynical friend, relieved that the girls hadn't pressed her on her own love life. Clearly, her sickly sweet answer on their night out about needing to heal herself had hit the mark.

Jo returned to clear the plates and take their cake orders. The café was quiet, bar a few customers picking up orders of home-made mince pies and Yuletide chocolate logs for the big day.

'What are your plans for tomorrow, Jo?' asked Jinnie. 'Are you spending it with family?'

Jo shook her head, a fleeting look of sadness crossing her face.

'No, my folks died a long time ago and I don't have any siblings, so it'll be a quiet one at home, with a shop-bought roast dinner and Christmas pudding for one.' She smiled.

'You needn't pull those faces. I'm perfectly happy slobbing in my onesie and catching up on the shows I've been meaning to watch all year. I'll probably pop into the pub tonight for a bit of human company.'

Left with their cakes, the girls exchanged gifts. Jinnie put hers aside to open tomorrow, but neither Hannah nor Shona were willing to wait. 'Bugger that for a game of soldiers!' exclaimed Hannah, tearing the shiny gold paper off her present with all the fervour of an overexcited toddler. 'Aw, thanks, hon. It's lovely.'

Jinnie had bought them both scarf rings she'd found in a tiny boutique near her parents' home. Inexpensive but pretty, they could either secure a scarf or be worn on a chain as a necklace.

'Right, what's the plan of action?' declared Shona, looking at her watch. 'It's just after two, so should we head back to yours for a while?'

Eek! Jinnie hadn't considered that her friends might want to visit. Short of dashing ahead and stuffing Dhassim in the broom cupboard, it was an absolute no-no. 'Sorry, the place is a tip,' she said. 'Knickers drying everywhere, and I don't think there's a clean cup or glass to be had.' Jinnie's cheeks glowed red at the outright lie. Her friends all knew she was something of a neat freak, if not a fan of dusting and vacuuming.

'Standards slipping out in the sticks, eh?' Hannah tutted, digging out her purse to pay her share of the bill. 'OK, so it's a whistle-stop tour of Cranley then off to the pub. Will we get to meet the enigmatic Sam and the energetic Ed?'

When chatting and texting to Hannah, Jinnie had mentioned the two men a couple of times, Well, maybe more than a couple. But she'd been adamant there was more chance of her persuading Prince Harry to dump Meghan than for them to be anything other than friends.

'They'll be there, along with most of the village. Bye, Jo.' Jinnie waved, and the trio exited in a flurry of giggles and pre-Christmas excitement.

* * *

By four o'clock the pub was jumping. Ed had been excused from bar duty for half an hour, and was currently charming the pants off Hannah and Shona. Peggy from the salon came over to admire Jinnie's hair, and insisted she'd be happy to give it 'a wee trim' when required. There was no sign yet of Sam. Jinnie was officially on holiday from the shop from now until January 4th, since Out of the Attics Antiques closed during the festive period. He'd given her a generous bonus despite her protestations, and she had to admit the money was very welcome.

'Another?' Ed picked up Jinnie's empty glass of mulled wine. It was totally scrumptious, infused with spices and no doubt laced with something lethal.

'Better not for now, or you'll have to carry me home,' she joked, feeling distinctly hot and bothered when Ed gave her an exaggerated lingering look.

'Party pooper,' screeched Hannah, shoving both her and Shona's empty glasses towards Ed. At the rate they were going, Ed might have to pour them onto their train later.

Testing her legs — still steady, thankfully — Jinnie headed over to the buffet table, laden with nuts, crisps and more substantial nibbles all provided by Ken. An empty shoebox with a slot cut in the lid acted as a makeshift charity box, all proceeds going to Alzheimer's research. Jinnie stuffed in a tenner and filled a paper plate with a selection of savouries.

'Thanks, love.' Ken appeared at her shoulder, closely followed by Mags.

'Ooh, how lovely to see some new faces here on

Christmas Eve,' she enthused, her gaze taking in Hannah, Shona, and Jinnie. 'We don't get many visitors at this time of year, do we, darling?'

Ken's face briefly crumpled before he kissed his wife on the cheek and gave Jinnie an apologetic look. 'That's true. Lucky we have three wise women to grace us with their presence, eh?'

Jinnie wasn't sure about the 'wise' bit. Hannah was now guzzling her fourth glass, and giving Ed either a sports massage or a grope. Shona was swaying to the loo and casting lascivious glances at all the menfolk on the way, regardless of age or infirmity. Maybe she could get them out of here by seven, and spend the rest of the evening bopping around with Dhassim...

'Penny for them.' Suddenly Sam was there, his presence as welcome as a hot bath after a long day.

'Not sure they're worth that much,' stammered Jinnie.

He ran a hand through freshly-shorn hair, a stray piece stubbornly sticking up like a horn. Jinnie resisted the urge to smooth it down, instead absent-mindedly flicking her own forward.

'I let Peggy loose with the clippers,' said Sam. 'A bargain at a fiver, but I feel like Shaun the Sheep.' He paused, squinting at Jinnie's hair. 'Whereas you look stunning. Great hair, great outfit. Now, where can a man get a drink around here?'

'Hello! You must be Sam.' Hannah appeared as if by magic, brandishing two glasses of mulled wine. A little slopped over the sides as she handed them over, hindered by her full body sweep of Jinnie's boss. 'My dad loves *Antiques Roadshow*, cos he fancies Fiona Bruce, but I can't recall many experts looking like you.'

Let the ground now split asunder and swallow up Hannah, and maybe Jinnie too. Jinnie took a sip, unable to look Sam in the eye.

A raucous laugh signalled the arrival of Shona, who entwined herself around Sam, coming perilously close to burying his face in her bosom. 'Sam the man, I do believe,' she simpered. 'Pleasure to meet you.'

Much as Jinnie loved her friends, they often behaved like bitches on heat when faced with a new male of the species. Leaving them to fawn over Sam, she fetched another glass of mulled wine and piled a mini mountain of sausage rolls on a plate.

'Here you go,' she said, glad to see that Hannah and Shona had stopped examining Sam, and were now slumped in their seats.

'Thanks, and cheers.' They clinked glasses, Jinnie nobbling a sausage roll and cramming it in her mouth.

'I am a total sucker for party food,' she said, hoping she hadn't sprayed Sam with pastry crumbs.

'Me too,' he replied, 'which is why I have several frozen boxes lined up for tomorrow. Bung 'em in the oven, dish them up, rinse and repeat.'

Jinnie hadn't asked what Sam would be doing on Christmas Day. She'd assumed he'd be spending it with Sean, or maybe other family and friends. 'Aren't you seeing your son, or someone…?'

'In the legendary words of Joan Armatrading, it will be "Me, Myself, I." Sean's with his mum and her partner. I'll see him on Boxing Day, hopefully, or thereabouts.'

Jinnie thought of her own plans, spending the day with family and adhering to traditions she was reluctant to let go of. She knew there would come a time when Wilma wasn't around, or when she had a husband, children and a whole new set of Christmas rituals. Her throat seized up at the thought, and she swallowed a lukewarm mouthful of mulled wine.

The hands on the pub clock seemed to whizz by. People

were still piling in, but it was time for Hannah and Shona to catch the train. Ed appeared, like a knight in shining armour, swinging car keys and offering them a lift to the station.

'Love you,' slurred Hannah, as Shona propped her up — or was it the other way round?

'Love you too,' replied Jinnie, blinking away tears she hadn't expected. Could she wish for everyone she loved to be happy, healthy and with people they cared about? Or was that too much to ask?

As 'It'll Be Lonely This Christmas' blared from the juke-box, Jinnie watched her friends leave. A headache threatened, her bed beckoned and she wanted nothing more than deep, deep sleep.

'Leaving already?' Sam appeared as she fetched her coat from the cloakroom by the main door.

'I'm exhausted, and I need my bed,' Jinnie said, reaching for her hooded, fur-lined coat. Sam unhooked it and slid it over her shoulders. For a moment they tussled, Jinnie's arm failing to synchronise with the sleeve. Sam pulled her closer, his face inches from hers.

'Merry Christmas,' Jinnie breathed, inhibitions scattered to the winds. She aimed for Sam's cheek, but her lips had other ideas. Like heat-seeking missiles they found their target and … boom! *We're kissing. And it feels pretty damn amazing.*

'Jinnie…' Sam's voice broke her reverie. Jinnie flailed her way to the surface, lost in the moment and unwilling to return to the real world. He was holding her hand, pulling her outside. But his demeanour was that of a caring parent escorting a belligerent child from a candy-fuelled outing, with a full-blown tantrum on the horizon.

'Merry Christmas.' They were already outside Jinnie's home, the intervening minutes a blur. Jinnie didn't know whether to drag Sam over the threshold (praying that

Dhassim was already fast asleep), or accept that what had happened was a one-off. And throwing herself down on the pavement, fists pounding and screams echoing, wouldn't change a thing.

'Do you want me...?' *Oh, what an ambiguous question.* Except Jinnie knew that Sam was being the perfect gentleman, offering nothing more than to see her safely inside. Anything else was down to her fevered imagination.

'I'm fine, thank you.' Jinnie slipped her key in the lock, and opened the door. Sam walked away, hands buried deep in his pockets.

She closed the door and slid down the wall to the floor, humiliation gnawing at her core. Now what?

CHAPTER 26

Rob sang loudly in his rich baritone about dreaming of a snow-filled Christmas, giving his carving knife a final buff.

Kath joined in, polishing a cut-glass wine glass, her face flushed from a combination of cooking and two glasses of pre-lunch champagne.

'Huh, dream on, cos it's pissing down out there,' sniped Archie. Which was true. Instead of delightfully fluffy flakes of snow, the sky was leaden grey and rain hammered against the windows.

'Who invited The Grinch?' retorted Jinnie. She'd arrived just moments ago, the train journey a blur as she revisited *that* moment again and again. It had been the most fleeting of kisses, she and Sam going in for a peck on the cheek after he'd helped her put on her coat. They'd misjudged which side to aim for, and their lips had met. Well, that wasn't *quite* true, but Jinnie didn't want to dwell on the fact she'd instigated the kiss. Until Sam pulled away and escorted her home. The perfect gentleman, but not the result she'd hoped for.

'Bah, humbug,' Archie replied. He was wearing a scraggy

pair of tracksuit bottoms and a T-shirt covered in stains. Jinnie hoped he'd brought something else to wear. Or, more likely, Mum had bought him clothes as part of his present and he'd reluctantly change before they sat down to eat.

'You look pretty,' declared Rob, gesturing at Jinnie's crimson wrap dress and favourite boots. The dress was a hand-me-down from Hannah. At their last get-together, she'd given Jinnie a bag of clothes she didn't like any more, or had decided didn't suit her. 'Much more your colouring,' she'd said. 'When you're as peely-wally as me, red makes you look like you need a blood transfusion.'

'Thanks, Dad.' Jinnie gave her still-damp but perfectly-coiffed hair a shake, then rummaged in her bag for the family gifts to place under the tree. Perfume for her mum, after-shave for her dad, a boxed set of horror DVDs for Archie, and a selection of fancy teas for Wilma. Nothing had cost more than twenty pounds, which still made a sizeable dent in her budget. But it was Christmas, and the season of goodwill to all men. Even Archie.

'Give us a hand with the sprouts, Jinnie,' said Kath. 'Dad's just popping out to pick up Wilma. He'd have picked you up too, love. You only have to ask.'

Side by side in the kitchen, trimming and cutting crosses in the sprouts, Jinnie wondered how Sam was doing. And Ed. And Dhassim. The three men who featured most in her life. Sam was spending Christmas alone. At least, he said he was. She had no reason to doubt him, and in any case, what he did was his business. That kiss had been an aberration, a mistake. They'd brush it off when they next saw each other, or simply not mention it at all. Ed? Well, Jinnie couldn't pretend she didn't like him. What she found difficult was working out if she liked him in a 'I really, really *like* you' way, or more like a brother. Not an annoying, rude, useless one like Archie — a kind, caring one who'd always protect her, make her smile, keep her on track…

'Ouch!' Jinnie yelped as the razor-sharp vegetable knife sliced into her finger.

'Oh dear. Run it under the tap and I'll fetch a plaster,' said Kath.

Archie appeared in the doorway, smirking as Jinnie watched blood trickle down the plughole. 'Why we have to eat those green abominations is a mystery to me.' He sidled closer, picking up a fork and using it like a pool cue. 'Bam! That's one out the way. He shoots, he scores, he —'

'Gets the flip out of the kitchen.' Jinnie sucked her wounded finger.

Kath returned and wrapped a plaster around the cut. It stung like buggery, but she'd live.

'Hello! Merry Christmas!' Wilma's voice echoed through the hallway, followed by a bout of coughing which suggested a lung might have come loose. Jinnie rushed out to greet her, then grinned at her gran's choice of outfit. Full on elf: green leggings, waistcoat with gold buttons and a jaunty cap with a bell. Gran didn't do things by halves. A couple of years ago she'd come as a sexy Santa, all fishnets and cantilevered bosom. Archie had gawped before taking a photo and uploading it on Instagram.

'Let me just put the stash under the tree, then you can fetch me a wee glass of fizz, Jinnie love.' Wilma was carrying an enormous carrier bag, filled to the brim with presents which looked as if they'd been wrapped in the dark. Corners protruded where the hastily applied Sellotape had failed to stick. Glimpses of the contents were visible where Wilma had cut the paper too short. And two of the packages bore the wording 'Happy Birthday'.

'Ach, I ran oot of time and patience,' she said, placing the last present. 'Anyway, nothin' wrong with a bit of crap wrap seein' as you'll have it all ripped off in minutes.'

Tradition in the Cooper household dictated that they did the presents first, aided by plenty of champagne (or beer, in Archie's case). More often than not, Wilma would nod off shortly afterwards — although she always protested she was just 'resting my eyes' — and Jinnie and Kath would add the finishing touches to the meal. Archie was in charge of setting the table, which involved a lot of clattering, banging and cursing under his breath. Rob had turkey carving down to a fine art, and spent a good chunk of Christmas Eve sharpening his knife in preparation.

As they took up their positions around the tree — everyone on the floor except Wilma, who argued she'd never get up again — Jinnie hoped Dhassim was OK. He hadn't been impressed when he realised he'd be spending Christmas on his own, not that he'd ever celebrated it before. Still, he'd perked up at the sight of Jinnie's miniature Christmas tree (artificial, with tiny, flashing lights) and the enormous tin of Quality Street chocolates she'd left for him. There was also a turkey ready meal and a box of mince pies for afters. And he'd been thrilled with his gift: a pair of reindeer-patterned socks that played 'Jingle Bells' when you pressed a little button.

The unwrapping commenced. Predictably, Archie received a pair of navy chinos and a smart polo shirt and was despatched to get changed. Jinnie adored the silver constellation earrings and deep purple silk scarf from her mum and dad. But her heart nearly stopped when she opened her present from Wilma. Nestled in a satin-lined box, it looked a lot like a —

'It's a facial massage wand,' her gran announced. 'The wee lass in Boots said it was the dog's bollocks for smoothing out fine lines and wrinkles. No' that you've got many, but better tae start early. Too late for me, mind.' Catching Jinnie's look of relief, she cackled. 'Don't tell me you thought I'd bought you a vib —'

'More champagne?' Jinnie leapt to her feet, aware her face was as purple as the new scarf.

The lunch was a triumph. Home-made Scotch broth to start, meltingly tender turkey with all the trimmings, and the Christmas pudding Kath always made on Stir Up Sunday, just before Advent. Everything was washed down with plenty of wine — and water, to ensure they weren't asleep before the Queen's Speech. Wilma, amazingly, hadn't needed a nap, instead nipping out of the back door a couple of times for a roll-up.

Archie was wriggling in his chair, a mound of Brussels sprouts piled up on his side plate, and his dessert bowl miraculously empty. He was supposed to be on clean-up duty too, but seemed more intent on performing a peculiar bottom shuffle.

'What's up?' enquired Jinnie, helping herself to pudding. 'Got ants in your pants?'

Archie stood up and gave his groin a good scratch. Eurgh! Jinnie pitied the poor girl who ever succumbed to her brother's dubious charms. She'd need the patience of a saint, and a high tolerance for revolting habits.

'Got a bad case of jock itch,' Archie replied. 'Must be that new washing powder you're using, Mum. That cheap stuff is giving me a rotten rash.'

Try doing your own blooming washing, thought Jinnie.

'Isn't he a tennis player?' added Kath, stacking up dirty plates. 'You know the one, good-looking, think he's won Wimbledon a few times.'

Both Jinnie and her dad howled with laughter. 'I think you mean Djokovic,' said Rob. 'And I don't think Archie's condition and a top-seeded tennis player have much in common.'

'New balls, please!' shrieked Jinnie, doubling over in hysterics.

'You lot are a disgrace,' huffed Wilma. 'Now can we get this table cleared and listen to what Her Majesty has to say?'

Her Majesty had much to say. The usual blend of the positive — new additions to the royal family — and concern for a world filled with so much hatred and division. Rob nodded sombrely, Kath sniffed (too much champagne made her weepy), and Wilma commented that Betty's jumper was an unflattering colour. Archie, meanwhile, had sloped off to snooze and scratch himself in private.

Jinnie wished again that Dhassim had the power to right all the world's wrongs. But it could never be that simple. Only mankind had the means to reverse the damage done; but the world seemed hell-bent on further destruction. The threat of another war loomed constantly, and an end to poverty and famine remained a faint and unlikely hope.

Jinnie was staying the night. Her old bedroom was largely unchanged, with patches on the walls where she'd stuck up posters of Justin Timberlake and Orlando Bloom. The double bed was made up with her favourite navy and cream checked linen, well-worn and faded, but deliciously soft and fragrant. Her mum had placed a bottle of water by the bedside, and would ensure the electric blanket was switched on before Jinnie said her goodnights. She laid out her pyjamas on the pillow and arranged her toiletries in the bathroom before heading down to rejoin the family fun.

Much later, after several raucous rounds of charades — Wilma acting out *Groundhog Day* was a particular highlight — and a mountain of sausage rolls, sandwiches and more bubbly, Jinnie was shattered. She helped her mum load the dishwasher for the second time, the two of them gulping down mugs of tea. Archie had headed out to the pub to see some mates, and Rob was trying to persuade a very tipsy Wilma that it was time for home.

'Ach, you're a right party pooper,' she complained, the bell on her cap drooping alarmingly. 'Guess I'll just need to fix mysel' a wee nightcap at home and watch the *Strictly* special on catch-up.'

'A great day as always, Mum,' said Jinnie, packing away the leftovers in the fridge.

'Thanks for coming, love,' said Kath, wiping down the worktops and wringing out the cloth. No matter the hour or how tired she was, Jinnie's mum never went to bed until the kitchen was spotless.

'Of course I came,' replied Jinnie. 'I've never wanted to be anywhere at Christmas except here.' Despite being in her thirties, Jinnie always spent the day with her family. It had caused friction with Mark, who thought they should alternate between his parents and hers, or take themselves off to a five-star hotel for fine dining and lots of sex. Hannah said she was insane turning down such an offer. 'Jeez, if I had a choice between hanging with the wrinklies and eating shrivelled-up dead bird, or being waited on hand and foot *and* getting laid … it's a no-brainer!'

New Year's Eve, or Hogmanay as they called it in Scotland, was a different matter. Since her early twenties Jinnie had either partied with the girls or stayed home alone, watching Jools Holland or the televised celebrations in Edinburgh. She and Mark had gone once, braving the bitter cold and icy rain. She'd hated it, fingers wrapped around a mulled wine for warmth as Mark and his cronies brayed at each other, cracking jokes that only they found funny. As for this year…

Tucked up with the blanket cranked to the max (Jinnie hoped she'd remember to turn it off or she'd be a puddle by morning), her mind drifted ahead. The start of another year.

New beginnings, more wishes. She'd volunteered to work a shift at the pub, the promise of double wages sealing the deal. The whole village would be there, counting down as the clock approached midnight. *Ten, nine ... Ed ... eight, seven, six ... Sam ... five, four, three, two, one ...*

CHAPTER 27

Ed had enjoyed a quiet Christmas Day with his parents. After the sixth text message from Cheryl, he'd switched off his phone. Yes, he was being an ostrich, but burying his head in the sand was preferable to the ear-bashing Cheryl would subject him to, given half a chance. Not playing the adoring boyfriend over Christmas *and* New Year was grounds for the coldest of cold shoulders.

Ed had sent her a voucher for her favourite shop, knowing she was hankering after a new handbag to add to the dozen or so she already owned. She'd sent him absolutely nothing, apart from a terse message. *Merry Christmas. Guess I'll see you when I see you*, minus kisses and emojis. The later messages had been shorter, sharper and all pointing the way to a not very happy ending.

Ken and Mags always opened on Boxing Day. Their reasoning was that not everyone had family or friends to spend Christmas with. It could be a lonely day if your only company was the TV, and crackers were a waste of money when you had no one to pull them with. Even in a village as small as Cranley, they knew there were many who saw

Christmas as an ordeal to be endured. The day after meant some return to normality.

Mags had been on decent form. Ken took charge of the cooking, and the only drama had been when she got vaguely hysterical about the dress that no longer fitted. With infinite patience, Ken had rifled through the wardrobe and produced a butter-soft cashmere knit that he'd bought as a present and hung up instead of wrapped.

'When did I buy this?' Mags had asked, stroking the wool. 'I can't remember.' Ed stepped forward, pretending to tuck in the label as he twisted off the price tag.

Today, Mags was resting and Ken and Ed were running the show, with help from Jinnie. As it wasn't yet too busy, Ed left the customers to sup their pints and complain good-naturedly about the preceding twenty-four hours, and wandered outside.

A couple were vaping, an old man waited as his grizzled dog did its business, and a woman sat huddled over a bench. It took Ed a few seconds to realise it was Jamie's mum, Angela. She was smoking a cigarette and staring at the sky.

Ed approached, wary of encroaching on her private space. Yet she exuded loneliness, and a vulnerability that propelled him forward. 'Hiya.'

Angela looked startled, stubbed out her cigarette and sat upright. She wore a knitted hat pulled down over her fore-head. The watery moonlight illuminated her face, high-lighting the dark shadows under her eyes. 'Hey. Sorry, I was miles away. Well, wishing I was miles away, but here I am. Fancy keeping a miserable cow company?'

Ed sat down. He didn't have a jacket and it was bitterly cold, but he couldn't just walk away. Just a few minutes, then he'd make his excuses. 'It would be my pleasure. I'm all ears, if you feel like chatting.'

Angela pulled out her packet of cigarettes and sparked up

another. Ed shivered and stuck his hands between his legs in a futile attempt to keep warm. Angela seemed oblivious, lost in a nicotine-fuelled memory. 'I guess you know who I am?', she said suddenly.

Ed nodded. He'd recognised her straight away, but they'd never spoken before. She struck him as someone who didn't open up readily. A single mum to the sullen Jamie, shrouded in whispers and rumours in a community with too much time on its hands.

'Truth is, I don't get out much.' Angela let out a barking laugh. 'Being skint does that to a person. And dropping by the local pub isn't the ideal outing for an alcoholic. Still, I like it here. People are nice … well, most of them.' She related how kind Sam had been a few days earlier. Ed nodded, although he didn't know the man well himself. Jinnie seemed to like him, as did his mum and dad. He shuffled in his seat, praying his privates didn't retreat permanently in the sub-zero temperature.

'I woke up one day knowing things needed to change. Yes, my life sucks, but so does a lot of people's. And wallowing in a puddle of booze and misery doesn't help.' Angela inhaled deeply, blowing out a steady plume of smoke. 'And these are next to go. One vice at a time, eh?'

Ed hadn't smoked in years, but he took a cigarette from Angela's proffered pack. The first draw made him cough, the second reminded him of the old days: huddled outside a bar with his mates, winding each other up about a girl, or how badly the Scottish rugby team had performed that day.

'How did you quit?' Ed asked, genuinely curious. He didn't consider himself a heavy drinker, although he'd certainly downed way more than the recommended number of units in his twenties. 'I know AA works for a lot of people, but it's not for everyone.'

Angela shook her head, the pom-pom on her woolly hat shaking too. 'I went to a couple of meetings, but I'm rubbish at talking about myself. No, really!' She swiped Ed with the end of her scarf. 'This is different. Less intimidating, I guess. I downloaded a book, believe it or not, and it just hit a nerve. Made me realise I was in charge, not the alcohol. It didn't happen overnight — if only — but I knew I was sick and tired of *feeling* sick and tired.'

Angela stubbed out her cigarette and pulled her hat further down over her ears. In the subdued exterior lighting she looked ethereal: all angular features and seductive shadows. Wait a minute, *seductive?* That had come totally out of nowhere. And yet... Ed felt himself shuffle closer, drawn to this woman like a moth to the proverbial flame. She was revealing herself, bit by bit, in a way that captivated him. By comparison, Cheryl was more like a spider's web, in which he'd become entangled.

'I used to hide bottles all over the place. Vodka in the bathroom drawer. Whisky in the kitchen, tucked behind the cereal packets. Even a couple of miniatures stuffed under the dirty laundry, because who'd ever look there?' Angela's laugh was strained, her eyes refusing to meet Ed's.

'Hey, don't be so hard on yourself.' He nudged her chin upwards, forcing her to look at him. 'I take my hat off to you. Well, I would if I was wearing one.' Ed tugged gently at the edge of Angela's beanie, glad to see her smile in return. 'Beating an addiction, whatever it is, is no mean feat. And you've raised a child single-handed. I can't imagine ever being responsible for a child. I'd probably leave it in the supermarket, or something.'

Before Angela could reply, the crunch of gravel signalled someone approaching. It was Jinnie, carrying a tray to collect the empties. She looked tired and out-of-sorts, her smile refusing to stay on her face. She'd come in at short notice, after Rose called in sick. 'If you want anything else you'd better hurry, because it's last orders,' she said.

Ed sprang to his feet, draping an arm around Jinnie's trembling shoulders. 'What's up, gorgeous?' he asked.

Jinnie shrugged and nodded hello to Angela. 'Just a dose of the post-Christmas blues, I guess. I always find this week a downer after all the festivities.'

'Me too,' said Angela, tightening the belt of her coat. 'Roll on springtime and warmer weather. Well, as warm as it gets on the east coast.' She smiled. 'Hey, why don't we get together soon, have a girlie day out or something? If you're not too busy, that is.'

Ed watched Jinnie's reaction, which was definitely lacking in the 'whoop whoop, fab idea' stakes. They were very different people, but didn't the 'opposites attract' saying apply to friendships as well as romances? He sensed — knew — that Angela could do with some female support, and as for Jinnie… She was harder to read, but he couldn't deny he enjoyed her company. A lot. He'd detected a closeness between her and Sam too, but couldn't be sure if it was work-related or … something else.

'I could do something a week tomorrow. That's just before I start back at Sam's.' Jinnie's teeth were now chattering, so Ed and Angela followed her back inside. 'We could head into Edinburgh and grab some lunch, do a bit of shopping?'

'Sounds like a plan. Shall we meet at the station, say midday?'

Jinnie agreed, and as neither Ed nor Angela wanted anything else from the bar, they bade Jinnie goodnight and left.

'If I wear high heels and shave off my beard, can I come along too?' Ed strode along next to Angela, who walked surprisingly quickly for someone much shorter than himself.

'Nah. Doubt you'd be interested in browsing make-up and clothes, somehow.'

Ed did his best to look put out. He actually enjoyed shopping, but was more into niche vinyl record stores and vintage clothing shops.

'Shame, I might even have treated you to a tattoo and got another one myself,' he retorted. 'Anyway, I need to spend time with Mum, and get some work done before my boss flips out over my extended absence.'

Angela pulled a sad face as they approached the small terraced house she shared with Jamie. Its faded blue front door bore a tatty Christmas wreath with several pine cones missing. 'Well, thanks for keeping me company. Hopefully I'll see you soon.' She fumbled in her bag for the house keys as the door swung open.

Jamie stood in the dimly lit hallway. 'Hiya,' he grunted, looking none too pleased to see Ed. 'All right?'

'All good,' replied Angela. 'Ed walked me home and I would kill for a cuppa, so…'

Without another word Jamie turned and disappeared, presumably to put the kettle on.

'I'd ask you in,' Angela said apologetically, 'but I can tell he's in one of his moods, so best not.'

Ed shrugged to show he wasn't bothered. He wouldn't have minded spending more time with her, but having a monosyllabic, grouchy teen acting as a chaperone wasn't his idea of fun.

'By the way,' added Angela, 'I've been tempted in the past to get a tattoo, but I've never had the courage. Don't they hurt a lot?'

Ed considered lying, since his last one had stung like buggery for days, but Angela's openness and honesty had genuinely touched him. 'A bit,' he said. 'Well, quite a lot, actually, but I don't think some fleeting pain would be a problem for you. You're one tough lady, and I know exactly what you should choose if you ever change your mind.'

Angela's nose crinkled in puzzlement. 'What's that, then?'

'You should choose the word *Brave.*'

CHAPTER 28

NEW YEAR'S EVE

TWO HOURS TO GO TILL MIDNIGHT, AND THE JEKYLL AND Hyde was crammed to capacity. Everyone was dressed to the nines, with many of the men in kilts and the women sporting tartan accessories. Ken had enlisted the services of an old schoolfriend to play the bagpipes when the bells signalled the start of the New Year. He was currently performing a few practice tunes which suggested he hadn't picked up the instrument for some time.

Jinnie had been working flat out since seven, alongside Rose, Ken and Jamie. At times the queue at the bar had been four deep, the whole of Cranley out in force to celebrate 'The Bells', as Hogmanay was also known.

'I hope he improves before "Auld Lang Syne,"' yelled Rose over the hubbub. 'Right now it sounds like he's squeezing an asthmatic donkey.'

Jinnie skimmed the head off a pint and giggled. She needed a few laughs; her mood was distinctly on the dark side. She still hadn't shaken off the mortification of Sam rejecting her advances. How had she got it so terribly wrong? And there was still no sign of Ed tonight. Her feelings for the two men flipped around constantly. *Maybe I should leave Cranley*, she thought. *Bunk up with Hannah again, and put some distance between the pair of them.* But that would involve taking Dhassim with her, and Jinnie knew that wasn't an option.

'Crikey, Janette's pulling out all the stops,' said Ken. He was oozing bonhomie, but beneath the 'host with the most' exterior, his face betrayed his inner turmoil. Mags was resting upstairs. She'd been down earlier, completely confused by the Hogmanay celebrations and convinced that they were about to enter the millennium. 'Everything's going to crash, they say,' she'd whispered to Jinnie. 'I'm not sure what that means, but it sounds bad.'

Janette had produced a couple of tape measures and criss-crossed them on the floor like Highland swords. She was jigging merrily over them, arms aloft and pseudo-kilt flapping alarmingly. Luckily, unlike the menfolk — who according to tradition should wear nothing under their kilts — Janette was sporting a pair of Bridget Jones-style pants which were visible each time she twirled and whooped.

'Ooh, Sam's arrived.' Rose's eyelashes went into full-on flutter mode. She was only twenty-one, but it seemed every woman with a pulse went a bit wobbly when the antiques man paid a visit. Jinnie's pulse quickened too, because she didn't know how to deal with him.

'Hi, Jinnie.' Sam reached the bar, the regulars parting like the Red Sea in his wake. Was he really that important? In a tiny community like Cranley, he probably was. A big fish in a small pond. And Jinnie had been reeled in by his presence; caught hook, line and sinker by his easy charm and kind words, which she now realised were not exclusive to her. *What an idiot I've been.*

'Hi, Sam.' Her voice was heavy with unspoken meaning. What she really wanted to say was: *Hi, Sam. Thanks for leading me up the garden path with a kiss that meant nothing to you, but sent me into a tailspin. Thanks for rebuffing me, and making me feel as important as an amoeba. But ... you're one of the nicest men I've ever met, and now I don't know how to act around you.*

'It's, erm, pretty lively,' said Sam, gesturing around him. The inhabitants of the tiny village were going hell for leather: some joining in with Janette's improvised jig, others joining arms and singing about old acquaintances being forgotten, or remembered. A bit early, perhaps, but they were fuelled with alcohol and a desire to turn the next page.

'Have you eaten?' Sam eyed the blackboard. On it was chalked traditional fare for the evening: Cock-a-Leekie soup, venison pie and Tipsy Laird trifle.

Jinnie shook her head. She'd been starving a few minutes before, but Sam's arrival had created a tight bubble of anxiety in her stomach. 'Not hungry,' she replied. 'And I'm kind of busy, so...'

Ignoring Sam's hurt expression, Jinnie dashed to the other end of the bar. Kylie and her posse were loitering there, wearing even less clothing than they had in the cocktail-making episode. To Jinnie's relief they'd already been served by Jamie, and each was supping a lethal-looking dark-green concoction. She didn't know if her cocktail skills still existed, but making gin and tonics and pouring beers was good enough right now.

Angela materialised at the bar. Wearing a fitted teal-blue dress and light make-up, she looked fresher and more relaxed than usual. 'Hi, Jinnie, good to see you. I'm looking forward to our trip into town.' She smiled, and Jinnie realised just how pretty she was. *Perhaps Angela's the reason why Sam isn't interested in me in that way.*

'Me too!' Jinnie hoped her enthusiastic response didn't sound as fake as it felt. If Sam was attracted to someone else, there was nothing she could do about it. Hadn't she told herself repeatedly that the last thing she needed was the complication of a man in her life? It was just a shame that the briefest of kisses had persuaded her otherwise.

At just after eleven Ken hustled her over to a table and plonked down a steaming bowl of soup and a basket of bread. 'Can't have you keeling over before the magic hour,' he chided, returning a moment later with a large glass of wine. 'Now get that lot down you. I'm off to check on Mags, but Rose and Jamie can hold the fort for a wee while.'

As he headed off Jinnie spied Jo, huddled in a corner with a group of people. They waved at each other, Jo giving a subtle eye-roll suggesting she was desperate to escape. Jinnie took a piece of bread, tore a chunk off, and dunked it in the soup. It tasted divine; just right to settle her wobbly stomach. She was just raising a spoonful to her lips when —

'Do you mind if I join you?' Sam stood before her, pint in hand, with an apprehensive look on his face.

Jinnie's instinct was to say, *Yes, I do mind. Please take your annoying good looks and charm somewhere else.* But that would sound churlish, and for now, he was still her boss.

'Sure. Knock yourself out.' That didn't sound *remotely* churlish, did it?

Jinnie slurped her soup noisily, and contemplated throwing in an Archie-style burp for good measure. Then again, she didn't need to make herself seem unattractive. Sam couldn't have made it clearer the other day that he didn't fancy her. He'd literally *ducked* when she'd got too close (not that she'd been aiming for another kiss, absolutely not), holding her at arm's-length and mumbling about getting back to do some writing.

'Jinnie.' Sam sat down — clearly he had a hide like a rhino — and looked directly at her. Jinnie stared back, remembering the staring competitions she'd had with Archie when they were younger. She'd always won, since Archie couldn't focus for more than twenty seconds. She wasn't going to blink, or give the slightest hint that this was an awkward encounter. Yes, her eyes were watering and her brain was shrieking 'I'm a nonentity, get me out of here!', but she would stand her ground.

'Listen, I'm so sorry about what happened. I mean the kiss.'

I know what you mean. I'm not totally stupid. And please don't make this more awkward than it is.

'It's not you, it's me.' *OK, cliché klaxon on full red alert.*

'I like you, Jinnie. I really, really like you, but it's not that easy. I'm a divorced man with a difficult ex-wife, and a son I adore but worry about constantly. You're a young woman with the world at your feet, and I just don't want to —'

'How are two of my favourite people in the cosy enclave of Cranley getting on?' Jo looked flushed and a tiny bit sozzled. She pulled up a chair, sat down, and regarded them both with slightly glassy eyes.

'We're just tickety-boo,' answered Jinnie. Now she was morphing into a creature from a bygone era. Was it the flapper period? *The Great Gatsby,* complete with swinging pearls and headbands? Glancing at her watch, she realised they were moments from the Bells. And still no sign of Ed. *So what? Is he my back-up plan? The fall guy if the main man doesn't step up to the plate?*

Jinnie looked at her rapidly congealing bowl of soup and pushed it aside. She saw Ken, circulating with a tray of fizz. 'Need to go and help with the champers,' she announced, and got up.

The countdown began, the whole pub watching the screen as Edinburgh prepared to welcome in the New Year. That irritating woman from Scottish TV was screeching above the roar of the crowds and the fireworks, and Janette was snuggling up to the bagpipe man.

'Three … two … one… Happy New Year, everybody!' Ken

announced, his arm around Mags — who looked bewildered — and Jo on his other side. He kissed them both in turn, Jinnie noticing he lingered a little longer with Jo. Angela and Jamie were standing together, and everyone linked arms with the person next to them. Glasses were downed in one, the crowd kissing and hugging as they bade the old year farewell. The bagpipes were quickly drowned out by music from the TV, and the atmosphere was both festive and contemplative.

'Happy New Year!' The doors opened, and a tall, dark, rather handsome man walked in carrying something small and black, with a bottle of whisky tucked under his arm and a bag slung over his shoulder.

'Ed!' Mags rushed over, closely followed by Ken. A group hug ensued, the rest of the room cheering the late arrival. Tradition stated that a male of the species blessed with good looks would stride into the gathering just after midnight, bearing a piece of coal, a bottle of Scotland's finest, some shortbread, and black bun — a dark fruitcake encased in pastry.

'I couldn't find any black bun, but I hope some leftover Mr Kipling will do the job.' He winked at Ken, who relieved his son of his offerings and poured him a generous measure of something peaty and potent.

'Cheers. Happy New Year to one and all!' Ed raised his glass, his glance sweeping the room. It rested on Jinnie, fiddling with the stem of her glass. Then it moved to Angela, who looked down and shuffled awkwardly.

Sam was nowhere to be seen — had Jinnie inadvertently wished for him to vanish? No, that kind of wish didn't work, and she felt a sudden urge to dash back to Dhassim and give him an enormous cuddle. He'd been super-sulky when Jinnie had said she was leaving him home alone *again* for an event he couldn't participate in. She had only been able to leave him with a relatively clear conscience by downloading every Jennifer Aniston film she could find.

'Happy New Year, Ed.' Jinnie clinked her glass with his, leaning in for a kiss. 'Where have you been?'

'Happy New Year, Jinnie,' he replied. 'Dad needed a tall, dark, handsome stranger, and as George Clooney wasn't available —'

Jinnie laughed, and linked arms with him as the crowd assembled to sing 'Auld Lang Syne'. She turned to her other side, and realised that Sam was right next to her.

He hesitated briefly before taking her arm. As the song started — the bagpipe man giving it his all — Sam leaned over and whispered in her ear. 'Friends?'

Could she do it? Pack away the errant feelings she had and just be friends? It had to be worth a try.

> *'And there's a hand, my trusty fiere!*
> *and gie's a hand o' thine!*
> *And we'll tak' a right gude-willie waught,*
> *for auld lang syne.'*

The lyrics spoke of friendship and of days gone by. Jinnie hadn't known Sam very long, but she was certain he would be a true and loyal friend. And those weren't always easy to find.

'Absolutely,' she whispered back, ignoring the sharp pang of loss in her heart.

CHAPTER 29

'HAPPY NEW YEAR, DHASSIM.'

It was just after 2 am on January 1, and Jinnie had arrived home to find him snuggled up on the sofa watching *Leprechaun.* Not his favourite actress's finest moment.

'Hmm, Happy New Year,' he replied, muting the volume. 'Although celebrating the start of another year isn't a big deal when you've been kicking around as long as I have.'

Jinnie cosied up next to him and gave him the cuddle she'd thought about earlier. He reciprocated, Jinnie detecting a whiff of the Jo Malone bath oil Hannah had given her for Christmas. She really needed to buy him some cheap manly toiletries before he plundered any more of her expensive stuff.

'Are you hungry?' Liz had parcelled up generous portions of the venison pie and trifle before Jinnie left. They would keep for a day or two, as Jinnie was having lunch with her family later. Her mum and dad had been delighted when she said she'd make the trip, and Wilma would also be in attendance.

Dhassim eyed the food parcels with disdain. He sniffed

the pie, his nose crinkling up, before moving on to the trifle. 'I will partake of a small bowlful of that,' he announced. 'That macaroni cheese concoction you left was barely enough to feed a mouse.'

A mouse the size of a small bungalow, thought Jinnie. It had been a family size pack, on special at Janette's because it was a few days out of date. Sighing, she served Dhassim half the trifle and a small helping for herself.

'So, did you wish for something when the year changed?' asked Dhassim, spooning the trifle in with barely a pause for breath. 'If you did, you must repeat it so that we — he gestured to his WIFI, lined up neatly with the TV remote — 'can work our magic.'

On the wish-making front, Jinnie was proving spectacularly hopeless. If Hannah had got her mitts on Dhassim's lamp she would have had a list as long as her arm. No more leg or armpit fuzz (Hannah's body hair grew at a terrifying rate). A hot date with actor Tom Hardy, preferably leading to marriage — the small matter of him already being married wouldn't deter her. And a lifetime supply of vintage champagne, delivered to her fridge on a weekly basis. Those would be just for starters.

'Nope, I didn't make a wish.' Wishing for things to be different between her and Sam was a non-starter. Anyway, Jinnie didn't want to rely on a genie and his gizmo to find true love. Surely it was better the old-fashioned way; boy meets girl and sparks fly?

'Do not fret, mon petit chou,' replied Dhassim.

Great, now she'd progressed from a pumpkin to a small cabbage. Or was that a backward step? Too tired to reprimand him again, Jinnie gathered up the empty bowls and dumped them in the kitchen sink. She was due at her parents' in nine hours, and sleep beckoned.

'I was wondering…' continued Dhassim, sneaking a toffee finger from the leftover box of Christmas chocolates.

This sounds ominous, thought Jinnie.

'If you can't think of anything — and there's no rush, I'm not going anywhere — maaaybe you could grant a little wish for me.' He fluttered his enviably long eyelashes at Jinnie. Hers were stumpy little things, reliant on liberal coatings of mascara to lengthen them. Should she wish for better eyelashes? No, that definitely came into the category of frivolous.

'And what would that be?' she asked, hoping she didn't sound as nervous as she felt. Perhaps Dhassim was pining for love himself, although she wasn't prepared to upload his profile to Tinder. Mind you, he'd probably adore posing for a shirtless shot and giving a come-hither look. And how would he describe himself? *Mythological, manic and prone to hissy fits?* Jinnie wasn't even sure if he preferred men or women, or if genies were permitted to have relationships beyond the master/servant double act.

'Well, I don't get out much, as you know, and I've been on my ownio a lot recently…' This remark was accompanied by a look befitting a puppy scolded for chewing a slipper.

Sheesh, if I don't get my jim-jams on soon, I'll be nose-down in my lunch. 'Look, can we discuss this properly after I've been to see my folks? I am knackered, and I need some serious shut-eye.'

Dhassim strode from the kitchen, harem pants flapping in harmony with his peeved mood. Come to think of it, they hadn't been washed since he'd emerged from the lamp, which probably accounted for their slightly crispy appearance. Jinnie could offer to wash them, but doubted Cranley's only boutique offered much in the way of replacement. She couldn't see Dhassim taking kindly to polyester pantaloons in day-glo orange.

'Night night,' she called.

There was no reply: just the sound of the TV volume being cranked up, the maniacal cackles of the leprechaun following Jinnie upstairs.

* * *

'WILMA'S NOT DOING TOO WELL.' Jinnie's mum ushered her into the kitchen, where the table was already set for lunch. 'Your dad popped round to see her last night, and found her passed out on the living room floor.'

'Why didn't you call me?' Jinnie felt shocked to the core. 'Where is she now, in hospital?'

'No sweetheart, I'm right here, and there's nowt wrong with me.' Her gran stood in the doorway, hands on hips, face a picture of defiance. 'I just took a wee tumble, that's all. I wisnae passed out, just took me a while to get my bearings.'

Jinnie rushed over and hugged her gran tightly. She inhaled her familiar scent, laced with something not so familiar —

'Gran, how come you smell of bubblegum?' Jinnie sniffed again; there was definitely a hint of the chewy confection.

Wilma produced something from the pocket of her cardigan. 'Your father decided that I should try *this*' — she waggled what Jinnie realised was an e-cigarette — 'to get me to kick the fags. And he very thoughtfully bought two different flavours for me to try. Lemon cheesecake, and this one.' Wilma sucked hard on the device, and emitted a fragrant plume of steam. 'Absolutely disgusting.' She made a face. 'Right, I'm off out the back for a proper smoke.'

With a sigh of resignation, Kath began serving up pot roast and vegetables. 'Stubborn as a mule. Honestly, Jinnie, she was grey as can be when your dad brought her here. Point blank refused to see the doctor, but at least she agreed to stay the night.' She shouted to Rob and Archie to come and eat, then took Jinnie's hands, smiling wanly. 'Happy New Year, darling. How was your evening?'

Jinnie gave a short recap of the Hogmanay events at the pub, and how nice it had been to be part of the local celebrations.

They were laughing together at Janette's tape-measure swords when Rob and Archie appeared. 'Happy New Year.' Rob pulled Jinnie in for a cuddle.

Archie bumped shoulders with her and helped himself to a beer from the fridge. 'Hope it's a good one, sis. Looking pretty epic for me, if I say so myself.'

When they were all seated round the table, Archie piled his plate high and smirked. No one paid any attention, so he stood up, tapped his glass with a fork, and waited.

'What's up?' Rob asked. 'Do you want us to say the Lord's Prayer?'

'Is your jock itch still causing you grief?' added Jinnie.

'Can we not just get stuck in? My stomach thinks my throat's cut,' said Wilma, reaching for the wine bottle.

'Well, ye of little faith, I just wanted to announce that a certain *big name*' — Archie did finger waggle quote marks — 'has been following my music. And he's very interested in collaborating with me on some pretty amazing stuff.'

Silence followed; apart from Wilma coughing with gusto, and Kath leaping to her feet to fetch the forgotten gravy.

'Do tell, darling brother.' Jinnie was deeply cynical about Archie achieving anything that involved effort on his part. So much so that she wouldn't be surprised if their mum had given Will.i.am a call. She was a huge fan of 'The Voice', even if she hadn't a clue what he was on about.

'It's Über Jean, and he's massive right now. Everyone wants to work with him. And he contacted *me!*' Archie looked more animated than Jinnie had ever seen him.

'Why would someone call themselves after a vegetable?' Kath plonked down the gravy boat. 'Nasty slimy things. Tried to make a moussaka once, but couldn't stomach them. They were horrible, weren't they Rob?'

As her dad muttered in agreement, Jinnie gave a high five to Archie. She'd actually heard of Über Jean; his collaborations with famous artists had pushed his profile sky-high. If, somehow, he saw something of value in Archie's work, good on him.

'The meat's a bit chewy, but the carrots are delicious,' said Wilma. 'Pass the gravy, Rob, there's a love.'

The rest of lunch passed in usual Cooper fashion. Wilma caused a minor uproar when she revealed she'd received photos of male genitalia on her Twitter account. 'Aye, willie shots, right there on the screen. Like I want to see somebody's scrotum in close up!'

'Dick pics,' added Archie, scrolling through his phone and humming under his breath.

'I dinnae know what his name is, but he can do one!' Wilma huffed indignantly, oblivious to the reaction around the table. 'And as for all thae US military chaps wanting to find love, they'd better look somewhere else. All I need is a nice cup of tea. Speaking of which, anyone fancy a reading?'

Miffed at no takers — and not remotely remorseful at using Charlize Theron's photo as her Twitter profile — Wilma took herself off to the lounge, hacking and spluttering all the way.

Jinnie helped her mum clear up. 'Gran doesn't sound great,' she said quietly. 'Can't we find a way to *drag* her to the doctor's?' As soon as she spoke, she realised how impossible that would be. Wilma was a hardy Scotswoman, born in an era when men were men and women just got on with it.

'You know what she's like,' sighed Kath. 'Wilma's always said the only way they'll get her out of that bungalow is in a coffin. And the way she *is* coughing — excuse the pun — I fear that's exactly what will happen.'

A judder of fear ran down Jinnie's spine. She knew her gran couldn't live forever, but she wasn't ready to lose her yet.

CHAPTER 30

'HAVE YOU EVER BEEN IN LOVE, DHASSIM?' *I COULD ASK MYSELF that*, Jinnie thought. And she was pretty sure the answer was no. Sure, she'd been smitten by Mark; but with the benefit of hindsight she realised she'd been more in love with the idea than the man himself. If he hadn't dumped her, Jinnie was certain they'd have parted ways sooner rather than later. Unless she'd done the whole stupid 'marry in haste, repent at leisure' thing. She shuddered at the thought.

'Have I ever been in love?' Dhassim repeated the question, digging his hands into the pockets of an old pair of Jinnie's jogging bottoms. She'd finally persuaded him that the harem pants needed a wash, and they were now drying over a radiator. Much to her chagrin, he looked better in her trackies than she did. Dhassim's pert little bottom filled out the fleecy fabric perfectly, whereas Jinnie's post-Christmas rear resembled a couple of overfilled balloons. And sticking a pin in them wasn't going to do the trick.

'Still waiting,' she said, figuring one more mince pie wouldn't do too much damage. After all, they were at their use-by date and Jinnie hated throwing food away. She removed the foil from the last two in the pack and zapped them in the microwave. 'Want cream with yours?'

Settled at the table, Jinnie bashed the top of her mince pie to let the dollop of cream sink in. Dhassim, who normally ate at warp speed, etched patterns on the plate. What looked suspiciously like a heart drizzled around his pie, his usually cheerful face tinged with sadness.

'Yes, I was in love once. It was a very long time ago.' As Dhassim's perception of time was a bit different from that of mere mortals, Jinnie didn't know if he meant a couple of decades or several centuries. Either way, unless she'd been blessed with the gift of eternal youth, Dhassim's sweetheart was either knocking on a bit or pushing up the daisies.

'So, spill the beans.'

Dhassim's brow creased. He pushed his plate aside untouched, went to the cabinet, and reached for a can of Heinz's finest. 'You want me to do something with these? Is this some kind of ritual? If I upend the contents, will the love of my life appear?'

Oh, for fuck's sake! Talk about being literal...

'It's a figure of speech, Dhassim. Put the can back, and just tell me who she was and what happened.'

'Her name was Aaliyah.' Dhassim whispered the word, as if just saying it would cause incredible pain. 'She was the most beautiful creature I ever laid eyes on, but the powers that be decreed that we could never be together.'

'What powers that be?' asked Jinnie. She'd never really thought about how genies came to be, and who decided they should spend eternity operating out of a lamp. Clearly someone with little regard for health and safety, or consideration for anyone with claustrophobia issues.

'I cannot say, for I truly do not know.' Dhassim unearthed a tissue from the pocket of the jogging bottoms. Jinnie watched as he dabbed his eyes, not wanting to spoil the moment by saying she *might* have blown her nose on it. 'My master chose my fate, as Aaliyah's fate was chosen for her. Had it not been for a strange coincidence when our lamps arrived at the same destination, we would never have met.'

Hang on a minute! Was Dhassim saying that the woman of his dreams was a genie like himself? Jinnie hadn't bothered researching his mystical origins, but she'd never heard of female genies. Were they even called the same thing? Perhaps one referred to them as 'geniuses'. She snorted at the thought. Of course *everyone* knew that women were smarter than men. Except men. Which kind of proved the theory, duh.

'You are laughing, Jinnie, which hurts me.' Dhassim tried to unfold the tissue, which remained defiantly welded together with —

'I'm not! Well, I am, but not for the reason you think.' Jinnie snatched away the offending item and fetched a box of tissues from the lounge. 'Tell me more, Dhassim. Was it love at first sight?' Pushing aside images of John Travolta and Olivia Newton John, Jinnie sat opposite him and gave his hand a quick squeeze.

'It was.' Dhassim looked taken aback at Jinnie's gesture, but gave her a watery smile. 'As I said, by some curious twist of fate we found ourselves in the same household. Fortuitously, we were allowed to serve together, at least for a while.'

Wow, double wishes! Not that Jinnie needed an extra helping, considering how pathetic she'd been so far.

'So, were your feelings reciprocated?' Perhaps the bootylicious Aaliyah preferred her men with a bit more meat on their bones. Despite his passion for eating, Dhassim was still skinny as a rake. He clearly possessed a metabolism Jinnie and her friends would kill for.

'She loved me as much as I loved her,' Dhassim replied.

'We were kindred souls, our hearts two halves of a whole. She was the yin to my yang, the sunset to my dawn, the Rachel to my Ross —'

'OK, OK, I get it,' interrupted Jinnie, a wave of nausea sweeping over her. Maybe the mince pie had been rancid after all. 'What happened? Did she grant her wishes before you did and get sucked back into her lamp?' Again, Jinnie didn't know what the protocol was when a genie gave out all their allotted wishes. As it stood, she'd be collecting her bus pass before Dhassim shimmied out of her life. Although he *had* said two months, if she remembered correctly.

'No.' Dhassim shook his head, a fresh bout of tears threatening. 'One day she was there, the next she was gone. Our master — the one who summoned us from the lamps — would not explain. However, I suspect he sold Aaliyah and her lamp, along with other items from the house. He was not a rich man, though he had a good heart.'

Not *that* good, if he'd chosen gaining a quick buck over Dhassim and Aaliyah's happiness. Why couldn't love be simple? Boy meets girl, they accept each other's flaws, instead of dredging them up years down the line, and in later life they settle into a comfortable routine of gently bickering about which TV show to watch. Like her mum and dad, in fact. Jinnie no longer believed that love was all about headboard-thumping sex, exotic holiday locations and eye-popping diamonds. Speaking of which, she still hadn't decided what to do with the ring that glinted at her mockingly each time she opened her jewellery box. Nor could she deny her confusion over Sam and Ed, her emotions flip-flopping back and forth every time she saw them. But that wasn't love, no sirree. Just good old-fashioned lust — or fancying the pants off someone, as Wilma would say.

'Listen, you need cheering up,' said Jinnie. 'I'm not working till Friday, so let's do something nice together. How about I teach you to play Scrabble? Or we could watch TV together?' *As long as it doesn't feature Jennifer bloody Aniston, even if my hair is now swishier than hers.*

Dhassim watched as Jinnie fetched the Scrabble set, and opened the box. He rubbed his goatee pensively as she tipped out the plastic letters and unfolded the board. Bending over, Dhassim scooped up a handful of tiles and peered at them. 'Are these runes?' he asked. 'Do they have magical powers?' He scattered the letters across the board, watching as they landed randomly.

'Erm, no,' Jinnie replied patiently. 'It's a game. You try to make words with the letters you're dealt, and the person with the highest score is the winner.' She pointed at the coloured squares. 'Look, if you place a letter *here* you get a double-letter score. Each tile has its own number of points. Q and Z have the highest, because they're the most difficult to use —'

She stopped talking. Dhassim wasn't listening to a word she said, his focus on laying out a sequence of tiles. Still stroking his beard — Jinnie needed to buy him a razor, as his use of hers had resulted in a few nasty underarm nicks — he sat back with a sigh. She read what he'd spelled out. *A-A-L-I-Y-A-H.* Not a bad word score, even if proper names were not allowed.

'Jinnie, I do not think I want to play a game or watch television.' Dhassim gazed at her with pleading eyes. 'I would like you to make my wish come true. Please can we go out together into the real world, just for a little while?'

Oh, help. Jinnie had hoped Dhassim would forget about escaping the confines of Brae Cottage. Clearly not. And she did owe him. So far, she'd aced cocktail making, gained a massive TV, taken an incredible magic carpet ride, and now had hair that even a soggy Scottish day couldn't destroy. Still, there were a few teeny tiny details that needed addressing before they could venture further than her front door…

CHAPTER 31

Jo stamped her feet, wishing she'd worn thicker socks. The temperature was below zero, the sky a dazzling blue. She was waiting for the train into Edinburgh, having decided to make the most of her last day before the café reopened. A spot of lunch, and retail therapy. The sales were well underway and she hoped to snaffle a few bargain jumpers and a new winter coat.

Ken had dropped by several times in the past few weeks. Mainly at the café, where they'd chatted with their usual ease. With customers coming and going, Jo could convince herself he was just one of the regulars, interested in nothing more than her home-baked goods and the welcoming smile and cheery banter she prided herself on.

It was the other three times — or was it four? — when he'd visited her at home that gave her cause for concern. Not because anything had *happened,* absolutely not. But now they messaged each other every couple of days: just silly, inconsequential things. And the fact that Mags was no longer their main topic of conversation wasn't relevant, either. Jo told herself it was a *good* thing. Ken needed an escape, somewhere to go where the burden of his wife's decline wasn't at the forefront of his thoughts.

Her initial qualms about seeing him had died down a little, dampened by the knowledge that they made a good team. Ken always said he felt better after seeing Jo, more able to cope with the reality of home life. And Jo, for the first time in longer than she cared to remember, felt needed. Wanted, even. Except she couldn't ignore the butterflies in her stomach, set in motion by wondering when she'd see him again. Nor could she pretend that Ken's demeanour didn't brighten a little more each time he walked through her door.

'Hey, Jo!' Lost in thought, Jo started at hearing her name. She'd been the only person on the station platform apart from an elderly gentleman who'd bade her good morning.

'Fancy meeting you here.' Jinnie gave her a quick hug, rekindling Jo's guilt that she hadn't made more of an effort to get together with the girl.

Angela stood apart, her face barely visible between a beanie hat pulled low and a coat collar zipped up high. 'Hiya,' she said, 'how's it going? Off to do something nice?'

It turned out they had similar plans: finding somewhere decent to eat, then making their way along Princes Street with an eye out for the 70% off banners.

The train approached, with only a couple of carriages and largely empty. Jo, Jinnie and Angela climbed in, grateful for the meagre heat that greeted them. They sat together — Jo felt awkward but didn't want to appear rude — and Jinnie produced a flask from her bag. 'Thought we might need a wee warm-up, so I made some hot chocolate. And you're in luck, Jo, cos I happen to have a spare cup. Always the Girl Guide, be prepared!'

Jinnie doled out the sweet, steaming liquid, and they sipped away quietly. The journey to the city was short, and soon they were stepping into the heart of the capital. A lone piper played a rousing Scottish tune, the cap at his feet already brimming with coins. Tourists gathered in clusters, listening intently to guides explaining the historical sites, and workers scuttled by oblivious to their surroundings.

'Just say if you'd rather do your own thing, but you're welcome to join us,' said Jinnie, tossing some loose change into the piper's cap. 'It'd be great to have a natter together. Right, Angela?'

If Angela were a poker player, she'd be raking it in. Her expression didn't change, even though her mouth formed the word 'Sure.'

Jo considered inventing a friend, or an appointment she'd suddenly remembered. Playing gooseberry didn't fill her with delight, but she liked Jinnie and knew from the rumour mill that Angela had her fair share of troubles.

'That would be great, thank you.' And with coats buttoned up and gloves unearthed from pockets, they set off.

* * *

'FANCY HARVEY NICKS FOR LUNCH?' said Jo. They'd popped into Jenners department store for a quick look which ended up taking over forty minutes. Jinnie emerged with a couple of tops and a pair of leggings with a faux-leather trim, all reduced to less than half price.

'Hmm, I'm not sure this coat is doing it for me,' Jo added. 'Cinching in at the waist is great if you *have* a waist to start with.'

'Don't be daft,' replied Jinnie. 'You've got an amazing figure, which we can go forth and destroy with two courses and a glass of fizz. Ooh, and Harvey Nicks sounds fab.'

Angela looked up from her perch on a chair. She'd given the sales rails a perfunctory glance before sitting down and scowling at her phone. 'Sorry, count me out; a toastie and a cuppa is all I need. Can't be doing with fancy stuff. We can hook up again after, if you like.'

Jo didn't consider herself a candidate for Mensa, though smart enough to deal with most of life's problems. What she *was* pretty good at was picking up underlying, unsaid messages. Angela's gruff response might fool some people, but it wasn't fooling Jo. 'You know, that sounds even better. Something light for now, then how's about I treat you both to afternoon tea before we head home?'

Decision made, they wandered along Edinburgh's main drag, Jo holding back until Angela was ahead and Jinnie was by her side.

'Is she having a hard time money-wise?' Jo looked at Jinnie, who nodded.

'I'm not exactly rolling in it myself, but I've two jobs and parents who deserve sainthood for the amount of times they've helped me out,' she replied. 'Getting Angela to open up isn't easy, but she said this morning her landlord was bumping up the rent.'

'Does she have a job?' Jo wasn't sure what Angela did, besides providing house space for Jamie the not-so-chatty barman.

'She told me she does the odd bit of tailoring. Taking up hems and making alterations. Certainly not enough to pay the bills. I guess she's on benefits, but I've no idea how that really works.'

They headed up a side street with several basement-level cafes displaying boards of lunchtime specials. *Freshly made toasties. Jacket potatoes. Salads. Selection of quiches.*

'This one looks OK.' Jo squeezed past a couple of smokers huddled over an overflowing ashtray. 'What do you think, ladies?'

Inside, the atmosphere was warm and convivial. Most tables were already occupied, but Jinnie spotted a raised bar area by the window with three free stools. 'Perfect,' said Jo. 'Right, I could eat a scabby dug, so let's hurry up and order.'

Both Jinnie and Angela burst out laughing at Jo's phrase. 'That's a new one for me, even with a gran fluent in all manner of strange expressions,' said Jinnie. 'I'm guessing it means you're a wee bit hungry?'

Jo grinned, and stabbed a finger impatiently at the menu. 'Cheese and ham toastie and a Diet Coke for me.'

Jinnie went to place their order at the counter. Angela opted for the same as Jo, while Jinnie dithered between quiche and a baked potato with egg mayonnaise.

'It's nice in here, isn't it?' Jo looked around the room, decorated with vintage movie posters. A retro jukebox played hits from the fifties and beyond, and the young staff buzzed around with broad smiles and enthusiasm.

'Here we go.' Jinnie plonked down three Diet Cokes. 'I couldn't make up my mind, so it's toasties all round. Should only be a few minutes.'

The conversation turned to plans for the coming year.

'The only resolution I make is to never make resolutions,' announced Jinnie. 'I have the willpower of an amoeba. Diets are doomed to failure within days and as for dry January — Why would anyone choose to give up booze during the most miserable month of the year?' She eyed her drink wistfully. 'Do you think we should get shots of rum in these?'

Jo shook her head, aware of Angela's discomfort. It was fairly common knowledge that she had had issues with alcohol, but perhaps the news hadn't reached Jinnie.

'I'd love to,' said Angela, 'but one shot would never be enough. Right now I've never been more tempted to throw myself off the wagon.'

She explained her financial plight. 'I lost a few jobs because of my addiction, not that I'm qualified for much. I do receive some government help, but barely enough to keep afloat. Jamie tries his best to help and Ken offered me some part-time bar work too, but I don't trust myself serving drinks. Being served is one thing, but having all those bottles at my fingertips…'

Just then, the jukebox blasted out Christine Aguilera's 'Genie in a Bottle'. Jinnie started to sing along, a curious expression on her face. Jo realised she was replacing the word 'bottle' with 'lamp', which didn't really fit the rhythm of the song.

'Are you OK?' Maybe Jinnie *had* laced her drink with something. She was giggling, and mumbling about genies being far more suited to lamps.

'What? Oh, sorry. Yes, I'm fine.' Jinnie wiped grease from her chin with a napkin. 'Should we head back to the shops before we do the coffee and cake thing?'

They went for a stroll along George Street which boasted a nice selection of boutiques. Jo spied a chocolate-brown wool coat with a broad shawl collar, marked down from mind-bogglingly expensive to mildly eye-watering. It fitted like a dream, and she cradled the tissue-wrapped package as lovingly as a mother nursing her firstborn. *Would Ken like it?* She swatted away the thought like a pesky fly. Whether he liked it or not was irrelevant —

'If I'm speaking out of turn, tell me to shut up.'

Jo tripped over a protruding paving stone, and grabbed Angela's arm for support. 'Oof, nearly came a cropper there.' She steadied herself, then waited for Angela to continue.

'I know I'm crap at most things, but I wondered… Well, you run A Bit of Crumpet on your own. I mean, I've never seen anyone else working there.'

It was true. Well, pretty much. Over the years Jo had hired the occasional part-timer, but the place was small and she couldn't really justify the cost of taking someone on more permanently. Yes, there were days when she regretted her fierce independence. Juggling all the tasks involved in running the business left her wrung out and often in bed by nine. And now... Business was solid, and Jo had been toying with the idea of expanding a little. Outside catering, on a small scale. Perhaps children's birthday parties — cake, savoury bits, all hand-made, and far removed from the pre-packaged stuff the supermarkets sold. Cranley was tiny, but Jo had her van and could easily travel a few miles in any direction.

'Have you any experience in catering?'

Angela shrugged and tugged off a glove to scratch the back of her head. 'Not really, but I used to bake a lot when I was young, with my mum. It was a Friday afternoon ritual when I finished school. Highlight of the week, because I bloody hated school.'

Jo felt sorry for the woman. Life hadn't dealt her a generous hand, and she suspected further unhappy secrets lurked beneath the surface. Did she *really* want to take on someone like that? Jo enjoyed an uncomplicated life. Well, she had done, until recently...

'That skirt has my name on it.' Jinnie was outside a shop, nose pressed to the window. Jo and Angela followed her gaze, focussed on a multi-coloured confection in a damask fabric. 'OK, I'm going to try it on. Are you coming in?'

Jo and Angela shook their heads in unison. 'We'll carry on a bit, and you can catch up with us,' said Jo. 'Unless you need our expert opinion?'

Jinnie grinned and dashed inside, leaving the other two to wander on. Before she could change her mind, Jo blurted out, 'Why don't you come in Saturday morning for a few hours and see how it goes? I'll get you up to speed with the hot drinks and serving. It'll be busy after the holidays, so an extra pair of hands would be useful.'

Angela managed to look both incredulous and delighted.

'Thank you! Thank you so much! I won't let you down, I promise.' And she hugged Jo tightly just as Jinnie appeared, toting another carrier bag.

'What's all this about?' she asked. 'Actually, don't tell me. You can reveal all over afternoon tea. And just to be clear, the jam goes on first, *then* the cream. We can't be friends otherwise!'

CHAPTER 32

'I KNOW THIS IS GOING TO SOUND A LITTLE STRANGE, BUT —'
Jinnie undid the knot of her scarf, then retied it again.

Sam had texted her on New Year's Day to say she didn't
need to come in until the afternoon of the fourth. Part of her
hadn't wanted to come in at all, but she wasn't in a position
to quit just yet. And in truth, the thought of not seeing Sam
hurt a lot more than the knowledge that they could only be
friends.

'What's up?' Sam moved closer, so close she could see
where he'd missed a bit shaving —*I must buy a pack of cheap
razors for Dhassim*, she thought. She caught a whiff of his
cologne, and noted a small hole on the sleeve of his jumper.
He needs the love of a good woman, she thought, then gave
herself the mental equivalent of a kick up the arse. Sam was
an adult, capable of darning his own holes — did anyone
actually *do* that nowadays? — and Jinnie needed to get a grip
and say what needed to be said.

'Well, I was just wondering … wanted to ask … if I could
borrow some of your clothes?' *There, she'd said it. And it didn't
sound remotely weird. Nope, a totally normal request.*

'Sorry, did you just say that you wanted to borrow my clothes?' Sam looked himself up and down, then back at Jinnie with a bemused (or was it amused?) expression. Threadbare jumper aside, his attire was perfectly acceptable. Jinnie had already decided Sam was the stereotypical author; a little bit shabby, but he'd scrub up well when the occasion warranted it. She could imagine him at some swanky writers' gathering, dressed in a tuxedo and waxing lyrical about his latest book with a martini in his hand. Oh, and Jinnie just *happened* to be next to him, all off-the-shoulder slinkiness and sequins, gazing adoringly at his chiselled jawline —

'Jinnie?' Suddenly Sam was perilously close, his mouth inches from her face. He'd clearly been chewing gum, a waft of mint tickling her nostrils. Memories of *the kiss* came flooding back, although their mutual breath had been more mulled wine than fragrant herb. 'You were saying…'

'Yes. Yes! It's because of my, erm, cousin. Who's just arrived unexpectedly. And … his bag got lost on the way so he doesn't have a thing to wear.' *Apart from harem pants or girlie joggers.*

Sam carried on staring at her, the corners of his mouth twitching. Why, oh why hadn't she prepared a spiel before she started this? Now she'd have to wing it and hope Sam didn't see through her transparent lies (and glow-in-the-dark cheeks).

'He's not *really* my cousin, more of a second cousin twice — or maybe three times — removed. We're friends on Facebook, and he messaged to say he'd like to come and visit me. In Scotland. Because he's from… He's from…' *Hell's bells and buckets of blood!* Another favourite expression of Wilma's. The woman should write a book: *Miscellaneous Swearwords And Colloquialisms For All Occasions.* 'Jersey. He's from Jersey.'

'As in the Channel Islands?'

Jinnie wasn't entirely sure. She had a vague recollection

of her parents showing her re-runs of a TV show featuring a detective with a pretty cool car, but was that Jersey, or Guernsey? And where *were* the Channel Islands exactly? Well, she'd started, so she'd better finish.

'That's it. He's only here for a couple of days and rather than have to buy new stuff, I thought he could borrow some of yours. Otherwise he'll have to wear my gear, and he's not too keen on that idea.' *Although I might have to wrestle him out of my trackies.*

'If he's only here for a couple of days, can't he just wash his stuff?' Sam took a step back, his brow still creased. 'Not that I mind lending you some of my clothes, but I'd have to pop home first. Not a problem, if you can hold the fort for a little while.'

'That's fine.' As customers were hardly beating down the door in search of collectable curiosities, Jinnie could probably hold the fort for a week without breaking a sweat. Ooh, there was an idea!

'He — my sort-of cousin — is terribly sweaty. Honestly, you would not *believe* the damp patches under his arms when he arrived! And I don't have a tumble drier, so I'd never be able to dry his stuff in time.' For someone totally crap at lying, Jinnie felt she was doing pretty well. Even her scarlet cheeks had cooled down. Although as Sam touched her shoulder reassuringly, she felt a heat rising that had nothing to do with telling fibs.

'I'll grab a couple of pairs of trousers, T-shirts and a jumper or two,' he said. 'I might have an unopened pack of boxers and socks too, as I'm guessing your cousin wouldn't be too happy wearing someone else's underwear. Are we roughly the same size?'

Only if Dhassim grew an extra foot (height-wise, not adding another actual foot), and bulked up a bit. Still, genies can't be choosers.

'He's smaller than you, but trouser legs can be rolled up and baggy is fine. He'll be grateful for your help,' said Jinnie. She drew the line at asking to borrow a pair of Sam's shoes. Firstly because his feet — all two of them — were clearly several sizes bigger than Dhassim's dainty ones. Secondly, because asking to wear someone else's shoes was, well, a step too far. He couldn't go out in his pointy slippers, so he'd have to wear Jinnie's hiking boots or trainers. Both were in pristine condition, as Jinnie didn't hike and certainly didn't run. Not unless someone was chasing her.

Promising to be back in under an hour, Sam left. His parting words were: 'Why don't you drop the stuff at home when I get back, then bring your cousin to the shop? I'd love to meet … what did you say his name was?'

Caught on the hop again. A name like Dhassim might raise questions about his origins, as would his exotic appearance, but maybe Jinnie could persuade him to adopt a new persona. Perhaps something a little … French?

'David. His name's David, but pronounced the French way. *Daaa-veed*. I think his mum was French, or came from a French-speaking country.'

In the end Sam was back within forty-five minutes. Jinnie was wrapping up a cut-glass ashtray and decanter for a customer when he burst in.

'Thanks. Have a good day!' Jinnie trilled, glad that Sam had arrived while she was busy. Unlike ten minutes earlier, when she'd been scrolling through Facebook and sharing cute dog photos.

'Here you go.' Sam hefted a large carrier bag onto the counter. 'Hopefully there's everything David will need. I also stuck in some cologne and body wash I got for Christmas, which I'll never use.'

Before she could protest, Sam hustled Jinnie out of the shop. 'Bring your cousin back with you. We can have a brew here, then show him the Cranley highlights. Or at least treat him to a drink or two at the pub.'

Striding back to the cottage, Jinnie psyched herself up for what lay ahead. A crash course in a new identity, a quick change of clothing, then introducing Dhassim first to Sam, then the staff and customers of The Jekyll and Hyde. Really, it couldn't be *that* difficult to pull it off. Could it?

CHAPTER 33

'HMM, SO MY NAME IS DAVID, MY MOTHER IS FROM TUNISIA and I live in a place called Jersey.' Dhassim and Jinnie gazed at a map, red pen circling his alleged country of birth and current place of residence. 'And I am here because…?'

'You wanted to visit Scotland,' repeated Jinnie for the umpteenth time. 'And your luggage got lost, so that's why Sam's lent you his things.' Unfortunately, a quick internet search at the shop revealed there were no direct flights from Jersey to Edinburgh during the winter season. Jinnie prayed that Sam wouldn't know this and question Dhassim on his travel schedule.

'I am not feeling comfortable in these.' Dhassim tugged at the waistband of Sam's jeans, a plaid shirt tucked in haphazardly. One of Jinnie's belts was cinched to the max, reminding her that ol' snake-hips Dhassim was narrower round the middle than she was. Maybe she could use up another wish to become a perfect size ten for evermore, but instantly dismissed the thought. Her wishes so far had been fairly shallow. However many were left, Jinnie decided they would be more meaningful than nice hair or a smaller arse.

'You look fine,' she scolded, rolling up the trouser legs a little more. 'Channelling your inner lumberjack. I'll explain what that is another time.' Dhassim might not look capable of snapping a twig, never mind chopping down a tree, but he'd have to do. Jinnie laced up her hiking boots for him like a mother getting her child ready for school, as Dhassim stared at them in bafflement. 'There, you're good to go. Now pop this on,' — Jinnie helped him into an ancient coat she'd pinched from her dad years ago — 'and let's get going.' Ignoring Dhassim's muttering that the shirt was making him itch, she dragged him into the street.

'Hey, good to meet you, David!' Sam extended his hand and shook Dhassim's vigorously. His pronunciation was spot-on, but his handshake provoked a squeak of pain. Jinnie suppressed an eye-roll and announced that she would stick the kettle on. Not that she *wanted* to leave them alone, but hovering around Dhassim like a mother hen might look a bit suspicious.

'It's a shame you're only here a short time,' Sam said, as Jinnie sidled off, ear cocked for any cock-ups. 'I've never been to Jersey, but I visited Guernsey once years ago. Have you lived there long?'

'I believe so,' replied Dhassim. 'The passing of time is not something I choose to dwell upon. We are all mere specks in the universe, adrift on a tide we cannot control. Our destiny is written in the stars.' He tapped his nose in a knowing manner. 'Although some of us are able to play —'

'Scrabble!' Jinnie scuttled back, clutching a handful of tea bags and a packet of Hobnobs. 'Dha — David is pretty nifty at Scrabble. Beat me hands-down the other night. He's very spiritual too. Into yoga and karma and — stuff.' She juggled the tea bags and biscuits, deftly kicking Dhassim in the shin at the same time.

'Ouch!' He fixed Jinnie with a wounded glare, while Sam appeared not to have noticed her brief assault.

'I'll make the tea, and you can give David the grand tour of the shop,' he said, relieving Jinnie of her burden. 'Don't worry, David, it won't take long. If anything catches your eye, I'll do you a good price.' Sam winked and went into the back room.

'You were about to reveal yourself!' hissed Jinnie. 'And I don't mean in *that* way,' she added, as Dhassim checked his flies. 'Remember you're a mere mortal here, and being able to play a hand in people's fates is *not* something you share. Got it?'

With a petulant nod, Dhassim gave his shin a rub and sashayed over to a display of costume jewellery. He flicked through pendants and bracelets, pausing to hold a diamante-encrusted medallion up to his chest. 'What do you think, Jinnie?' he purred, unbuttoning the shirt a fraction to reveal his baby-smooth skin. 'It gives me a certain *je ne sais quoi*, don't you agree?'

Jinnie thought it made him look like a seventies porn star, but he couldn't buy it anyway. Dhassim might have a wish-granting gizmo and an enviable bottom, but genies weren't equipped with wallets and credit cards. 'Put it back,' she ordered. 'Sam will come through in a minute and you need to act normally. Say as little as possible, and put your WIFI on silent mode.' The device had an annoying habit of making pinging and beeping noises, often competing with Dhassim's snoring to keep Jinnie awake.

'I left it behind,' Dhassim retorted, stroking the medallion once more before hanging it up. 'Do not worry your pretty little head, I shall be on my best behaviour. Ah, here is Sam now.'

They gulped down their tea. At least, Jinnie and Sam did,

while Dhassim sniffed his suspiciously and focused on devouring half a pack of Hobnobs. He kept his answers to Sam's questions brief, and Sam didn't press too hard for information.

'Right, shall we adjourn to the pub?' he said. Jinnie nodded gratefully, feeling a stiff drink might be necessary to calm her fear of Dhassim putting his trainer-clad foot in it. It was just after five, and unlikely any more customers would appear. 'Oh, I forgot to mention, Jinnie, but I unearthed a couple of boxes in the back room earlier.'

Jinnie frowned, wondering where this was going. Dhassim was already back at the jewellery stand, fingering the medallion with barely disguised longing. 'You can have it,' said Sam. He walked over and unhooked the hideous object, dropping it into Dhassim's outstretched palm. 'A little welcome-to-Scotland gift.'

'Thank you.' Dhassim gave a flamboyant bow, and fastened the medallion around his neck. 'You are a kind and generous man. Now I understand why Jinnie finds you —'

'A great boss and a good friend,' Jinnie said, wishing she could kick Dhassim again. 'Anyway, tell me about these boxes in the back.'

'I haven't had time for a proper look, but it's possible the second lamp I told you about is in there. I'll check later. Right, where's my wallet?' Sam rummaged in his pockets, and Jinnie walked to the door.

She turned to see Dhassim swaying like a sunflower in a breeze, his face ashen. Jinnie grabbed his elbow and guided him to a wing-backed chair.

'What's the matter?' asked Sam. He hurried to Dhassim's side, and placed a comforting arm around Jinnie's shoulders. She tried to ignore the frisson of excitement his contact evoked, and knelt to look Dhassim in the eye.

'Are you OK?' Jinnie didn't need to be Einstein to figure out the reason for his pallor. Not that Sam would understand, and she wasn't about to reveal the truth about her distant 'cousin'.

'I am a little shaken,' replied Dhassim. 'What if it is —'

'Jet lag!' Jinnie clapped her hands together, instead of placing them around Dhassim's throat. How many times did she have to cut him off mid-sentence before he put his size six foot in it?

'Erm, jet lag?' queried Sam. He still had his arm around Jinnie's shoulders, and she fought the urge to snuggle closer. 'He only flew from Jersey … or did you mean New Jersey?' He looked from Jinnie to Dhassim, a twinkle of amusement in his eyes.

'OK, maybe not jet lag, but exhaustion from the journey. He's not a frequent flyer.' Unless you counted magic-carpet rides. And he'd only taken her on one, although who knew how many other women he'd soared through the skies with?

'I'll get a glass of water,' said Sam, releasing his hold on Jinnie and heading to the small kitchen.

'Are you feeling better?' Jinnie asked. The colour had returned to Dhassim's cheeks. He still looked shaken, but gave a weak smile.

'Do you think this other lamp could be Aaliyah's?' he whispered, his face a picture of cautious optimism.

Jinnie didn't want to rain on his parade, but while possible, she thought it unlikely. How could the two lamps turn up *again* in the same place? But then who'd have believed a genie would come into her life? Now wasn't the time to dwell on such matters, though. The lure of alcohol was stronger than ever.

'Here you go.' Sam handed the water to Dhassim, who gulped it down in one. 'We could skip the pub if you'd rather go home and rest.'

'Absolutely not,' Jinnie declared. 'David is fine — aren't you, David? Something alcoholic will soon sort him out.' *Or send him staggering around the room, based on his last encounter with booze.*

Off they went, Sam striding ahead. Jinnie held back, not just to ogle his impressive rear view.

Dhassim shuffled along at her side, the sights of Cranley failing to inspire more than a random sigh. 'Quite attractive, but rather old, no?'

For a second Jinnie thought he was talking about the appearance of the high street, which could do with a lick or two of paint. Then she twigged that Dhassim was referring to Sam. 'He's only in his forties,' she replied indignantly. 'And that's rich, coming from someone older than Methuselah.' Ignoring Dhassim's blank look, she hustled him inside the pub, sending up a silent prayer that this outing wouldn't end in disaster.

CHAPTER 34

SAM'S GAZE FLITTED BETWEEN JINNIE AND DAVID. THEY'D ALL ordered cheeseburgers and chips, with a glass of Pinot Noir for Sam and Jinnie, and a half-pint of lager for David. He was spooning the froth off the top with his fork, and had already broken his burger down into its individual components. *Curiouser and curiouser.*

There was something not quite right about the whole distant cousin/lost baggage/Jersey story. Perhaps David was actually Jinnie's lover — but why the need to lie? And they didn't strike Sam as a couple, more like a harassed mother dealing with a stroppy child. At one point, Jinnie rapped David on the knuckles when he took a bite of gherkin and spat it out on the plate. As she did so, she caught Sam's eye and blushed. *God, she's pretty.* He batted away the thought, remembering that they'd agreed to be friends. Anything else would be a mistake. Sam's own baggage — difficult ex-wife, needy son and self-imposed solitude as a writer — couldn't disappear as easily as someone's belongings at an airport.

'Hey, how's it going?' Ed appeared, and both Sam and Jinnie gawped at him open-mouthed.

'You've shaved off your beard!' cried Jinnie. Sam noted resentfully that he was better-looking without it. In his experience, men often grew beards to hide weak chins or sagging jawlines. Not Ed. He looked like he could moonlight as a male model in a hipster magazine.

'Yeah.' Ed stroked his chin, clearly not used to the lack of hair. 'It started to freak Mum out, and she didn't recognise me sometimes, so I decided it ought to go.'

After brief introductions Jinnie followed Ed to the bar, where they stood for several minutes, chatting. A sour-faced Jamie served customers, his manner grouchier than ever. Sam attempted to engage David in a discussion about his relationship with Jinnie, but got no more than their alleged contact on Facebook and this subsequent visit. He sank back in his chair, still aware of Jinnie and Ed talking at the bar, and being far more tactile than he liked.

Finally Jinnie returned, shiny hair bobbing as she sat down. 'Sorry about that. Ed just wanted to put me in the picture about Mags. He's really worried about her; that's why he's taken more time off work.'

She explained that Mags's short-term memory was worsening, and things she used to enjoy were slipping away. 'Ed said she was always a huge reader. Now, she has piles of books that she can't remember starting. Ken bought her a Kindle, but she threw it in the bin. It's so sad, Sam. There's my gran, still sharp as a tack at eighty-six, and Mags is maybe thirty years younger and losing her grip a bit more every day.' Tears filled Jinnie's eyes, and Sam wanted nothing more than to pull her close. But he didn't. He *couldn't*.

'Can I get you something else to drink?' Sam asked David, who'd devoured his burger and was now staring at his beer.

'A soda water and lime would be good,' said Jinnie. 'And one for me too, if that's OK.'

Standing at the bar, Sam caught Ed's eye and placed the

order. 'Jinnie was telling me about your mum,' Sam said, as Ed added slices of lime to the drinks. 'That's rough. And it can't be easy for you, taking so much time off work to be here.' Assuming that Ed *was* purely around to help with Mags, and didn't have an ulterior motive. Sam had noticed more than once how Ed looked at Jinnie. Heck, the way most men with a pulse and semi-decent eyesight looked at Jinnie.

'To be honest, I'm planning on jacking in my job and finding something in Edinburgh. Then I can be closer to Mum and help Dad out more.' Ed accepted Sam's handful of coins and worked the till. 'My boss has been understanding, but I'm thinking of setting myself up as freelance, which will give me more flexibility.'

Returning with the drinks, Sam overheard David mumbling to Jinnie about a lamp. Surely he wasn't referring to the mysterious second lamp? Come to think of it, David's funny turn in the shop had happened the moment he'd mentioned it. And if his memory served him correctly, Jinnie had also had a strange reaction when Sam remembered they'd come as a pair. But what could possibly connect them to a battered old lamp? Might they suffer from some rare phobia? Wait — Jinnie didn't, as she'd happily taken the first one home with her.

On the pretext of visiting the bathroom, Sam took out his phone and did a quick Google search. Right, an irrational fear of lamps. *Dadaphobia,* or *Faxmetus.* The first sounded more like a fear of fathers, the other a rare medical condition. But the weirdest phobia, according to the website, was *anatidaephobia:* the fear that somewhere in the world a duck is watching you. That made an aversion to lamps seem quite normal.

Chuckling to himself, Sam rejoined Jinnie and David. 'When do you head home?' he asked. 'Jinnie said it was a short visit. Shame if you don't have time to see Edinburgh.'

'He leaves tomorrow,' said Jinnie. 'Work commitments, and all that.'

David nodded, otherwise engrossed in opening condiment sachets and squeezing the contents on to his fingers. 'Eurgh!' he exclaimed, after a mouthful of mustard. 'That is almost as vile as those green things.'

'David is a picky eater,' continued Jinnie, handing him a wad of napkins from the dispenser. 'He prefers sweet stuff.'

But he's never tasted mustard before, and doesn't know what a gherkin is? Sam was starting to wonder if David was from another planet, or had spent his life in some strange cult. 'What do you do for a living?' he enquired.

Jinnie had just taken a large mouthful of her drink, and proceeded to choke on it. Sam got up and slapped her on the back. Her face was puce, and she was gasping like a goldfish liberated from its bowl. 'Breathe, Jinnie!' he urged, aware that her distress was attracting attention around the pub.

'Aah, aah, ooooh!' Jinnie let out a sound somewhere between a hiccup and a gasp. Sam resumed his seat. David looked completely uninterested, instead perusing the dessert section of the menu.

'Sorry. About the choking and the … unattractive noises.' Relative calm resumed, and Jinnie fluttered her hands around in a general *I'm fine, move on, folks* gesture. Across the room, Ed gave a thumbs-up. Sam reciprocated, although a small, ridiculously petty part of him wanted to stick up two fingers.

'No problem. Now, where were we?' Sam was glad Jinnie had recovered. He was less glad to see Ed approaching, sleek jawline to the fore.

'All OK?' Ed crouched down in front of Jinnie and touched her cheek. 'You gave me a scare. Can't be having my favourite staff member keel over, can I?' Now Sam wanted to stick his fingers down his throat. Did Ed have to flirt so blatantly with Jinnie in front of him?

'Yes, my drink went down the wrong way. No need to call an ambulance!' Jinnie smiled.

David tapped Ed on the shoulder and pointed at the menu. 'Can I please have a chocolate fudge cake? With vanilla ice cream. Anyone else?' He looked at Jinnie and Sam, both of whom declined.

With Ed gone, Sam struggled to recall what they'd been talking about. Oh yes. How the downright odd David earned a crust. 'I didn't get to hear what your job is, David. Anything exciting?'

David appeared perplexed by the question. Jinnie coughed loudly, and poked him in the ribs. Perhaps he was unemployed, and embarrassed to admit it. Or he worked for some top-secret agency and couldn't talk about it —

'I grant wishes!' The words burst from his mouth, followed by a howl of either anguish or mirth from Jinnie. It was hard to tell, as she'd buried her face in her hands.

'OK. That's … very interesting.' Sam wasn't often lost for words, apart from the dreaded writer's block, but this one had him stumped. Either David was officially bonkers, or —

'That's right, he does, but not in a crazy fairytale way. Of course not, that would be insane. Goodness me, who would ever believe such a thing!' Jinnie sat bolt upright, her eyes glittering manically. 'David, you have such a funny way of saying things!'

Dessert arrived. Sam contemplated ordering more wine, then decided against it. He wanted to be clear-headed when he heard what David's job really was.

'The thing is … he works for a charity that makes dreams come true for … sick people.' Jinnie nodded with enthusiasm. 'Mainly sick children, but they sometimes help older people too. You know the kind of thing: a trip to Disneyland, swimming with dolphins, visiting Santa Claus in Lapland.'

Sam was convinced Jinnie was fibbing. David, meanwhile, was stuffing cake into his mouth, and merely nodded.

'He, erm, doesn't really like to talk about it,' she continued. 'So heartbreaking, all these little ones with life-threatening conditions. Such a worthwhile cause, but it takes its toll. Mentally, I mean.'

Sam suspected David was indeed a sandwich short of a picnic. Still, at least he was leaving the next day. He had no idea what the truth was, but his instinct told him that something was amiss.

'All finished? Great! Let's leave Sam in peace.' Jinnie had her coat on, and threw down some cash for the dessert. 'David's looking a bit peaky, so I'll take him home if that's OK. Come along, David.' And with lightning speed, they departed.

Sam headed to the bar, ordered another glass of wine, and knocked half of it back in one. What on earth had that been about?

CHAPTER 35

'You're good at this.' Jo smiled as Angela tipped out used coffee grounds and refilled the machine. Two pots of freshly brewed tea sat on trays alongside slices of apple pie, and jugs of pouring cream completed the order. Angela scribbled down requests for sausage baps, hot chocolate and fruitcake, then nipped out back to remove a batch of bread rolls from the oven.

'It's not rocket science, but yeah, it's all coming back to me now. Me and Mum baking up a storm in the kitchen, pretending it didn't matter when Dad staggered in complaining that his tea wasn't on the table.' Angela rubbed her eyes. Possibly because of the steam from the oven, or —

'Are they still around?' Jo wiped down the counter as Angela prepared more orders. 'Your parents, I mean.'

She waited as her new assistant darted out from behind the counter, helping an old lady who'd got her handbag strap entangled with the chair. Angela then held the door open for a young mum and her pushchair, bending down to pull silly faces at the wailing toddler.

'Right. Where were we? Hang on, let me get these out first.' Jo felt like the new kid on the block as Angela zipped from table to table. For someone with so little self-confidence, she handled the job like a seasoned pro. It had only been a couple of hours, but Jo's vision of offering outside catering seemed achievable. As long as Angela was interested…

'OK. You were asking about my folks.' Angela sipped from a glass of water, her gaze steady. 'My dad disappeared when I was fifteen, and we haven't heard a dicky bird from him since. Might be dead, and to be honest, I couldn't care less about the drunken bastard.'

Jo flinched at Angela's words. Not because she was shocked, more because the tremor in Angela's voice contradicted the statement. At a guess, it must be twenty years or so since Angela's father left. And if the gossip-mongers were to be believed, she'd had Jamie in her mid-teens and been left high and dry by the boy's father, too.

'And your mum?'

'She's still around, but we don't talk much these days.'

Another customer approached the counter, looking for a hot-water refill for their teapot. Jo obliged, and nodded at Angela to continue. 'She was good at the start, helping with Jamie. I guess I took advantage a bit — well, a lot — and left him with her more and more so I could hang out with my mates. He wasn't an easy baby, and he's still a handful, but I was only sixteen. Nowhere near ready for that kind of responsibility.'

Jo couldn't imagine how tough it had been. Abandoned by her father, pregnant in her mid-teens, watching her friends carry on with their lives. She couldn't blame Angela for wanting to escape, but felt sorry for her mum.

'How come you don't talk much now?'

'Mainly because of my drinking,' replied Angela. 'It got out of hand — "the apple doesn't fall far from the tree" was one of Mum's favourite sayings. I left school because of having Jamie, and it was easier to get hammered than face the fact that my life was a train wreck.'

Jo waited for Angela to continue, her heart going out to the young woman's plight.

'I'd take money from Mum's purse — not that she had much — and did a bit of shoplifting too. Nothing to be proud of, but I did what I needed to survive. I'm sober now, but whenever I hit a rough patch it's so tempting to start again. And with my landlord bumping up the rent, I'm not sure I can stay where I am much longer.'

After reassuring Angela that she'd pay her cash in hand for now (it jarred with Jo's conscience, but would only be short-term), they carried on working. In between serving and clearing up, Jo outlined her vague plans for expanding the business. Angela didn't drive, but she could help with preparing the food and perhaps run the café if Jo was out on a job.

'You're an angel, Jo.' Angela hugged her, just as new customers arrived.

'Hello! Could one of you visions of loveliness rustle up a milky coffee and something calorie-laden for a starving lad?' Neither Jo nor Angela had noticed Ed coming in.

Jinnie was right behind him. 'Great minds think alike, Ed. I need a serious cake and caffeine fix myself.' Jinnie scanned the cake display, then pointed at a chocolate brownie.

'Make that two,' said Ed. 'Actually, three. Two for me and one for Jinnie. I'm wasting away, you know!'

Taking in Ed's muscular physique and the way every woman in the café — Jinnie and Angela included — laughed in disbelief, Jo pulled a face and dished up the brownies.

Grabbing their plates and mugs, Ed and Jinnie settled in a quiet corner. On their day out in Edinburgh, Jinnie had mentioned her ex-fiancé, but given little else away about her love life. Watching them now, Jo wondered if there was something going on. Their body language suggested they were at ease with each other, but that might simply be friendship. Judging by the steely look on Angela's face as Jinnie punched Ed playfully on the shoulder, she too questioned their relationship status. And Jo would put the smart money on Angela hoping they weren't about to become an item.

Leaving Angela in charge, Jo retreated to her cupboard-size office space out back. Firing up her laptop, she clicked on the flyer she'd worked on yesterday. Her plan was to distribute copies around the village, and find ways to sneak it into places further afield. Admittedly, the logo needed some work; Jo's attempt at a crumpet suggested a mouldy cheese, or a pre-schooler's interpretation of the moon. Maybe she could ask Ed's advice; Ken had said he was a designer. Which reminded her — not that she *needed* reminding — he was due at her place on Tuesday. He'd texted to ask if he could drop by, and Jo hadn't had the heart to say no. *Damn, those bloody butterflies are at it again.* Jo tweaked the text on her flyer, trying out different fonts and wording, but it still looked amateurish. She closed the laptop and returned to the café.

Ed was now on his own. Only a few brownie crumbs remained on his plate, and he was stabbing furiously at his phone. After a few moments he slammed it down on the table and let out an enormous sigh. Jo hesitated, unsure whether she should ask if all was OK. Maybe it was to do with Mags. The thought of something awful happening to her sent shudders down Jo's spine, in tandem with a horrible feeling that it would leave the way clear for... The butterflies turned into stomach-churning guilt. Jo was no goody two-shoes, but she had never, *ever* wished harm on anyone. Not counting an unfulfilled urge to turn up on the doorstep of her ex Graham's mother and tell the old bat exactly what she thought of her.

'Ed looks in need of more coffee,' murmured Angela, zipping past Jo with a mug in hand. 'I'll sit with him a few minutes, if you don't mind?'

Jo nodded, seeing Ed's face light up as Angela plonked down the mug and pulled up a chair. He showed Angela something on his phone, and she pulled a face before reaching over to squeeze his arm. *Is Ed interested in Jinnie, or Angela or both? Is it any of my business?* Jo asked herself. *Absolutely not. Is my 'relationship' with Ed's dad anyone else's business?* She swallowed. *It can't be.* Tempted as she'd been to confide in Jinnie on their day out, the words had stuck in her throat. Jo wasn't a fool. To an outsider, any attempt to justify seeing Ken in secret would imply something to hide. Nothing untoward had happened, but Jo wasn't sure she trusted herself — or Ken — to keep it that way.

'Ed's girlfriend just dumped him,' Angela announced, as said dumped boyfriend left with a wave to them both.

'Oh dear. Is he pretty cut up about it?' Jo didn't think he had the demeanour of a man crushed by rejection; he'd looked positively chirpy during the short time he'd been talking to Angela. And she was mightily relieved that the phone-banging had nothing to do with his mum.

'Nah, don't think so. He said it was on the cards, and things hadn't been great for a while.' Angela tried and failed not to grin. 'Mind you, giving someone the heave-ho by text is a bit brutal, don't you think?'

Leaving Angela to deal with a couple of pensioners dithering over cake choices, Jo nipped to the loo. As she washed her hands, she caught her reflection in the age-spotted mirror. The frown lines she tried to erase with jars of expensive cream and facial exercises seemed deeper than ever. She patted the pocket of her apron where her mobile sat. A quick text to Ken, saying it was better they didn't see each other anymore. That was all it would take. Except... Jo left the phone where it was, and ignored the little voice of dissent in her head.

CHAPTER 36

'DID DAVID GET OFF OK?' SAM ASKED WHEN JINNIE ARRIVED at the shop on Monday morning.

'Who?' Momentarily flustered, she lobbed an A Bit of Crumpet paper bag in Sam's direction. 'Ah, yes. A bit of a flight delay but he's back home safe and sound. And hopefully not suffering from jet lag, ha ha!'

Sam upended the bag and two Danish pastries glistening with sugar and dried fruit landed on the counter.

'I'll fetch some plates,' Jinnie said breezily, in contrast to the deepening pink of her cheeks, and disappeared into the back.

Sam knew her well enough to recognise that something was rotten in the state of Cranley. He'd spent a sizeable chunk of the weekend mulling over the strange encounter with her crackpot cousin, unable to come up with any rational explanation. A terse exchange with his publisher over his request for a deadline extension hadn't helped his mood. And an out-of-the-blue text message from Lucy asking if she could come and see him had completed the trilogy of headache-inducing scenarios.

'You look a bit pale.' Jinnie placed the pastries on plates, eyeing Sam sympathetically. 'Is everything all right?'

Was it? For the first time in years Sam didn't know what the honest answer was. He still loved writing, always would, but his mojo seemed to have left the building. The words were there; they just refused to emerge in any semblance of order. As for Out of the Attic Antiques, Sam had always treated it as a hobby. A harmless sideline, carried on in honour of his father. The shop barely made a profit, and he couldn't really justify employing Jinnie. On the other hand, he couldn't imagine letting her go. And not just in the job sense.

'Yeah, I'm fine. A few bumps in the road to negotiate, but nothing major.' Sam took a bite of pastry and allowed its sinful sugariness to soothe his worries for a moment.

'Can I ask you something?' Jinnie twirled her pastry round and round, staring at it as if it held the answers to the universe.

'Sure, go ahead.' Sam wondered for a moment if she was going to mention The Kiss again. It had attained capitalisation status in his mind over the past two weeks. *It was only A Kiss. We're friends, we can get past The Kiss.* Except that for Sam it had been a moment he would never forget; not least because of his stupid, knee-jerk reaction to it.

'I've still got my engagement ring. From when I was engaged, duh.' Jinnie pulled a comic face.

Sam knew a little of her failed relationship, privately thinking her ex-fiancé sounded like a prize jerk. If you were lucky enough to meet someone like Jinnie, you didn't let her go. 'Right. So you didn't toss it in the tosser's face?'

'It would be tempting,' admitted Jinnie. 'I guess I was just so stunned when Mark dumped me that it didn't cross my mind.'

Jinnie related how Mark had said he didn't find her

attractive any more, then quickly moved on to another staff member at the agency where they worked. All the time she fiddled self-consciously with her naked ring finger, the pastry forgotten. Sam finished his and fought down the urge to drive to Edinburgh, storm through the agency doors and punch her ex in the face.

'It's been in my jewellery box ever since, and I can't decide what to do with it,' she continued. 'I thought about selling it — it must be worth quite a bit — but that doesn't feel right. Unless I gave the money to charity, or something.'

Sam wondered if Jinnie was still hung up on Mark. The break-up hadn't been long ago. Maybe she had kept the ring in the hope they'd get back together…

'In case you're thinking I'd ever want him back' — *clearly mind-reading was one of her skills* — 'there's absolutely no way. If I fall in love again it will be with someone who loves me just the way I am.' Jinnie ceased her finger-twiddling and gave Sam a look so achingly raw he longed to kiss her again. On the forehead, as a father would kiss a sobbing child — Heck, who was he kidding? He wanted to return to that fateful night and not make a pig's ear of it this time.

'Jinnie, only you can decide what's the right thing to do, but for what it's worth, I think you should give it back. Gain closure, although I bloody hate that expression.'

Jinnie was silent for a few moments. Probably the thought of facing Mark again filled her with dread. Sam toyed with the idea of offering to drive her there himself, then figured he might end up facing a charge of grievous bodily harm.

'You're right.' Jinnie stood up purposefully and crammed a chunk of the pastry in her mouth. She chewed, swallowed, then spoke again. 'I'll call the agency later, check if he's in tomorrow, and get it over with. Thanks, Sam.' Before he could reply a couple of customers wandered in, and Jinnie bounded over to greet them.

* * *

'PLEASE PLEASE *PLEASE* CAN I come with you?' Dhassim clasped his hands together in prayer, his amber eyes piercing Jinnie's conscience. She'd been frostier than a neglected freezer over the weekend, furious at how many times their cover story had almost come unstuck. Sam undoubtedly smelt a rat, and the last thing they needed was to be clocked together by someone in the village. *David* was supposed to be back in Jersey, making wishes come true for the sick and vulnerable. Not skipping off to Edinburgh with Jinnie to confront Mark and commit God knows how many faux pas.

'No, no and *no!*' Jinnie stirred the pan of scrambled eggs she'd prepared for their dinner. 'You had your little trip on Friday, and that went *really* well, didn't it?'

Her oozing sarcasm was wasted on Dhassim. He'd dodged her glacial stares and barbed comments since meeting Sam, more intent on vacuuming, dusting and making Brae Cottage shine like the proverbial new penny. Tiring of Jennifer Aniston, he'd now developed a crush on Reese Witherspoon. *Legally Blonde* had played on a loop, with the rest of her back catalogue lined up for his delectation.

'I thought it did, Jinnie. Your Sam most definitely liked me, although I suspect he likes you a little more.' Dhassim wrapped his arms around himself and made irritating 'mwah, mwah' noises.

'Firstly he's not *my* Sam, and secondly I'm sure he thought you'd escaped from an asylum.' Jinnie buttered toast aggressively and dumped spoonfuls of egg on top. 'Eat this, I need to figure out what I'm going to wear tomorrow.'

Jinnie stomped up the stairs, shovelling in eggs as she

went. Her call to the agency had confirmed that Mark would be in the office, and she'd made an appointment for 11 am under a false name and the pretext of discussing properties in the half a million plus bracket. Jinnie imagined Mark salivating at the thought of a well-heeled prospective client, his eyes glittering at the potential commission. Boy, was he in for a surprise.

'I promise I'll be good.' Dhassim stood on the threshold of Jinnie's bedroom, clutching a packet of Maltesers. He lobbed one in the air, and caught it in his mouth. 'It will take my mind off the lamp, and my dream of seeing Aaliyah again. Ah, Jinnie, she was truly more beautiful than Jennifer and Reese combined.'

Dammit! Jinnie had forgotten to ask Sam about the lamp. She'd been too focused on her own problems, too keen to seek Sam's wise counsel. She felt a wave of guilt at her self-centredness. Almost a week had passed since lunch at her parents', and she'd only managed a couple of texts to check on Wilma's health. *Still coughing and refusing to see the doctor,* her mum had replied. And Hannah had messaged her several times, demanding to know when they could meet up again. *Any luck with Sam or Ed?* she'd written. *Or have you lost the key to your chastity belt? LOL xxx*

Jinnie crouched down, opened her mouth, and caught a Malteser. She high-fived Dhassim, then pulled out the little black dress she'd bought all those weeks ago. Only worn once, and — quick sniff — still good to go. It seemed fitting that she wear it as she strode into Mark's office —

'Please, Jinnie?' Dhassim did an Olympic gymnast-worthy roll across the floor and under the abdominal trainer. 'My time here is coming to an end, and I would like to experience one more visit to the outside world.' He tilted his knees towards his chest, and performed a rapid series of crunches.

The small pile of Sam's borrowed clothes still lay in the

corner. She hadn't got round to washing and returning them. Maybe if Dhassim borrowed a knitted hat and pulled it down a long way (preferably over his face), they might get away with a quick jaunt to the city. Jinnie also had a pair of enormous fake-designer sunglasses she'd bought in a bid to appear a bit glamorous and Hollywood. Mark had taken one look and said she resembled a giant fly.

'OK, you can come with me.' Jinnie dropped the dress on the bed as Dhassim catapulted upright and squeezed her tight. She hugged him back, with a lump in her throat that had nothing to do with a trapped chocolate ball. *My time here is coming to an end.* Did she have any wishes left? Not that she could think of. Apart from wishing that the clock wasn't ticking for her genie friend.

CHAPTER 37

By some miracle Jinnie and Dhassim boarded the train into Edinburgh without being spotted. There was one nerve-jangling moment when Janette rounded a corner, resplendent in a bright blue top and leggings that made her legs look like sausages on the brink of explosion. Desperate not to be dragged into conversation, Jinnie tugged Dhassim behind a line of wheelie bins, where they crouched until the coast was clear. 'Eugh, this place smells!' Dhassim protested, Jinnie shushing him furiously.

With the coast clear, they legged it to the platform and reached the city without further incident apart from Dhassim complaining that the hat made his ears itch (although he kept admiring his reflection wearing Jinnie's sunglasses).

It was a crisp, clear day, the sky an unspoiled blue. Dhassim clung to Jinnie's arm, intimidated by the volume of people crowding the streets. She pointed out the landmarks they'd soared above on their magic-carpet ride, although Dhassim seemed more impressed with the shops lining Princes Street. 'What is all this colourful fabric?' he enquired as they stopped outside a tourist trap with a lurid window display of bargain kilts and plaid throws. Jinnie explained about tartan, and how different clans had their own distinct colours and patterns.

They wandered inside, and Jinnie took great delight in winding Dhassim up when he came upon a shelf of furry toys. 'Those are replicas of haggis — plural "haggi" — which roam the highlands of Scotland,' she told him. 'Sadly, they are killed for their meat, which you're rather partial to.'

Dhassim turned light green and dropped the similarly hued toy he'd picked up. 'That is barbaric!' he cried. 'Why did you not tell me this, Jinnie? I will never eat haggis again.'

Giggling at his face when she confessed it was a big fat fib, Jinnie caved in when he begged her to buy him a cheap sporran. Dhassim dangled it over his groin and performed a little jig.

Checking her watch, Jinnie realised she had only ten minutes until her appointment with Mark. 'Come on, we need to go,' she urged. His office was only a couple of streets away, but Jinnie needed to deposit Dhassim some-where. There was no way she'd get through this with Dhassim sticking his oar in. 'Here's some cash.' Jinnie handed him a fiver and hustled him into a quiet café. 'Get yourself a coffee or something and stay put until I get back. And do *not* speak to anyone … well, apart from whoever takes your order.'

A few minutes later Jinnie stood at the entrance of the agency. She popped on another pair of cheap sunglasses and tucked her hair into a baker boy cap. *Deep breaths,* she told herself. *And suck your tummy in.* She marched in, head held high, and approached the reception desk. 'Jennifer Wither-spoon to see Mark Mitchell,' Jinnie announced.

The receptionist — luckily a new one, otherwise Jinnie's cover might have been blown — smiled sweetly and picked up her phone to buzz Mark. A moment later, she pointed at the closed door of Mark's office. *OK, this is it. Show time.*

Jinnie knocked once, heard Mark's familiar deep voice say 'Enter', and strode in. He had his back to her, and was rifling through a stack of lever-arch files. 'Just give me a second, Ms Witherspoon, and I'll be right —'

Mark swivelled round in his chair, and his jaw dropped in a manner befitting a cartoon character.

Jinnie sat down opposite and waited for him to regain his composure, which took some moments. 'What are you doing here?' he said, staring at her. 'And why did you pretend to be someone else?'

Seeing Mark flustered and wrong-footed gave Jinnie a buzz of delight. He'd always been so in control (and controlling, if she was totally honest). 'Nice to see you too, Mark,' she said, her voice oozing sarcasm. 'I thought it was time I returned something that really doesn't belong to me.' Jinnie opened her bag and produced the ring, its perfect diamond glinting in the overhead lights. 'Sorry about the subterfuge, but I wasn't sure you'd want to see someone so *unattractive.*' She tugged off the cap and sunglasses, delighted to feel her hair fall perfectly into position.

Mark flinched at her words, tugging at his mauve and pink silk tie. A present from Jinnie, if she wasn't mistaken. 'Yes, with hindsight, I know I didn't handle our break-up very well and … well, I'm sorry.' He regarded her with those hazel puppy-dog eyes which had once reduced her to jelly. Now, she felt absolutely nothing. He wasn't even *that* good-looking compared to someone like Sam —

'Listen, Jinnie, keep the ring. I don't want it back. Maybe you can get the stone made into a necklace or something.' Mark got up and walked around the desk. 'Think of it as a gift: an apology. And can I just add that you look pretty spectacular.' He moved closer, Jinnie catching a whiff of garlic from his breath. 'Did you find a new hairdresser? And that dress really suits you...'

Jinnie wriggled off the chair, still clutching the ring. What an oily, arrogant piece of work. She reached out to toss the ring on the table —

'Oops! Didn't know you were with a client, darling. Should have knocked.' There stood Kimberley, holding a takeaway cup and wearing a bodycon dress so tight that Jinnie wondered if they had the same number of internal organs. Sod it! She stopped sucking in her tummy and let it all hang out. Not that there was much *to* hang out, but compared to the stick insect Jinnie felt distinctly blobby. *But happy and blobby.* She grinned.

'We were just finishing up,' replied Mark smoothly. 'Sadly we don't have anything to offer Ms Witherspoon at present, but I sincerely hope she'll be back in touch soon.' He gave Jinnie one of his finest *I am a love god, worship at my feet* smiles. Jinnie's organs shrivelled on the spot.

'That would be wonderful!' cooed Kimberley, insincerity seeping from every honed and toned pore. Then she did a double-take. 'Wait a minute, aren't you —?' She placed her cup on Mark's desk, revealing a ring on her engagement finger — an itsy bitsy diamond that could have been the runt of the litter spawned by Jinnie's ostentatious offering. Bitchy, but Jinnie couldn't care less. She watched as Kimberley removed the lid and perched on the end of the desk. 'It's Jinnie, right? Why are you pretending to be someone else?'

Jinnie ignored the question. 'Do you still take two sugars?' she asked Mark. He shook his head and opened his mouth to speak —

'There you go!' She lobbed the ring into the coffee, suppressing a laugh as it splashed hot liquid directly into Mark's lap. 'Hope that sweetens things nicely. Cheerio!'

Outside, Jinnie gave a little fist pump, Mark's roar of pain and outrage still ringing in her ears. She'd love to be a fly on the wall when his new fiancée clocked the size disparity between the two gems.

* * *

'ALL DONE!' Jinnie found Dhassim sitting in a corner, still wearing her sunglasses and drinking a Coke. 'Think I need a drink myself to celebrate.' She caught the attention of a waitress and ordered an Aperol Spritz and two bags of peanuts.

Dhassim eyed the lurid orange drink when it arrived, and Jinnie allowed him a sip. 'Euch! That is disgusting,' he declared, washing away the taste with a mouthful of Coke. 'Like the urine of a camel, although I have fortunately only sampled it once.'

Jinnie had no desire to know more of Dhassim's experiences with camel pee. Now that the euphoria of putting Mark in his place had worn off, she wanted to get home and put her feet up.

'Why do we have to leave so soon?' whined Dhassim as they did battle against the tide of shoppers and tourists en route to the station.

Jinnie was about to reply, when a familiar figure came into view. Walking towards them, head down and puffing a cigarette, was Angela. *Shit!*

'Get in there now!' Jinnie manhandled Dhassim into a shop doorway, ripped the hat from his head and tossed it at his feet. 'Sit down, look sad and stay put till I sort this.' Damn it, Angela had spotted her.

'Angela!' Jinnie threw her arms out wide, nearly knocking down an old lady with a walking frame. 'Gosh, sorry, are you OK?' The genteel-looking pensioner muttered an expletive and shuffled on by.

'Hey, Jinnie. How are things?' They moved to the side of

the road, Angela stubbing out her cigarette on a bin by the bus stop. Her eyes were puffy, her hair flat and greasy.

'Good, thanks,' Jinnie replied. She shot a glance at the doorway, but Dhassim was hidden by a mass of bodies. 'And you?'

Angela shrugged listlessly. 'Life's just dumping on me from high, as usual. There's no way I can afford my landlord's rent hike, and I've a pile of bills that need paying.'

Praying that Dhassim wouldn't wander off and get into trouble, Jinnie took Angela's arm and guided her towards a street vendor selling hot drinks and snacks. 'What do you fancy?' she asked, the delicious smell of sizzling bacon and sausages filling in the air.

Two sausage butties ordered, they took a seat in Princes Street Gardens. Angela guzzled hers ravenously, Jinnie nibbling the edges, impatient to get back to Dhassim.

'Aren't you working at Jo's now?' Jinnie said, cursing as a dollop of brown sauce plopped on to her dress. She dabbed at it with a napkin, hoping the stain wouldn't mean an expensive dry-cleaning bill.

'Yeah, Jo's been really kind and wants to offer me more stuff, but it's bolting the stable door after the horse has gone.' Angela kicked at a loose stone with her scuffed shoe. 'I'm looking at renting a cheap bedsit in Edinburgh, maybe finding some work doing alterations or whatever. I'm not lazy, Jinnie, I'm just desperate.'

Jinnie wondered how Jamie would feel if his mum moved out of Cranley. More to the point, where would *he* live?

'Anyway, you don't want to hear me droning on about my sad little life.' Angela crumpled the buttie wrapper and got up. 'Thanks for this. See you around.'

Jinnie watched Angela's retreating back. She vanished in a throng of people, and Jinnie sat back with a sigh. Shredding the remainder of her buttie, she tossed the crumbs to a handful of delighted pigeons. If only she could help, but Jinnie wasn't living the champagne lifestyle herself. More fur coat and nae knickers, as Wilma would say.

She experienced a brief moment of panic when Dhassim wasn't where she'd left him. Relief kicked in when Jinnie spotted him two doorways further along, chatting animatedly to a homeless man swathed in manky blankets. A well-groomed dog of indeterminate breed languished at his feet — or rather, foot, since he had one leg missing.

'Jinnie, this is my new friend, William,' Dhassim said, beaming broadly. 'He lives here, which is strange, but no stranger than living in a lamp, I suppose.' William grinned and saluted Jinnie, his other hand rotating a finger beside his head in the universal 'got a screw loose' sign.

'Nice to meet you, William.' Jinnie patted the dog, its tail beating a tattoo on the pavement. Digging out some small change, she placed it in the tin box in front of William. 'Sorry, but I need to take my, erm, charge back to his … facility. Care in the community, and all that.'

Dhassim leapt to his feet, producing his woolly hat from his pocket, and with a flourish, he tipped its contents into William's tin. Several one and two-pound coins landed with a clatter. 'I do not know why people gave me money, Jinnie, but there is much I do not understand in your world. Goodbye, William!'

Seated on the train, Jinnie rested her head against the window and closed her eyes. Poor Angela. Jinnie wished she could do something. And a seedling of an idea sprouted in her mind…

CHAPTER 38

'How's Mags?'

It was good to open with a question about Ken's wife. It set the tone, cleared the air. Nothing could be misconstrued; a boundary was clearly marked out between them.

'Up and down,' replied Ken, hanging his coat up, then passing Jo a bottle of wine. 'She had a good couple of days, then this afternoon she got agitated about going to see her sister Eileen.'

'Wouldn't that be a good thing?' asked Jo, peeling cling film off a tuna and bean salad she'd made earlier. 'Maybe spending time with family might trigger some happy memories. Not that I'm an expert, or anything.'

Ken rummaged in the drawer for a corkscrew — he knew his way around Jo's kitchen now — and opened the bottle. He poured two glasses, and raised his in a toast. But there was nothing celebratory about his expression.

'Eileen died over twenty years ago in a car accident, Jo. I tried to get Mags to understand, but she burst into tears. Then she went looking for her old address book to find Eileen's number.'

'Oh.' Jo didn't know what to say. She stirred the salad, her heart aching both for the loss of Mags's sister and the fact she believed she was still alive. Looking up, she felt the familiar internal somersault as Ken watched her, his eyes filled with pain.

'Should you be here?' Jo knew her tone was brusque, but she was angry at herself. Angry at the way her body was reacting, while her brain was screaming at her to call a halt to it all. 'If your wife is upset, shouldn't you be with her?'

Ken slumped in a chair and massaged his scalp. Jo noticed for the first time that his hairline was receding just a little, creeping back above each temple. 'Her friends Lindsay and Ruth are with her. They're going to watch some TV, play cards, or something. And no, I probably shouldn't be here, Jo. But I'm not a saint, and I certainly don't have the patience of one.'

The two of them picked at the food. Jo put on the radio, and 'Don't You Forget About Me' by Simple Minds drifted over the airwaves. Jo loved the song, but it added an extra layer of poignancy to the evening. Bit by bit Mags was forgetting, her memories slipping away and unlikely ever to be retrieved. Jo had often wondered which would be worse: being physically incapacitated, or losing one's mental faculties. On balance, she thought the latter. Becoming frail was one thing; becoming increasingly confused, distressed and unable to function was another. If Jo made it to a ripe old age she hoped she'd still be sharp as a tack, even if her body was crumbling.

'This is delicious,' said Ken, as the music switched to a jollier number. 'What's in the dressing?'

As Jo listed the ingredients — garlic, lemon juice, tarragon and mustard — she wished things had turned out differently all those years ago. Not that she had gone ahead and married Graham, and gained the mother-in-law from hell, of course. No, Jo wished she'd met someone else and they'd shared a life together, both good times and bad. That they were sitting here now, eating quietly, in that way of couples who were comfortable with each other. Just as she and Ken were doing, without the long, shared history. Was that partly why she was drawn to him? *In less than five years I'll be fifty. Fifty, and probably still single.* The thought had never really bothered her before. 'Gettin' old is better than the alternative, hen,' Janette from the corner shop had sagely told her on more than one occasion. But maybe deep down Jo hankered to be with someone after all.

'Ed's packed in his job.' Ken's voice broke Jo's reverie. She looked up, aware she'd hardly touched her meal. 'Handed in his notice yesterday, apparently.'

'Do you think he's made the right decision?' Never having had kids, and unlikely to do so now, Jo wondered if parents ever stopped fretting about their children's choices. Ed was probably in his thirties now, but she could see how they both doted on him. He was a nice boy — man — and had a girl-friend. No, he'd been dumped, Jo recalled.

'Who knows?' Ken refilled the wine glasses and looked questioningly at Jo's almost-full plate. She nodded, and he tipped the contents on to his own. 'He's young, free and single at the moment, so I guess he can please himself.'

'Do you think he'd be interested in an older woman?' Time to lighten the mood, get back to the joking and good-natured joshing that was their trademark.

'If you're thinking of Janette again, I really can't picture them as a couple.' Ken laughed and Jo joined in.

'Actually, I was thinking more of myself. I'm only, what, five years older than Ed —'

Ken laughed harder. Jo stood up, and swatted him with a tea towel, but he grabbed the end and pulled her closer. She stumbled, and Ken caught her. They were inches apart, the air between them charged and terrifying. Jo wasn't drunk, so she couldn't blame what happened next on alcohol. She couldn't blame it on anything, other than a longing that left her dizzy with desire.

'Jo.' She didn't want to hear words, didn't want to think about what was happening. They were achingly close, the stubble on Ken's chin grazing her cheek. Jo turned her head, her lips touching his, and they remained like that for what seemed minutes. Just touching, Ken's eyes boring into hers. Who would instigate the next move?

The answer came swiftly. Jo pulled away, hot shame replacing the yearning that had turned her briefly into the kind of person she knew she could never be.

'Jo.' Ken spoke again, and this time Jo listened. 'I want to kiss you. There's nothing I want more right now. But I can't. You know that. We both know that.' The longing she'd seen mirrored in his eyes was replaced with sadness and regret.

'And I want to kiss you.' Jo took Ken's hand and scrutinised it. Solid, warm and slightly calloused from years of lugging beer kegs. His wedding ring needed a polish, she noted. 'In another world, in different circumstances, there's nothing I'd like more.'

They sat together, Jo stroking Ken's hand in gentle, circular motions. He didn't stop her, and minutes ticked away with only the chatter of the excitable DJ piercing the silence. Finally Jo got up and switched on the kettle.

'I won't stay,' said Ken. 'It's been lovely, as always, Jo, but I almost crossed a line tonight. And I'm sorry.'

Jo lobbed a tea bag into a mug. She kept her back to Ken, afraid he'd see the disappointment in her eyes. But she'd done the right thing. They'd teetered on the brink, yet managed to avoid a mistake they'd always regret.

'You don't have to go,' she replied. 'And you don't have to apologise. Nothing happened. Everything's fine.' Although it would be best if Ken did go, and left her to deal with her inner turmoil.

Seeing him to the door, Jo kept her arms by her sides. 'Don't be a stranger!' she trilled lightly.

In response, Ken raised her right hand to his lips and kissed it. 'There's no chance of that. Not having you in my life isn't an option. As long as you want me around, that is.'

Jo promised that she'd see him soon, but that it was better to meet on the neutral ground of the café. Ken agreed, and he headed for home.

Sitting with her tea, Jo choked back a sob as Donna Summer's 'Love's Unkind' filled the room. *Yes, it really, really was.*

CHAPTER 39

'Gran, you've got your finger over the camera ... Right, now you've flipped it so I can only see the living room... OK, I think you've muted me...' Cue mime to indicate problem with sound — 'Ah, that's better.'

For a woman so well-versed in social media, Wilma struggled with conducting a face-to-face conversation on her mobile phone. Jinnie had called her before she headed into work on Friday, knowing that her gran was an early to bed, early to rise creature.

'Ach, I'm absolutely fine,' Wilma huffed when Jinnie asked how she was feeling. 'Couldnae be doing with any more nagging, so I went to see the doctor. Not Dr Ritchie, he retired last year. Shame, I used to enjoy sharing a wee snout with him back when there was none of that politically correct crap.'

The good old days — in Wilma's eyes, anyway. Filling the consulting room with acrid plumes of smoke, doctor and patient puffing away in blissful harmony.

'So this wee slip of a girl — only looked about twenty — gave me the old lecture about lookin' after myself and said my blood pressure was too high. Aye, it would be when you're telt to stick to one glass of wine a night and knock the fags on the head!'

Now on a week-long course of antibiotics to clear her chest, and armed with enough nicotine patches and gum to fill an entire shelf of Boots, Wilma was not a happy camper. But still a devious one. 'Mind you, she didnae say what size glass, so I bought myself an extra-large one. And the odd wee roll-up won't kill me.'

It probably won't, thought Jinnie. She pictured Wilma receiving her one-hundredth-birthday telegram from the Queen, tweeting about it to her ardent followers, and posting selfies with a ciggie in one hand and a drink in the other.

'When are you going to come and see me?' asked Wilma. 'It's been a while since I last read your leaves. What was it last time?'

A wish coming true. Almost six weeks had passed since that reading. The next day Dhassim had come into her life and wishes *had* come true. Now Jinnie had the chance to make a real difference to someone's life. Dhassim, however, had taken some persuading.

* * *

'HMM. I am not sure, Jinnie. It is a noble thought, but my WIFI is — how do you say? — on the blink again.' Sure enough, said device now emitted only feeble flashes and pitiful whining sounds. If it conked out completely, would that be the end of the whole genie/wish thing?

Jinnie's brainwave about Angela and her financial plight depended on Dhassim stepping up to the plate. That, and his bloody useless piece of kit doing what it was supposed to do.

'I thought if Angela could win some money with a scratch card or something, that would solve her problems,' she said.

'Well, some of them, at least.' A small windfall would help Jinnie too, but she didn't want to wish for that. She was getting by, whereas Angela was sinking fast.

'I'm not talking millions,' she continued, as Dhassim squirted more WD40 and frowned. 'Maybe 20K or so.'

'I do not know what this *scratch card* is, or the 20K to which you refer.' Dhassim gave his WIFI a vigorous shake, and it mewed like an abandoned kitten.

It was a quarter to nine, and Jinnie had the shop to open. She'd barely seen Sam since Monday, and she wasn't working at the pub again until tomorrow evening. Was Sam avoiding her? He'd been out and about most of Wednesday, and had been extremely secretive about his whereabouts today. 'Just stuff to deal with,' he'd said, after taking a phone call. Whoever it was, Sam hadn't wanted Jinnie to hear. He'd gone into the back room and closed the door firmly.

'I have to go,' Jinnie said, checking her keys were in her bag. 'Be a good genie and get your WIFI working. I should be home by five at latest.'

Three hours and two customers later, Jinnie was bored out of her skull. She'd rejigged some displays, priced a box of items Sam had left out, and played several rounds of Candy Crush on her phone. She'd also called Hannah, and endured twenty minutes of squealing as her best friend described the 'total hottie' she'd met on the tram.

'Honest, Jinnie, he's like the double of that M & S model guy. You know the one; mean and moody and fills out underpants better than Beckham. Not that I've *seen* Simon in his underpants, but give a girl some time!'

Jinnie hadn't seen any man in a state of undress for some time. Well, apart from Dhassim stripped to the waist in his harem pants, and Archie sloping around their parents' house in saggy Y-fronts looking for clean clothes. She doubted she would any time soon. Maybe she should ogle a few shots on the M & S website —

'Been fighting them off with a stick again?'

Jinnie hastily put down her phone. Sam approached, his handsome face tired and drawn. *What's he on about?* Surely he didn't know she'd been thinking about men, and just about to check out images and ponder whether any sock-stuffing had been involved? Ha, Jinnie would have to *chase* a man with a stick at this rate... Oh, Sam meant *customers.*

'Ha ha. Nope, it's been super quiet. Erm, are you OK?' He looked exhausted, as if he'd been up all night researching gruesome ways to commit a murder. For his books, obviously. Or maybe there was another reason for his jaw-dislocating yawn.

'I'm fine. Didn't sleep too well, that's all.' Sam collapsed into a chair, long legs stretched out and arms folded behind his head. 'Stuff going on, but I won't bore you with the details.'

Please do. Jinnie wanted to get into Sam's headspace. Figure out what made him tick. Even if his tick was out of synch with her tock.

'Go home, Jinnie.' Sam yawned again. 'Do something nice with the rest of the day. I'll stay here and catch up with some paperwork.'

Jinnie didn't want to go home. No doubt Dhassim would still be fiddling with his WIFI and expect her to rustle up some food. She'd left him a can of tomato soup and half a loaf of bread, which would have to do.

'If you're sure. Or I could treat you to lunch at the Jekyll and Hyde?' Liz's legendary Lancashire hotpot was a Friday favourite. Jinnie drooled at the thought of those juicy chunks of lamb, smothered in crispy potato —

'Sounds lovely, Jinnie, but I don't think I'd be good

company today. See you Monday?' Sam's phone buzzed and he frowned at the screen.

'OK, have a nice weekend.' Jinnie gathered up her stuff and left, pausing to look back as she opened the door. Sam didn't look up, and she swallowed the bitter taste of rejection.

Aware that she was perilously close to busting her meagre monthly budget, Jinnie decided to swing by A Bit of Crumpet. A Scotch pie would suffice, and she could have a natter with Jo. However, on entering she spotted Angela behind the counter, ladling soup into bowls. Jinnie waited her turn while the couple in front of her debated whether to have scones or doughnuts with their tea.

'Hiya,' said Angela, when Jinnie reached the counter. 'What can I get you?' She looked better than when they'd bumped into each other in Edinburgh, but only marginally.

'A Scotch pie, please, and a coffee to go.' Jinnie pulled out her purse, but Angela shook her head and produced a handful of change from her apron pocket.

'This one's on me. You treated me last time, remember?' She counted the coins into the till before bagging the pie and fitting a lid on the coffee cup.

'Jo not around?'

'Nah, she's off touting for business for her new venture. Outside catering. Already got a couple of bookings on the back of this.' Angela pointed at a small pile of flyers on the counter. 'They don't look too brilliant at the moment, but Ed's going to work his design magic on them.'

At the mention of Ed, Angela's face changed from glum to glowing. *Alrighty*, thought Jinnie. Definitely interest there. Whether it was reciprocated, though, was another matter.

'That's good news then,' she replied, unable to resist taking a bite of pie. Sod the calories, Jo's pies were a little slice of heaven. 'More business means more money, right?'

Angela shrugged as she filled milk jugs for another order. 'Unless Jo bags a deal to feed the Scottish Parliament, it won't change my situation.' She looked past Jinnie. 'Sorry, was that two cappuccinos and one tea?'

Back on the high street, Jinnie dithered about what to do next. She could visit her family, but her dad would be at work and her mum often volunteered at the local charity shop on Fridays. Wilma would be around, but Jinnie didn't feel up to another tea-reading session. She'd go and see them next week.

Dismissing the idea of popping into the pub for a cheeky drink, Jinnie reluctantly decided that an afternoon with her genie pal would have to do. Dragging her heels, she shuffled back to Brae Cottage. Her route took her past Sam's place, also a cottage, but on a considerably grander scale. Its sandstone façade spoke of a genteel past, the front door a discreet powder blue complete with polished lion's-head knocker. Jinnie had never been inside — why would she? — but she was curious about the kind of home a man like Sam would have. She imagined a full-length wall of bookcases, an enormous squishy sofa, a tidy but dated kitchen well-stocked with fine wine but lacking in cupboard essentials. As for his bedroom —

Eek! Jinnie's thoughts of a super king-size bed made up with masculine grey linen were replaced with horror as the front door opened a fraction. She scurried across the road and into an alley, half-mortified that Sam might think she had stalker tendencies, half-wondering why he was already home. Unless … unless he'd been burgled, and said thieving bastards were about to emerge with armfuls of swag.

Heart thumping, Jinnie pressed herself against the alley wall. Whichever scenario it turned out to be, she didn't want to be clocked by either Sam or some wild-eyed chancer wielding a kitchen knife. Eventually curiosity won the day, and she peered around the corner. No stocking-over-the-head felon. Instead, an immaculately-groomed female who might well be wearing stockings, but on her impossibly long legs. Auburn hair, piled up in one of those buns designed to look effortless but requiring piles of pins and manual dexterity. She had a large holdall slung over her shoulder, and for a moment Jinnie thought she might be Sam's cleaner. Until Sam appeared behind her, and she turned and rested her head on his chest. *Probably not his cleaner, then.*

Jinnie felt sick, willing herself to look away. But like a rubbernecker passing a road accident, she couldn't help but watch. Sam raised the woman's chin with one finger, then kissed her on the forehead.

Unable to stomach any more, Jinnie took off at a gallop as a taxi pulled up outside Sam's place. All she wanted was to lock herself in her bedroom and reflect on what an idiot she was. *As if Sam could ever be interested in someone like me. Dull, dumped and woefully unambitious.* She worked for Sam, and he'd been kind to her. End of story. One misjudged kiss, and she'd built it up into something that could never be.

CHAPTER 40

'You are sad, Jinnie.'

Ten out of ten for observation. Was the pile of sodden tissues crumpled all around her the giveaway? Or the fact that she'd stormed into the cottage, thundered upstairs and wailed, 'I am never coming out of this room, ever!' at the top of her voice? That in itself should have warned Dhassim to keep his distance. But no. Her genie possessed many skills, but recognising when someone really wanted to be alone wasn't one of them.

'Yes, I'm sad. And there's nothing you can do about it.' Jinnie honked into another tissue. Granted, he'd let her be for a couple of hours before barging into the bedroom with a peanut-butter sandwich in one hand and a mug of tea in the other. She'd tried to snooze, but the sound of Johnny Cash singing 'Ring of Fire' as he wooed June (Reese) had kept her awake. Now Jinnie's nose was aflame, and her mind kept snapping back to the image of Sam with another woman.

'My WIFI is working.' Dhassim nudged the sandwich closer. 'Please eat, Jinnie.'

Jinnie took an unenthusiastic bite, then nearly spat it

back onto the plate. Who, in the name of the wee man, mixed mayonnaise with peanut butter?

'Is it because of Sam?' Dhassim sat cross-legged at the end of the bed. 'If you like, you can wish for him to —'

'No!' Jinnie lunged forward before Dhassim could touch his WIFI, sending the mug of tea flying. 'I'm not going to wish for him to love me. That's just pathetic. Ugh. I'm sad and lonely, but I'm not desperate.'

Watching as Dhassim mopped up the spilled tea with a discarded T-shirt, Jinnie pulled the duvet up to her chin. She'd got it hopelessly wrong, and she couldn't see a way to make it right. The thought of walking into the shop and pretending everything was fine, made her shudder. Working alongside Sam and seeing him gambolling around like a spring lamb would be torture.

'If your WIFI is functioning again, can we do the thing for Angela?'

Dhassim ceased mopping and returned to his position on the bed. 'The screech card?' *Close enough.* 'If that is your wish, then it is my command.'

Huddled together, Jinnie said the words — 'I wish for Angela to win money' — and Dhassim gave a thumbs-up to signal all was well. Oops, Jinnie hadn't specified how *much* money. She hoped Angela didn't do the EuroMillions and suddenly find herself hounded by gold-digging Lotharios. Although she might be happy beating them off with a wodge of crisp hundred-pound notes.

'Thank you.' Jinnie kissed Dhassim on the cheek. A fresh bout of tears threatened when he wrapped his arms around her. She squeezed him tight, aware that soon he'd be out of her life too.

Then Jinnie pulled away. 'I have to go.' She needed to splash some water on her face, put on a bit of slap and drag her weary body out of the door. How she would convince

Angela to pop to the corner shop and buy a scratch card was something she'd figure out on the way.

* * *

AFTER KNOCKING FOR SEVERAL MINUTES, Jinnie turned to leave. Then the door opened and Angela appeared, her expression stony.

'Hi. Sorry if it's a bad time, but I was just passing and wondered if you fancied a walk?' *Well, that sounded totally convincing.*

'Walk to where?' Angela replied. 'I think back to happiness might be a stretch.' She smiled, but it was a lacklustre effort.

'Oh, I dunno. Just a wander along the high street. We could check out the boutique, see how the refurb's gone.'

The boutique had closed down just after Christmas, and re-opened a few days ago with a new owner. Rumour had it that the tent-style dresses and forgiving waistbands had been replaced by more attractive and modern stock.

Angela shrugged, unhooked a jacket from behind the door and stepped out.

'Aren't you going to lock up?' asked Jinnie. Cranley wasn't the crime capital of the region, but Jinnie was always vigilant about making sure all windows and doors were secure.

'Nah,' said Angela, patting her pocket and producing a shabby purse. 'Jamie's in his kip and one look at him naked will scare anyone off.'

They ambled along, Angela revealing she had a couple of bedsits to view in the city early next week. 'I'll have to give my landlord a month's notice and I guess that'll be the end of the line with Jo too. As for Jamie—'

Stopping at the boutique, they admired the dramatically different window display. Pastel jumpers draped over wickerwork chairs; multi-hued scarves threaded through a lattice frame, and glittering items of costume jewellery hung from tree-shaped metal stands.

'Bit of an improvement, eh?' said Jinnie, heading inside. They were greeted by the new owner, Alison Gale, who explained she was originally from the village, but had moved to Aberdeen many years ago.

'My husband died a few months ago,' she said. 'I've been living in the small flat upstairs here, but hopefully I'll buy something bigger in due course. Now, can I offer you ladies a wee glass of something to celebrate my opening?' Alison produced a bottle of champagne and two plastic flutes. Angela declined, and Jinnie hesitated before saying yes.

'This is pretty.' Angela fingered a double-layered moss green top with a chiffony piece poking out at the bottom. 'It's been ages since I bought anything new to wear.'

Overhearing her, Alison glided over and flipped the price tag. 'Fifty per cent off for opening week,' she declared. 'An absolute bargain, and that colour is perfect for you!'

'Fifty per cent is still too much when you've got nothing in the pot,' muttered Angela out of Alison's earshot. 'Come on, let's go. Unless you've got your eye on something.'

Waving goodbye to a crestfallen Alison, they made their way to the corner shop.

'When life gives you lemons, you need chocolate,' said Jinnie. 'Ooh, and maybe a little flutter. You never know when Lady Luck might be smiling on you.' *Smooth, Jinnie, very smooth.*

Janette was arranging newspapers and magazines when they arrived. Balanced on a stepladder, she tutted over a copy of *GQ* featuring a scantily clad model with whipped cream on her nipples.

'Whit a waste o' cream, that,' she grumbled. 'Mind you, I'd

need a whole can to hide my puppies. Hello, girls. What can I get you?'

Jinnie selected a Wispa bar and a bag of chocolate-coated raisins. Angela went for a Crunchie, and pulled out her purse.

'Wait!' This was it. Crunch — or Crunchie — time. 'What do you recommend on the scratch card front, Janette? I mean, in terms of winning a decent prize.'

'Well, hen, I've no' had much luck here. Senga McArthur in the next village had a £200,000 winner last year and jings, did she go to town with it. Posters in the windae and her photo in the local paper.'

Janette drew a finger down the display case of cards promising prizes to change your life, or at least gild it a little. 'The Diamond Mine's a popular one. Only two quid, and you can win up to £50,000. Peggy at the salon bought one and bagged a hundred quid. Wisnae worth a poster, mind. Got a wee Polaroid taken. Think it's pinned up next to the basins at her place.'

Before Angela could speak, Jinnie slapped down a tenner. 'Two Diamond Mine cards, please.' Much as she itched for Angela to do the deed straight away, Jinnie decided it was better to give her time. 'Here, this one's for you.' Batting away Angela's protests, she thrust a card into her hand. 'Save it for later. And if you win a hundred, you can treat me to lunch at Jo's.'

They parted ways, both munching on their chocolate. Angela tucked the scratch card in her pocket, thanked Jinnie again and ambled off.

Now what? Jinnie could hardly loiter outside Angela's place waiting to hear her screams of delight. Anyway, she had a feeling the card would languish unscratched for a few hours. When you hit rock bottom, it was difficult to imagine anything good ever happening. Tempted as she was to visit the pub and maybe have a chat with Ed, Jinnie turned the other way and headed home.

'Your friend, was she excited to win the money?' Dhassim bounded up to her like a puppy who'd just heard the word 'walkies'.

'I don't know. She didn't scratch it right away,' Jinnie replied. 'I got one too.' Pulling out the card and a ten pence coin, she scratched off the foil covering. 'Woo hoo. Won a tenner, so I'm all square.'

Ignoring Dhassim's protests that she should have wished for some money herself, Jinnie wandered into the kitchen. A notepad lay on the worktop next to the coffee and tea jars. On it was her current 'To Do' list. It included visiting her family, setting up a get-together with Hannah and co, and —

Uncapping a biro, Jinnie added: *Find a new job. Leave Cranley. Start afresh.* A tear splashed on to the paper, smudging the ink. She tore off the page, stared at the next, blank one, and began to write a letter of resignation...

CHAPTER 41

'Why the long face?' Ed put down the glass he was drying as Jinnie arrived for her shift. 'I'd much rather have happy smiley Jinnie working alongside me than this imposter with a coupon that'd turn milk sour.'

In spite of her black mood, Jinnie giggled at Ed's description of her downcast expression. 'It's nothing. At least, nothing you can help with.' She went to the far end of the bar to serve a couple of regulars their usual.

Liz appeared, looking harassed and trumpeting into a hankie. 'Keep your distance, love,' she said. 'I'm coming down with the lurgy, so Ray's flying solo in the kitchen tonight. It's Lemsip and early bed for me.'

Jamie emerged from the back, having already finished his shift. Judging by his equally miserable face, Jinnie doubted Angela had so much as glanced at the card. Or — horrible thought — the wish hadn't worked and she'd won diddly squat.

'How's your mum?' she asked brightly.

'Same as usual,' Jamie replied. 'Except she's looking at

some crap bedsits in the city with barely room to swing a cat.'

'That's not good,' interjected Ed. 'I'd hate to see her — well, both of you — have to leave here.'

With a noncommittal grunt, Jamie took off. Jinnie was no authority on reading people's feelings, but she sensed Ed's sadness ran deeper than concern for the wellbeing of a staff member and his mum.

'Are your folks not around tonight?' Jinnie pulled a couple of pints, aware she was watching the door in case Sam dropped in. She'd slid the note into the shop letterbox on her way to the pub. Cowardly, but Jinnie couldn't stomach telling him face to face. She'd offered to work a week's notice, but made it clear she preferred a clean break.

…Much as I've appreciated your kindness and enjoyed the experience, I feel it's time for me to move on. I will drop off the clothes you kindly lent my cousin.

Yours, Jinnie

The moment the letter left her grasp, Jinnie was consumed with guilt. Sam hadn't done anything wrong. His only crime was not to return her feelings. Would he be confused by her actions? Disappointed, perhaps, or even angry?

'Jinnie, you're a million miles away.' Ed slung a friendly arm around her shoulder, bringing to mind the cocktail episode when she'd embarrassingly sniffed his armpit. Back then, Jinnie had felt a spark of attraction, but now…

'Mum and Dad have taken off for a few days.' Ed removed his arm and uncorked an open bottle of red. 'Large or small?' he asked the loved-up duo at the bar, who had prised themselves apart long enough to order.

'Where have they gone?' Jinnie could murder a large glass of red herself, but drinking on duty was a no-no. Unless sanctioned by the boss, which would be Ed this evening.

'Pitlochry. They stayed there yonks ago, when they were first married. Dad reckoned it might spark some good memories. He's been a bit strange these past few days, come to think of it.'

Jinnie felt a rush of gratitude that her own parents were both happy and healthy. Wilma too, despite her 'it's my body, and I'll do what I want to' attitude. Even Archie had come good, meeting up with Über Jean in London. Early days, but perhaps her little brother would surprise them all.

An hour passed, and Jinnie was glad of the Saturday-night surge of people keen to escape the confines of their homes and park their problems on the doorstep of The Jekyll and Hyde. The thought that moving on also meant leaving Ed, Ken, Mags and the regulars she'd come to know during her short time in Cranley gave her stomach cramps. And as for Dhassim...

'Rose is here.' Ed smiled at the young barmaid, who said a shy hello. She wasn't the chattiest girl on the planet, but her manner was pleasant and she worked hard. Jinnie knew Ken often gave her extra shifts, as she was saving up for a beautician's course. 'How about we give Ray a shout for a sharing platter, and you can tell me what's causing those nasty frown lines?' Ed dodged as Jinnie aimed a playful punch at him.

Minutes later they settled down with a mountain of chicken wings, cheese-topped nachos and stuffed mushrooms. Ed had a half pint, Jinnie a small glass of house red.

'As it's only been a week since your girlfriend binned you, how come you're so revoltingly upbeat?' Jinnie already knew the answer; that Ed and Cheryl's relationship had been wobbly for some time. She just wasn't ready to pour her heart out about her feelings for Sam and her plans to leave.

'She did me a favour, to be honest,' replied Ed, dipping a wing in a bowl of blue cheese sauce. 'We weren't exactly a match made in heaven, unlike *this* divine coupling.'

Contented sighs and slurping sounds followed. Jinnie scooped up some nachos, and strands of molten cheese dribbled down her chin. If dubious eating skills were a sign of compatibility, she and Ed were love's young dream.

'So, got your eye on anyone else?' Jinnie laughed as Ed mock-choked on his food. Once upon a very short time, she might have hoped for a lingering look that said: *Why, you, of course*. The look he gave her now was affectionate, but more one a doting brother would give to an upset sibling.

'Steady on, woman! Just because I'm not broken-hearted doesn't mean my ego's not bruised.' Jinnie doubted that. Ed's ego could probably withstand a hurricane, since it seemed as robust as his physical form.

'You didn't answer the question.' And it remained unanswered as the pub's door flew open and Angela charged towards them; cheeks flushed, eyes glittering and waving something aloft. She skidded to a halt in front of Ed and Jinnie, her lips moving but no sound coming out.

Ed grabbed another chair and guided Angela into it. 'What on earth's the matter? Has something bad happened?'

Quite the opposite, thought Jinnie.

Angela unfurled her fingers to reveal the scratch card, in all its scratched-to-bits glory.

'I won, Jinnie.' Her voice cracked, and she trembled from head to toe. 'I waited and waited to do it, because people like me never win.'

'That's amazing.' Ed pushed the plate of food in Angela's direction, but she ignored it. 'How much?'

'Fifty thousand pounds.' The words hung in the air, the only sound a gasp from Ed.

Jinnie downed the rest of her wine, sending up a prayer of thanks to Dhassim and his WIFI. Finally she'd made a wish that would change someone's life —

'And it's yours, Jinnie.'

Jinnie stared at her. *Eh, what?*

Angela nudged the card towards Jinnie. 'You paid for it. I think you're one of the loveliest people I've ever met, but — I can't keep it. It wouldn't be right.'

Ed chose that moment to head back to the bar. Jinnie didn't know what to say. Yes, technically she'd bought the card, but she'd given it to Angela. What she said next was so important.

'Angela, listen to me. The card was a gift. I didn't know it was a winner — how could I? — but the money is yours. Please. I'm thrilled for you and I want you to have it.'

Angela rested her head in her hands. The winning card lay between them, a ticking money bomb. When she looked up a minute later, tears streamed down her face. 'Last night I bought a cheap bottle of vodka and poured a glass. And I thought, "What's the point in being sober?" I stared at it for half an hour, held it to my lips, but I couldn't do it.'

Jinnie handed her a napkin and Angela roughly wiped her eyes. 'I poured the lot down the sink, and went to bed. Then I spent the day working at Jo's, mapping out what to do with my stupid life. It was only when I got home that I remembered the card, and —'

'Now you can stay!' Jinnie shoved the card back under Angela's nose. 'I don't want the money, honestly. It's all yours. You can pay your rent, treat yourself to some nice things, do whatever you want.' Despite her sadness over Sam, a warm bubble of joy tickled Jinnie's insides. She even managed a proper smile when Ed returned, holding a bottle and three glasses.

'Non-alcoholic fizz,' he declared, popping the cork.

'Give me a few minutes to tidy myself up.' Angela picked up her bag and took a step towards the toilets. Then she stopped, turned back to Jinnie, and wrapped her arms around her. 'You don't know how much this means to me,' she whispered. 'I thought I'd hit rock bottom, but now the only way is up. Thank you.'

'You are one hell of a woman, Jinnie Cooper.' Ed poured three drinks and gave her that cheeky grin which had female customers swooning. 'Maybe you could buy me a scratch card too, seeing as I'm pretty much unemployed at the moment?'

They waited for Angela. Ed fiddled with a beer mat, and Jinnie felt her brief euphoria seeping away. Before she could stop herself, she blurted out: 'Have you ever fallen in love with someone who doesn't feel the same way about you?' *Great. So much for not talking about Sam, and especially to Ed...*

'I'm not sure about falling in love.' Ed's gaze shifted to the door of the ladies, which remained closed. 'But I'd be lying if I said I wasn't interested in someone.' He studied her. 'I suspect your question relates to a certain man with a passion for old things. Present company excepted, of course. And I'm no expert, but I'd say he has more than a soft spot for you.'

Jinnie goggled at him. *Is that true?*

Before she could answer Angela returned, and they toasted her good fortune.

'What's the first thing you're going to do with all that dosh?' asked Ed. 'Apart from taking yours truly out for a slap-up meal, of course.'

Angela blushed before clinking her glass with Jinnie's. 'You're next in the queue after this amazing woman. But — there is *one* other thing I'd like to splash out on, Ed, if you don't mind helping me.'

Ed and Jinnie waited.

'It might sound crazy, but I kind of fancy getting a tattoo.'

CHAPTER 42

'Ach, you're looking awfy peely-wally, Jinnie.' Wilma regarded Jinnie sternly as they sat together in her kitchen. Clearly the liberal dusting of blusher she'd applied had failed to disguise her pallor.

It was Monday afternoon, and Jinnie should have been at Sam's. The weekend had passed without any word from him, despite Jinnie checking her phone at least twenty times a day. She'd wimped out of dropping off the borrowed clothes, figuring it could wait till she felt stronger.

'I'm OK, Gran. Just glad to see you looking better.' A few days into the course of antibiotics, Wilma radiated rude health. The dreadful cough had diminished to the odd splutter, and nicotine patches were plastered on both her arms.

'Are you meant to use more than one at a time?' Jinnie asked. 'I mean, can't you overdose on the stuff?'

Wilma harrumphed and defiantly stuffed a piece of gum in her mouth. 'Miss Prissy Pants at the surgery said I needed a strong dose to conquer the cravings. Seems to be working, although I did have a smoke this morning.'

Jinnie had swung by her mum and dad's en route to

Wilma's. They fussed over her as usual, and she left with a bagful of home-made food. Archie was still in London, living it up in a five-star hotel and mixing with the rich and famous. According to Kath, some of his music — 'Don't ask me what, it all gives me a migraine' — would feature on Über Jean's latest album.

Jinnie had also messaged Hannah to ask if she could crash at her place for a while. She'd offered no explanation, and ignored the barrage of question marks and WTFs that followed. Ed's comment about Sam having more than a soft spot for her plagued her mind. She didn't doubt that he liked her; but if he *really* liked her, why hadn't he been in touch? Round and round her thoughts went, until Dhassim distracted her on Sunday with an all-day Disney movie extravaganza. *Beauty and The Beast* and *Toy Story* had tickled his fancy, but he'd been singularly unimpressed by Robin Williams' blue genie in *Aladdin*.

'So, are you going to tell your old gran what's botherin' ye?' Wilma filled the kettle and reached for the tea caddy. 'I havnae seen you this glum since that chubby wee chap left that boy band.

Jinnie cringed at the memory of being devastated when Robbie quit Take That. She hadn't even reached her teens then, but she had sobbed for days.

'It's nothing, Gran,' she said, fetching the cups and saucers. 'I got hold of the wrong end of the stick about something — someone — and made a bit of a fool of myself.'

Wilma raised a badly-pencilled eyebrow and prepared the tea. 'A man, I'm guessing? Well, if he's daft enough no' to realise what a wee diamond you are, he can bugger off! Plenty more fish in the sea, an' all that.'

Jinnie wasn't in the mood to discuss her pathetic love life, or, for that matter, to hear what nonsense the tea leaves revealed. To add to her worries, she needed to give notice on the cottage, and inform Ken and Ed that she'd soon be leaving. They hadn't drawn up a formal contract, but Jinnie hated to let them down. Still, Wilma's heart was in the right place and it wouldn't hurt to humour her.

'Here we go.' Wilma performed the ritual, Jinnie playing her part.

They both peered at the contents of the cup. As usual, Jinnie couldn't see anything recognisable.

'Hmm,' mused Wilma, chomping loudly on her gum. 'That's a tricky one. Could ye fetch my reading glasses from the living room, sweetie? They're on top of my book.'

Jinnie found the glasses perched on a copy of *Sex After Seventy*, which Jinnie had no desire to flick through. She wondered if there was a follow-up — *Sex After Eighty* — or if that was considered a leg-over too far.

'Thanks, Jinnie. Right, let's have another gander.' Wilma pulled the cup closer, her nose grazing its rim. 'OK. I cannae be totally sure, but it looks a lot like … a horse's head.'

From where Jinnie stood it might well be a horse's arse, but either way, she couldn't imagine it was a good thing. A horse's head? All that sprang to mind was that horrible scene in *The Godfather* when a bloke woke up next to one. It was hardly a good omen, was it? 'Maybe we should just forget the tea leaves today, Gran. How about a nice cup of coffee inst—'

'Hawd yer wheesht, lass!' Wilma put the cup down and folded her arms triumphantly. 'A horse's head means a lover. A bit like the umbrella — or was it a kite? — the last time, but it's no' often I see animals in the leaves.'

Try as she might, Jinnie couldn't make the connection between the two. Maybe a bunny rabbit or another cute creature, but what did a horse's head have to do with love?

'The leaves are never wrong, sweetie.' Wilma nodded sagely and Jinnie kept schtum. Yes, the kite one had been near the mark in terms of a wish coming true, but this prediction of a new lover was way off.

'Gran, right now I'm more likely to fly in the air — *now was not the time to reveal she'd done precisely that* — than hook up with another man. Can we change the subject, please?'

* * *

WILMA'S TEA-LEAF reading played on Jinnie's mind all the way home. It was just superstitious nonsense. Wasn't it?

'Dhassim?' she shouted as she walked in the front door, but there was no reply.

For an awful moment Jinnie wondered if he'd gone walk-about. Then she heard the shower running and the dreadful caterwauling that passed for singing. She was desperate to tell him about Angela and ... something else. Something she'd dismissed before as pathetic, but now she wondered if it was worth a try. After all, what did she have to lose?

'Ah, Jinnie. You have run out of my favourite shower gel, and these towels are so harsh on my delicate skin.' Dhassim stood in the doorway, rubbing half-heartedly at his damp torso. Luckily his lower half was covered by Jinnie's jogging bottoms, which he now favoured over the harem pants. Would he wear her trackies when he vanished from her life forever? And would his next master or mistress wonder why a genie was a walking advertisement for Hollister?

'Listen. Your wish came true for Angela.' Dhassim nodded in a way that suggested he had never doubted its success. 'To the tune of 50K, which is a bit more than I expected, but —'

'Your friend is happy, yes?'

Jinnie grinned. 'She's over the moon. That's another way of saying she's really, really happy. Just in case you think Angela's zapping around in space, because I know you don't always understand what people are on about.'

Dhassim gave a little bow. God, she'd miss him, even when he was driving her up the wall with his pet names and petty gripes.

Jinnie took a deep breath, and asked Dhassim to sit down. He draped the damp towel over his shoulders, and waited for her to speak.

'I know I said before that I didn't want to wish for Sam to … you know… But I've thought about it more, and —'

'Now you are desperate?' Dhassim raised an eyebrow and produced his WIFI. Jinnie added his dubious talent for calling a spade a spade to her list of minor irritants. 'I fear this may be the final wish I can grant.'

He turned the screen to face Jinnie, revealing a digital clock on countdown. It appeared there were only six hours left. Did that mean Dhassim would slither back into his lamp? And what about the elusive Aaliyah? There was no guarantee that the second lamp housed Dhassim's dearly beloved, and Jinnie hadn't wanted to harp on about it to Sam.

'No, I'm not desperate. Actually, I am. Put it this way, wouldn't you wish to be reunited with Aaliyah?' The thought struck Jinnie that maybe her last wish should be just that, instead of using Dhassim's powers to force feelings on Sam that weren't real.

'I believe in karma, Jinnie. When something is meant to be, it will happen.' *Whit's fur ye'll no go by ye.* Wilma and Dhassim had a lot in common. Although Wilma wouldn't be seen dead in jogging bottoms.

'Karma aside, can we do this, please?' Jinnie didn't want to leave Cranley. In the short time she'd been here, she'd felt part of a community. Far more so than when she'd lived in Edinburgh, caught up in Mark's superficial world. Ken and Mags; Ed and Angela; Jo; even Janette. All people she'd grown fond of, and knew she could rely on. And then there was Sam…

'Your wish is my... OK, I think you know the drill by now.' Dhassim held the WIFI aloft and Jinnie took a deep breath.

'I wish … I wish for Sam to love me.'

She exhaled loudly, scared to look at the screen. The device emanated its familiar beeps and buzzes, then … silence.

Great. The bloody thing decides to give up the ghost on the home run. Jinnie suppressed a howl of despair, and resigned herself to the fact that —

'Jinnie, please open your eyes.' Jinnie obeyed, not realising they'd been tightly shut the whole time. 'Read what it says.'

Instead of the clock display, a message scrolled across the screen like a news ticker. *This wish cannot be granted. Object of wish concurs with desire of wishee.'*

Hesitating only to wonder if 'wishee' was a real word, Jinnie blinked and read it again. Did it mean what she thought it meant? Her brain struggled for another explanation, but those little grey cells kept bouncing back to one thing.

'I can't grant that wish, Jinnie.' Dhassim tossed the WIFI aside and gave a Cheshire Cat-like grin. 'Sam already loves you.'

CHAPTER 43

JINNIE HURTLED ALONG THE HIGH STREET, DRIVING RAIN lashing her face and soaking her cheap furry boots. She hadn't paused to change, but was oblivious to the curious glances she received as she pounded the pavement, calf muscles screaming in protest.

'Nice outfit, love!' hollered a passing van driver. For good measure, he tooted his horn and pulled closer to the kerb, sending an icy shower of water over Jinnie's lower half. She gasped, gave him the finger, and kept on running.

I can't grant that wish, Jinnie. Sam already loves you. Dhassim's words replayed over and over in her head. But … she'd seen Sam with that other woman. Pulling her close, the look in his eyes unbearably tender as he'd kissed her on the forehead. OK, no tongues had been involved, but — but — it all pointed to him being involved with someone else. And that someone had been everything Jinnie wasn't. Tall, elegant and unlikely to be seen dead in baggy trackie bottoms, a tartan pyjama top and squelchy fake Uggs.

Jinnie slowed as she approached Out of the Attic Antiques. She bent over and grasped her sodden thighs, wheezing painfully. She hadn't run so fast since she was fifteen and being chased round the school building by Rodney Fleming. She'd made the mistake of snogging him at the half-term disco, and he'd been after a repeat performance.

The shutter was pulled down and the shop was closed, which was strange at 10 am on a weekday. Since Jinnie had handed in her notice, she'd tried not to dwell on how Sam would cope without her. Her answer, *just fine,* tickled her tear ducts and made her stomach ache with what could never be.

It was possible he'd gone on a stock-finding mission, but he normally did those in the afternoon or at weekends. Maybe he was ill? Jinnie pictured Sam in bed, burning up with a fever, delirious and calling out her name. Then the image changed to the mystery woman placing a cold compress on Sam's brow, her beautiful features arranged in a look of devotion. Florence sodding Nightingale in designer gear, smelling of Chanel rather than disinfectant.

'Sam! Sam! Are you in there?' Jinnie hammered at the door with her fists. Her fingers were already turning blue from the damp and cold, and she'd lost all feeling in her feet. *Might as well make use of that*, she thought, and gave the door a hefty kick. 'Please, Sam, I need to talk to you.'

Still no response. Jinnie fumbled for her phone, then remembered she'd left it at home on charge. He wasn't there, the rain was coming down in buckets, and doubt dragged Jinnie's heart into her sodden boots. What if Dhassim's WIFI was knackered again? What if it had misinterpreted Sam's feelings? Jinnie knew he *liked* her, but it was a massive leap from liking someone to loving them. She turned to leave, resigned to the fact that neither she nor her genie pal were destined for a happy ever after —

'Jinnie?' She whirled round at Sam's voice. He stood in the

doorway, arms folded and reading glasses perched on his head. A set of headphones dangled around his neck, and tinny music echoed from within.

'Sam…' Jinnie tried but failed to put one foot in front of the other. Her ability to speak seemed to have frozen up too. A sudden gust of wind knocked her off balance, and Sam rushed to her side.

'God, you're soaked through,' he said. 'Get inside and take off your wet things. I mean, your coat, that is.' He blushed, and Jinnie nudged aside thoughts of doing a slow and soggy striptease. She wasn't here to seduce Sam. She just needed to know his true feelings once and for all.

Jinnie hung her coat up on the stand, watching water trickle from it and form a small puddle on the floor. She went to sit on the comfortable Chesterfield next to the counter, then decided against it. Leaving marks on its fine leather wasn't the best of ideas. She unfolded the cheap plastic stepladder Sam kept for reaching high places and perched on that instead. Off came her boots, then her socks. Crikey, her tootsies looked like she might be suffering from trench foot. Jinnie raised one leg into her lap — ouch! — and began massaging to restore the circulation.

Sam reappeared carrying two towels, one of which he gently placed round her shoulders. Jinnie took the other and rubbed her feet. Crinkly skin and bluish tinge notwithstanding, she was ridiculously pleased that she'd trimmed her nails and painted them recently.

'The kettle's on. I'll fix us a cuppa in a minute.' *Ah yes.* The great British cure-all for everything from broken hearts to bunions. No, that absolutely *wasn't* a bunion, her foot was just a bit puffy —

'Forgive me, Jinnie, but I'm not sure why you're here. In your note you made it pretty clear you didn't want to see me again.' Sam sat on the Chesterfield, his face downcast and his hands clasped between his thighs. 'I kind of understand, but I thought we'd got past the Christmas thing. I thought — I hoped — we were friends. Good friends.'

Before Jinnie could reply, he headed out back. She heard the clatter of the tea caddy, and the clinking of spoons. Leaving a note had been a cowardly thing to do. She should have been honest, explained that she'd seen Sam with *that* woman and jumped to conclusions. But that would have laid her feelings bare, and exposed her to yet another humiliating situation. She'd gone along with the *we're just friends* thing: admitting that seeing Sam with someone else had felt like a hammer blow to her heart was too much to reveal.

'Here you go. I added some sugar and a dash of whisky to warm you up a bit.' Sam passed Jinnie a mug, and she accepted it, wrapping her fingers around its heat.

'Thank you. And I'm sorry about the note. It wasn't a nice thing to do. I just didn't know how to explain —'

Damn it! Sam smacked his forehead and was off again! Did the man seriously have no clue what Jinnie was trying to say? Or rather, what she was hoping *he* would say? Not that Jinnie had any visions of him going down on one knee and begging her to marry him. And she wasn't planning on pouncing and locking lips, not in her current bedraggled state.

Sipping the tea, and getting a welcome buzz from the whisky, Jinnie listened as Sam clattered around. *What on earth is he doing?*

The answer came a moment later.

'I found it.' Sam held aloft a lamp which bore more than a passing resemblance to the one Dhassim had emerged from. 'I was going to give it to you the other day, but then you quit and… Well, you're here now and I'd like you to have it.'

Talk about bad timing! Jinnie was here to discover if Sam really loved her, not to gain ownership of a vessel that might contain a genie's long-lost squeeze. She reluctantly took the lamp from Sam. It was in better nick than Dhassim's, suggesting Sam had given it a bit of a clean. Which begged the question: how many rubs away was it from emanating the alluring Aaliyah? Assuming she was in there in the first place.

'Ah, thank you. It'll look lovely alongside the other one. The perfect pair.' Jinnie smiled at Sam, touched again by his thoughtfulness. 'It's so nice and shiny … I guess you gave it a bit of a buff?'

Sam laughed hard and long. He had the loveliest laugh, all deep and gurgly and infectious. Jinnie joined in, although she wasn't totally sure what they were laughing about.

'Jinnie … from the first day you walked into my life, you've enchanted, amused and downright bewildered me. You fill my thoughts when I wake in the morning, and distract me constantly when I'm trying to write. I've been so afraid to cross the line between friendship and… I thought I'd blown it completely, although I still don't know what I did to upset you.'

Discussing the mystery woman could wait. All Jinnie could do was hold her breath as Sam moved closer. They were inches apart, his hand reaching out to stroke her hair.

'You are something else, Jinnie Cooper,' he murmured. 'Stumbling in here like a drowned rat, but not a hair out of place.' *Oops, forgot about that.* 'And I know there's something odd about your cousin, and your obsession with the lamps, but I really, really don't care. When we kissed it was pure magic, but then I went and spoiled it…'

Much as Jinnie adored Sam's voice, and his laugh, and pretty much the whole package, she didn't want to talk any more. They stood together, Sam's arms embracing Jinnie, pulling her towards him. Jinnie closed her eyes, felt his lips on hers and …

Thump-thump-thump. Crikey, she knew her heart rate was up but —

'Did you feel that?' Sam drew back and looked down.

Jinnie hadn't realised she was hugging the lamp to her body when they embraced. Something had certainly moved — and sadly, it wasn't the earth. 'Erm, I think it was just my tummy rumbling. Skipped breakfast, and that whisky on top. Bad decision.'

Sam took a step forward, and Jinnie took a step back. If he'd already cleaned the lamp, and they'd accidentally rubbed it when they touched, then —

'Ooh! That does not feel good!' Jinnie doubled over dramatically, shifting the lamp behind her back. 'I'd better nip home and take some Rennies. Eat something, maybe.'

The lamp gave another shudder, and she gave an exaggerated groan of pain. 'I'll be right back, I promise. Soon.'

Before Sam could speak, Jinnie belted out of the door: coatless, bootless, and clueless as to what would happen next.

CHAPTER 44

'Is this Aaliyah's?'

Jinnie placed the lamp on the coffee table. Sprinting home like an out-of-condition athlete had left her wheezing and breathless. Her bare feet ached, and she felt she'd like nothing more than a hot shower and a lie down. Oh, and time to think about the things Sam had said, and what they really meant. But that had to wait.

'I am not certain.' Dhassim touched the lamp tentatively. 'It is possible, but how can it be that my lamp and Aaliyah's ended up in the same place?'

How, indeed? What was it called again? Serendipity, a word Jinnie had learned in her late teens when she watched the movie of the same name starring John Cusack. If someone had told Jinnie all those weeks ago that a genie would come into her life — or that a man like Sam would turn it upside down — she'd never have believed it. *Whit's fur ye'll no go by ye.* Sometimes all you had to do was wish hard enough.

'Well, there's only one way to find out.' Jinnie cracked her knuckles, making Dhassim wince. 'By my reckoning it only needs one more rub, so —'

Pulling her pyjama top over her hand, Jinnie gingerly raised the lamp and gave it a wipe. It made a pulsating sound before flying out of Jinnie's hand and landing at Dhassim's feet. They stood together, watching as the lamp gyrated furiously. Dhassim grabbed Jinnie's arm so tightly that she yelped, and he gave out a little squawk as a spinning cloud of silvery mist rose between them. As before, it dissipated, and a human form came into focus. A one-hundred-per-cent female form, with a long inky-black pigtail and a figure that brought to mind Jennifer Lopez.

'Aaliyah!' Dhassim relinquished his pincer-like grip on Jinnie's arm and reached out to the shimmering creature before them.

Jinnie watched in awe as Aaliyah solidified — was that the right term? — and performed what could best be described as a belly dance: hips gyrating, hands clasped and raised above her head. She had an astonishing midriff with not a spare ounce of flesh.

'Why aye, man!' Aaliyah shimmied towards Dhassim, her armfuls of gold bangles clanking and her pigtail swinging back and forth. 'Lookin' lush, as always.'

Good lord, the genie of Dhassim's dreams might resemble a famous singer and actress, but she sounded more like TV double act Ant and Dec. *What on earth —?*

'I do not understand what you are saying.' Dhassim turned to Jinnie, bafflement creasing his face. 'Which foreign land has she come from?'

The not-so-exotic city of Newcastle, judging by the accent, thought Jinnie. *Only 90 or so miles away, but with a language all of its own.*

'Alreet, pet.' Aaliyah ceased her shimmying and looked Jinnie up and down. 'Are you me man's mistress, like?'

Jinnie nodded, aware that Dhassim still hadn't a clue what his long-lost love was talking about. 'Yes, I am. Delighted to meet you.' She put out her hand, which Aaliyah shook limply. 'It's hard to believe that we found you after all this time.' Exactly how *much* time was a mystery, but clearly Aaliyah had spent time in the North East of England (or was a TV addict like Dhassim, but hooked on *I'm A Celebrity* or *Geordie Shore*).

'Can you remember where you met?' Jinnie wanted to keep the conversation going. Dhassim still had the countenance of a stuffed mullet. An animated one, though: mouth opening and closing, but nothing coming out.

Aaliyah shrugged. 'Who knows? It's not important. Our master sold me — 'e was a right wazzock — and I thought we'd never see each other again.' Her stunning honey-flecked eyes filled with tears, and Dhassim pulled her into his arms. They made an odd couple — statuesque and curvy versus short and wiry — but somehow they matched. *A bit like Ant and Dec*, thought Jinnie. *Two halves of a whole*. She couldn't fathom how they'd both ended up at some old dear's house in Musselburgh, and subsequently at Sam's, but it didn't matter. They'd found each other, and that was what counted.

'What happens now?' Dhassim and Aaliyah remained entwined, but they addressed Jinnie.

How the heck would I know? Dhassim's WIFI was working again, but her last wish, to make Sam love her, had failed. Or rather, it had been redundant because —

'I need to get back to the shop!' Caught up in the touching reunion, Jinnie had forgotten about poor Sam. They'd been *so* close to kissing, and this time it promised to be a full-on, not-coming-up-for-air number. If only Aaliyah hadn't chosen that moment to signal her presence...

'My beautiful, precious Aaliyah, I think we must co-ordinate our WIFIs and seek the answer to our fate.' Dhassim whipped his out, and Aaliyah delved down the front of her sequinned crop top to produce an even flashier device. Hers was rose gold and much slimmer, like the latest iPhone. At once the two WIFIs emitted a series of noises and a sequence of lights. A bit like in *Close Encounters of the Third Kind*, they seemed to be answering each other.

'Erm, can you hurry this up?' Jinnie itched to leave, afraid Sam might have deemed her certifiable. Taking off like that, minus coat and boots, didn't bode well for someone's sanity.

'It is hard to read,' said Dhassim. 'And I do not want to rush this now that we are together again.' He caressed Aaliyah's cheek, and she responded with a feline purr. *Yuck!*

Jinnie decided to leave them to it and get back to more important business. Well, more important in *her* eyes. She dashed upstairs, swapped her pyjama top for a fleece, and tugged on her trainers.

Back in the living room, she snatched up an ancient cagoule and paused by the front door. 'Right, you two. Behave yourselves, and I'll see you when I get back.' Jinnie waggled a mock-scolding finger. She didn't really care if Dhassim and his Geordie genie pal got up to hanky-panky in her absence, as long as they didn't use her bed…

'Bye bye,' cooed Aaliyah, giving Jinnie a dismissive wave. 'Now where's me scran, Dhassim? I'm clamming!'

Dhassim looked helplessly at Jinnie.

'I think she's hungry,' replied Jinnie. 'Feed her. And check out *Geordie Shore* on the TV. It might help.'

CHAPTER 45

Since Angela had bowled in, giddy with excitement over her win and begging to invest in the business, Jo had allowed herself time to sit back and take stock. A cash injection of twenty thousand pounds would go a long way towards getting the catering business on a strong footing. Better equipment, and perhaps a bigger vehicle to transport supplies to venues. Of course they'd need to draw up a proper contract to formalise the arrangement, but Angela's enthusiasm was infectious. And after all these years working solo, Jo felt perhaps it was time to share the workload.

The café had been open almost an hour, and customers were thin on the ground. The atrocious weather didn't help. It had been sleeting non-stop overnight, and the roads and pavements were treacherous. Only Janette had braved the elements so far, stopping in for a pea and mascarpone soup and roll to take away.

'That'll do nicely for my lunch,' she said, perching her dripping umbrella in the stand by the door. 'A wee zap in the micro, and Bob's your uncle.' They'd chatted briefly, Janette mentioning possible retirement in the coming months. 'I've squirreled away a fair bit of cash and my pension's half-decent, but I dinnae ken what I'll do with myself if I'm no' working.'

Jo remembered Ken's quip about Janette having a black belt in macramé. It seemed a lifetime since she'd last seen him, though only a week had passed. She wondered if he might be avoiding her. It was unusual for him not to drop into the café, whereas Jo wasn't a frequent visitor at the pub. She preferred to stock up on wine in the city, since Janette's meagre selection was of dubious quality, and drink a glass or two watching TV or listening to music. *The sad life of a lonely singleton.*

Sighing, Jo went to check on a batch of pasties baking in the oven. *Not quite ready yet.* She slammed the oven shut just as the café door swung open.

'Morning, Jo.' Ken brushed droplets of melted snow from his jacket, then ran a hand through his damp hair. 'Shocker of a day, eh?'

The bigger shock was seeing Ken, as if she'd conjured him up with her thoughts. Jo's errant heart did a little skip, and she prayed her face didn't give away the feelings that still ran deep.

'It is indeed,' she replied. 'You're my second customer so far. Assuming you're after something to eat or drink?' She couldn't help her snarky tone, or fail to notice Ken's wounded reaction.

'I could lie and say I'm here for one of your legendary chocolate éclairs and a strong coffee, but I really just wanted to see you.'

'Oh.' Jo snatched up a set of tongs and levered an éclair onto a plate. 'That's nice…'

Please, please don't say anything that gives me false hope, because I don't think I can take it.

'Jo, Mags is my wife, and I love her as much now as the

day we met. But you are one special lady who will always own a piece of my heart.'

Jo turned away under the pretence of filling a mug. She dug her teeth into her bottom lip, determined not to cry.

'I'm not a particularly brave man, and every day Mags deteriorates a little more I want to scream at the unfairness of it all. But as long as she's with me and needs me, I'll be there for her.'

As long as she's with me. Was Ken hinting that if the unthinkable happened, he'd want to be with Jo? No, he wasn't a callous man; he wouldn't hint. He possessed all the qualities Jo hoped she'd find in a partner one day. That day might not be this year, or the next, but The One was out there.

'Hey Dad, Jo, how's it going?' Ed was next through the door, his coat draped over his and Angela's heads. 'We're in dire need of warmth, sugar and a truckload of carbs.'

'Hey, business partner-to-be.' Jo hugged Angela.

She flinched. 'Sorry, my shoulder's a bit tender,' she said, by way of explanation.

'This girl is officially the coolest kid on the block,' added Ed, with a proud grin. 'Show 'em, Angela.'

With a roll of the eyes, Angela removed her coat, slid her jumper down and revealed a small tattoo on the back of her shoulder. A looping figure-of-eight with the words 'Be Brave' on one side and a trio of colourful birds in flight on the other.

'Very nice,' said Jo.

'Tasteful,' said Ken.

'He made me do it.' Angela pulled a mock put-upon face, and Ed responded with a peck on her cheek.

'Did not! Anyway, we've a few things to celebrate, haven't we, Angela? Jo, can we get two hot chocolates and a couple of slices of the cake with the most calories?'

As Jo fixed their order, Ed explained that he'd set things in motion as a freelance designer. Several loyal clients had already pledged their support, and his strong network meant he was confident of building a solid base quickly. 'And now that you two are combining your undoubted talents, A Bit of Crumpet is going to blow all the competition out of the water.' Jo doubted the handful of cafés and self-catering businesses in the immediate area would be quaking just yet, but Ed's optimism was reassuring.

'I need to take Jinnie out for a fab meal soon, to thank her for the winning card,' said Angela. 'But tonight I'm treating this one' — she grinned at Ed — 'to a night on the town.'

Watching the two of them chatting eagerly, Angela deftly wiping away Ed's whipped-cream moustache, Jo smiled. Life was a strange thing. She wouldn't have matched up Ed and Angela, but they appeared completely at ease with one another. Whereas Jinnie and Sam… Then again, Jo had no idea if that was just a product of her overactive imagination. And it was none of her business, either way.

'Right, we're off, see you later.' Ed plonked down a tenner and waved away the change. 'Here's to new beginnings, eh?'

Left alone, an awkward silence descended between Jo and Ken. To lighten the mood Jo switched the radio on, and the excitable chatter of Zoë Ball filled the air.

'I'd best be off too,' said Ken, finishing his tea. 'I meant what I said before, Jo. About needing you in my life. I have a wife and a son, but I don't have a lot of real friends. And they don't get any better than the beautiful person standing in front of me.'

Refusing his money — Ed's generosity just about covered the combined bill — Jo walked Ken to the door. 'Of course we're friends,' she said. 'I've barely enough myself to fill a phone box!'

Ken laughed, and tapped the end of her nose lightly. 'A

woman as wonderful as you deserves lots of friends, and an amazing man to take care of her. Not that you *need* taking care of. But I know you'll meet someone special one day.'

Once he'd left, Jo leaned against the closed door and drew a deep breath. 'I already have,' she whispered. 'Shame he's taken.'

CHAPTER 46

'Hello, I'm back!'

For a terrible moment Jinnie feared Sam had left, but the door was unlocked. She tiptoed inside, aware of how insane her departure had been. Perhaps she'd totally blown it. Sam was probably browsing the internet, looking up mental illness symptoms including fictitious relatives and fleeing buildings without footwear. Then she heard Sam's voice coming from the back room. He was talking to someone. On the phone? No, Jinnie could make out another voice, so unless the call was on loudspeaker —

'Jinnie?' Sam appeared, closely followed by a familiar and completely unwelcome figure. The glamorous woman she'd seen him with before; except she didn't look quite so glam now. Her face was blotchy, and the perfect bun was more collapsed doughnut.

'Sorry. I didn't know... I thought... I'll leave you to it,' Jinnie stammered. Quite *what* she was leaving them to made her nauseous, but also angry. How dare Sam kiss her when he already had someone on the go? Mr Nice Guy was showing his true colours, stringing Jinnie along when —

'This is Lucy, my ex-wife. Lucy, this is Jinnie, my...'

'Assistant. I work for Sam. Maybe he's talked about me. Or maybe not.'

Jinnie shook hands with Lucy and they exchanged polite greetings before Sam ushered Lucy to the door. 'Give me a minute,' he said to Jinnie.

Ten minutes later Jinnie had gathered together her dried-out boots and coat, taken a sneaky swig of whisky, and flicked through a pile of vinyl records from the 60s and 70s. She was just admiring one with a banana on the cover when Sam returned. 'Sorry, I wasn't expecting her. She turned up unannounced the other day too, but I thought we'd sorted things out.'

What things? Were they getting back together? And if so, why had Lucy looked so upset? Before Jinnie could speak, Sam pulled her into his arms. 'I hope you're feeling better, because all I want to do is carry on where we left off.'

Much as Jinnie wanted to do the same, she needed some answers. Gently, she eased away and took a seat. 'One of the reasons — the main reason — I wrote that note was because I saw you with Lucy. Before, outside your place. I thought she was someone you were seeing. Dating, whatever. And it hit me like a ton of bricks that I wanted us to be more than friends.' Jinnie gulped. 'Sam, I need to know where I stand. If you and Lucy want to make another go of it, I don't want to get in the way.'

Sam knelt before her, took her hands and stroked them with his thumbs. Jinnie tried to ignore the zinging sensation that crept through her whole body. 'Jinnie, Lucy and I are absolutely not getting back together. The phrase "when hell freezes over" springs to mind.' He carried on stroking, and Jinnie searched his face for any clue that he was lying. The longing in his eyes, and the smile that widened with each second, told her he was not.

'Lucy came by because she discovered her new partner was cheating on her. I'm not sure why she confided in me — well, it became a bit clearer today — but all I could do was try and comfort her. We have a son together, a shared history, and she'll always be part of my life. Just not in the way she suggested earlier.'

Oh. So Lucy had hoped for a reunion after all. And Sam had turned her down, hence her distressed appearance. Jinnie felt a *thump-thump-thump* again, but this time it had nothing to do with a genie in a lamp.

'I've been trying to figure out the rest of my life,' Sam said. 'This place, my writing, making sure Sean is happy and doing what he loves. I even wrote it all down.' He reached into his pocket and pulled out a folded sheet of paper. On it was a series of squiggles — he had appalling handwriting — most of which had a line through them. Jinnie squinted at it, but couldn't make out a word. Apart from... *Is that my name?*

'When I read your note it shook me to the core. It made me question what really mattered, and how I could fix things.' Sam crumpled up the piece of paper and lobbed it into the wastepaper basket. 'Jinnie, I put you on my to-do list, and crossed off everything else.'

JINNIE FLOATED home in a state of bliss. She half-expected to look down and discover she was treading on heart-shaped clouds, with tweeting birds flying around her bearing silk ribbons. Sam loved her! He'd said so, just before they kissed again. And this time they didn't come up for air in a hurry. It had been *perfect*, except for one small thing. Or rather, two things of differing sizes: Dhassim and Aaliyah. Much as Jinnie yearned to stay in a lip-lock with Sam, she needed to find out how their story ended. And she was dreading saying goodbye.

Sam, used to her erratic behaviour, didn't question Jinnie when she took off again. 'Whatever it is you need to do, go and do it,' he said. 'We have all the time in the world.' Then he'd kissed her again, and it took every ounce of willpower to tear herself away.

'It is time, Jinnie.' Entering the living room, Jinnie saw that both lamps were aligned on the coffee table. Dhassim sat cross-legged in front of his lamp with Aaliyah to his right, munching on a cheese and pickle sandwich.

'But I thought we had a little longer?' Jinnie's lip quivered, and her vision blurred. 'Can't you put it off for another day or two?'

'Nah, it's time te gan, pet,' said Aaliyah. 'War number's up.' She licked a dollop of pickle from her finger and pouted at Dhassim. He pointed at the two WIFIs by their feet, which displayed a starburst pattern pulsing across each screen.

'You are happy now, Jinnie? Sam is in love with you, I can tell by your aura. Just as we are in love' — Dhassim blew a kiss at Aaliyah — 'and thanks to you, we are together.'

Why couldn't happy moments be just that? Jinnie's joy was tempered with a deep sadness that soon her genie friend would disappear forever. Aaliyah she didn't know, and doubted she'd ever have counted her as a bestie, but still —

'Within the next few minutes we will return to the lamps.' Dhassim stood and clasped his hands beneath his chin. 'I am honoured to have served you, Jinnie, and I will never forget you. I hope you don't mind if I keep these.' Sure enough, Dhassim was wearing the jogging bottoms, the silken edge of his harem pants poking out from a pocket.

'Of course not, knock yourself out. Sorry, another silly expression.' Jinnie moved closer, and ignoring Aaliyah's grunt of disapproval, rested her head on Dhassim's shoulder and took in his familiar scent. He wrapped his arms around her waist, and they hugged for several moments.

Eventually Jinnie pulled away. 'What do I do with the lamps? I can't keep them, can I?' As she spoke, Jinnie realised Dhassim and Aaliyah were shimmering, their solid forms fading to a hazy mist.

'You must take us back to Sam,' replied Dhassim, his voice dwindling to a faint echo. 'It is where it began, and there is a reason for that. I do not know what it is, but perhaps it will be clear...'

Jinnie watched in dismay as both genies spun, shrank and hovered in mid-air before swooshing towards the lamps. There was an almighty clatter, then ... nothing. She sank to the floor, her legs unable to support her. Nervously, she prodded Dhassim's lamp with a trembling finger. It felt cold to the touch, and appeared to be exactly what she'd believed it was all those weeks ago. An old, slightly tatty, completely harmless oil lamp.

'Goodbye, Dhassim,' Jinnie murmured, 'I will miss you so much.' She drew a finger along the lamp's perimeter. It gave a tiny judder, then all was still.

CHAPTER 47

'WILL YOU BE MY VALENTINE?' SAM SWEPT INTO THE SHOP, A single red rose clenched between his teeth. Therefore what he said sounded more like 'Wey oo ee I arentine?'

Jinnie giggled, his distorted speech reminding her of Aaliyah and her Geordie-speak. 'I'll be yours, if you'll be mine,' she replied. From behind her back she whipped out an over-the-top padded card featuring a cute polar bear and a plethora of cupid's-bow lips. Jinnie had chosen it knowing it would amuse Sam.

'Tasteful,' said Sam. He handed Jinnie the rose, kissed her till she gestured that oxygen was required, and slapped a small white envelope on the counter. 'Open it, please.'

Jinnie tore open the flap and pulled out a card. It was the antithesis of hers; a single red heart and the words *I love you.* She looked inside. Sam's typical scrawl was hard to decipher, but one word leapt from the page: *Marry.* Or was it Harry?

'I know it's very soon, and there's absolutely no rush, but if you could think about it? Because I'm an impatient man and a decisive one, and I know without a doubt that I want to spend the rest of my life with you.'

Jinnie thought about it for all of three seconds, then threw herself into Sam's arms. 'Yes! The answer's yes! Unless you were referring to someone called Harry...?'

Sam gave one of his wonderful, gurgly laughs. 'Jinnie, did I happen to mention I love you? I may not be one for all that soppy Valentine stuff, but I'll make an exception for you. In fact, I'm thinking of making my next book a romance, believe it or not.'

'No way!' Jinnie had taken it upon herself to read a couple of Sam's books in the past month, and had quickly deduced they weren't for the faint-hearted. 'You mean no more "mur-rrder", just lots of lingering looks and a happy ever after?'

Sam scratched his chin thoughtfully, then shook his head. 'How about a gory crime thriller with an interwoven love story? But I promise not to kill off the sweethearts. Not unless I get bored with them.'

In the weeks since Dhassim and Aaliyah had departed, Jinnie had wrestled with Dhassim's assertion that they should be returned to Sam. Night after night she'd sat up in bed, looking at the two lamps, wondering what was the right thing to do. She'd contemplated tossing them in the river where she'd originally planned to dump her engagement ring, but she didn't want to be arrested for fly tipping. She could take them to another antiques shop — there were plenty dotted around Edinburgh — but her conscience screamed 'No!' Dhassim had granted her wishes, and the least she could do now was to carry out his request.

'You want me to have them back?' Sam's brow had furrowed when Jinnie unwrapped the lamps and placed them on the counter. She'd been particularly careful not to rub them in any way, in case the whole chain of genie-releasing events was set in motion again.

'They're lovely, but I think they'd be better off with a new home. A fresh start, so to speak.' She never asked where they went, and Sam didn't say. All Jinnie hoped was that they stayed together and found a way to escape the confines of their tiny metal cages.

Sam hadn't hesitated in asking Jinnie to move in with him. Thrilled as she was, she'd decided to stay at Brae Cottage for now. He'd accepted her decision, along with her desire to keep working at The Jekyll and Hyde for the time being. So much had happened that Jinnie needed space to process it all. Being Sam's wife would be the icing on the cake, but there was no rush. Sam wasn't going anywhere, and Jinnie knew what they had was built to last.

'I have something else for you.' Sam produced another envelope and handed it to Jinnie. She ripped it open to find a pair of plane tickets to Paris, departing in three days' time. Once upon a time, the sight of such a thing would have filled Jinnie with dread. Now, thanks to dear Dhassim, fear was replaced with unbridled joy. The City of Love, where romance blossoms — except this time Jinnie would stroll the historic streets hand-in-hand with Sam.

'Thank you so much,' she said. 'Did I happen to mention I love you too?'

Sam took her hand, kissed it and pulled her so close that she could feel every outline of his body. 'There is so much I want to learn about you,' he said. 'I want to savour every moment getting to know you, every delicious inch of you, inside and out. But … can we start with your cousin?'

'He wasn't really my cousin.' Jinnie faltered. 'But I promise I'll tell you all about it. One day.'

'OK. And I know there's a story behind the lamps, but I guess that can wait too?'

Jinnie didn't reply, and buried her head further into Sam's embrace.

'Don't worry, they've gone to a good home already.'

Jinnie raised an eyebrow. 'That was quick! Was it some random customer, or—?'

'Actually, it was Jo who bought them. Don't worry, I gave her an excellent deal. A fiver for both of them. She said they'd look good in the café.'

Jinnie gave a judder of terror. Should she say something to Jo? She thought about it for a moment, then decided against it. Whatever happened — or didn't — was out of her hands. Perhaps, if Dhassim and/or Aaliyah put in an appearance, Jo might just appreciate a few wishes coming true.

Arm in arm, Jinnie and Sam left the shop. A Valentine's Day bash was going on at the pub, with sickeningly-sweet cocktails on offer and a menu 'for lovers' concocted by Ray and Liz. Oysters — bleurgh! — and a few more palatable options. They would see everyone there, including Ed and Angela, who now shared Angela's cottage. Jamie planned to move into the pub, at least until he found a place of his own.

Pausing outside, Jinnie looked up at the shop sign: Out of the Attic Antiques. She still had Sam's business card in her purse. *Samuel A. Addin.* Sam had told her that his middle name was Alistair.

Al Addin.

Jinnie felt a little shock of recognition. Coincidence, or not? She leaned towards Sam for a kiss, and then she laughed.

THE END

ACKNOWLEDGMENTS

Book Three! Who would have thought it. I'm a wee bit stunned, and — dare I say it — rather proud to release this one into the wild.

A huge thanks to the talented Lisa Firth at Oliphant Author Services for the stunning cover. Isn't it gorgeous? It's so wonderful when a designer captures exactly what you were looking for.

Editing is vital to ensure a book emerges into the world in the best possible shape. Liz Hedgecock took on board my rough manuscript and kicked it into shape, in the nicest possible way. Any errors that remain are entirely down to me.

Thanks also to Laura Mae for the cute publisher logo on the title page.

Once again, I'd like to thank The Book Club (TBC) for introducing me to so many wonderful authors and dedicated book lovers. Reading other people's work is so important to the process of writing. Thanks also to beta readers Jody Morrow, Terri Harwood and Nicole Addie. Early feedback is both exciting and terrifying, and I'm so happy you enjoyed it and made a few suggestions.

If you haven't already read my other books, please check out my debut novel, A Clean Sweep and its short prequel, A Clean Break, as well as my second romcom novel, The Haunting of Hattie Hastings.

Finally (are you still awake)? can I just say thank you for reading this. When it's five o'clock in the morning and I'm clattering away at the keyboard, staring at the screen through tired eyes, it's you who keeps me going. Knowing that someone enjoys these stories I make up is a wonderful feeling, and I appreciate it more than you know.

If you have just a moment more, I really need your help. Today's blockbuster authors have publishers who don't mind spending millions promoting their books, but I have something better. I have you! If you enjoy what I write, you can play a huge part in keeping these stories flowing, simply by sharing.

Readers trust other readers. Would you please leave a review on whichever site you bought the book? (Reviews are the lifeblood of today's authors.) After that, if you're a social media user, please help to spread the word. Tell your friends, share your review, mention me over a cup of coffee. Whether it's Facebook, Twitter, Pinterest, Instagram or down the pub, I'd be eternally grateful if you'd be part of my team and help get the word out.

Thank you! ♥♥ Audrey

ABOUT THE AUTHOR

Audrey Davis is the author of romantic comedy A Clean Sweep and its short prequel A Clean Break. She originally released her second book The Haunting of Hattie Hastings as a novella trilogy between November 2017 and July 2018 before combining it into a standalone novel. A Wish For Jinnie is her third novel. A fourth is in the pipeline.

Audrey lives in Switzerland with her husband and enjoys shopping, cooking, eating and drinking red wine. And – of course – reading and writing. She gets quite giddy with excitement when readers make contact, so please feel free to get in touch through either Facebook or Twitter.

If you'd like to read the **free** short prequel to The Haunting of Hattie Hastings, just pop over to www.audrey-davisauthor.com to sign up for your copy of When Hattie Met Gary.

Printed in Great Britain
by Amazon

84489496R00157